Growing up on a steady diet of Ray Bradbury and *The Twilight Zone*, Jay R. Bonansinga began writing seriously after winning a short story contest in the eighth grade. He subsequently studied creative writing at Michigan State University and film directing at Columbia College Chicago. Since then he has directed numerous short films and music videos, winning the prestigious silver plaque at the Chicago International Film Festival for his science-fiction movie *City of Men*. His previous three novels, *The Killer's Game*, *Head Case* and *Bloodhound*, have also been published by Macmillan and Pan.

He currently resides in Evanston, Illinois, with his family and three antisocial cats.

Also by Jay R. Bonansinga

THE KILLER'S GAME

HEAD CASE

BLOODHOUND

JAY R. BONANSINGA

OBLIVION

PAN BOOKS

First published 2000 by Macmillan

This edition published 2001 by Pan Books
an imprint of Macmillan Publishers Ltd
25 Eccleston Place, London SW1W 9NF
Basingstoke and Oxford
Associated companies throughout the world
www.macmillan.com

ISBN 0 330 37611 X

1 3 5 7 9 8 6 4 2

A CIP catalogue record for this book is available from
the British Library.

Phototypeset by Intype London Ltd
Printed and bound in Great Britain by
Mackays of Chatham plc, Chatham, Kent

FOR BECKY JONES
MY FAVORITE DEMOCRAT

Acknowledgments

A special thanks to Irene Doyle-Sandler for outstanding research, and Lori Zuker and Bradford Smith of Overbrook Productions for helping shape the story. Also to Peter Lavery for cutting the fat. To Jocelyn and Lesly Pierre for the Haitian folklore and dialect. To Nate Maier for background. And to Matthew Snyder for being a big gun.

We are all ghosts, every one of us.
Henrik Ibsen

Prologue

THE FUNERAL

I'm twenty-nine years old, and I'm less than two years out of seminary school, and I'm watching my life piss away before my eyes.

Here it is, three o'clock in the afternoon on a blustery Saturday in May, and I'm standing outside Xavier Baptist in the overcast sun. The church is a poor one—a small stone edifice on the edge of a landfill—and there's a modest little cemetery adjacent to the building, crowded by huge, bare, spindly elms. There's an outdoor funeral going on, with a couple of dozen mourners, mostly black and poor, heads bowed in the pale sunlight. I'm standing at the rear like an idiot, in my collar and coat, trying to see over the tops of all the heads. The wind reeks of garbage and there's a horrible sound drifting on the breeze, a maintenance crew in the distance augering a hole into the ground. As the black preacher continues slogging through his litany, the machinery in the distance grinds on.

They're digging a hole for the boy.

' "Thou preparest a table before me," ' the preacher is wailing, ' "in the presence of my enemies." '

I look down at my shoes. They're scuffed black wingtips from a discount shoe store. Not much call for high fashion in my line of business, and especially in my archdiocese. But that's not why I keep staring at my shoes. I'm so damned ashamed of myself right now I find it hard to lift my head. The wind buffets my black trousers and I feel like I'm made of balsa wood—like I just might blow away at any moment.

The preacher's voice sings out in that soaring tone that seems to come naturally to black clergy: ' "Thou anointest my head with oil, my cup overfloweth!"'

I have to pay my respects—I owe the family that much. I have to go up there and say an aspiration to Saint Joseph, or a prayer for serenity, or maybe a quick Pater Noster. That's my job. I'm a priest. I should act like one. But my body won't hear of it. My body won't budge. All I can do is stand there at the rear, staring at my scuffed wingtips, listening to the Baptist minister declaim.

' "Surely, goodness and mercy shall follow me all the days of my life!"'

Okay, this is it. It's now or never. Through force of will, I urge my bull-legged self forward through the folding chairs, down the makeshift aisle, toward the front of the congregation, toward the small pine casket raised on cinderblocks. Little Eric Rivers is in that box. I can see his little navy-blue suit now, his delicate little caramel-colored hands folded across his chest. The sight of him sends gooseflesh across my scalp, across the backs of my arms and down my spine.

' "—and I shall dwell in the House of the Lord." Amen, thank you, Jesus!'

I finally make it to the front, and I can feel the mother's eyes on me as I approach the casket. I can see her in my peripheral vision, her ebony face ashen in the gray sunlight, her mouth gaping at the sight of me. She knows something that nobody else in that congregation knows. And now she is stricken at the sight of me—stricken speechless.

I wait my turn in the line, trying to avoid her deadly stare, her trembling face.

She's trying to say something.

I pause by the casket and gaze down at the little brown shell of a boy. Even in death, his round face and long lashes slice through my soul like a meat cleaver, his waxen hands folded so neatly across the breast of his Sunday-school suit. He's like a burned building, a charred remnant of some horrible, obscene maelstrom. A chill flutters through me. I can still sense the dark force that once infected his body, that ran through it like a current, manipulating his poor little face like a puppeteer. I can still hear it calling out—even in death.

'You!'

His mother's strangled voice behind me, piercing my renewed fear like a meat hook.

I turn around and look at her.

'You're the one!' she cries out, her face contorted with rage and mad grief. 'It's your fault! It's your fault!'

I try to say something, but I feel the hands of other men on my shoulders now, gentle but firm, coaxing me away. They don't know who I am, but they sure as hell don't want me making some kind of a scene. They don't want me making this day any worse than it already is. The mother is sobbing now, cursing me, wailing inarticulately, while older women hold her back, steadying her for fear she'll collapse into the dirt.

I start to turn away, to leave, when I see something out of the corner of my eye.

It happens so quickly, so discreetly, so furtively, that I know it's meant for my eyes only. And the moment it happens—the exact moment—I know it will stay with me for the rest of my life. Neither a challenge nor a taunt, it lasts only a second: A faint movement inside the casket, which could easily be explained by pathologists as merely a vestigial muscle contraction or gases escaping. But I know differently.

I know it's a warning.

As I'm turning away from the casket, the dead little boy's hand twitches upwards.

His finger is pointing directly at me.

Part I

THE PHONE CALL

Fate has a terrible power. You cannot escape it by wealth or war. No fort will keep it out, no ships outrun it.

Sophocles

CHAPTER ONE

The Man in the Burberry Coat

1. A Storm Brewing

Twenty years—that's how long it took for the dark force to find me. Just as I knew it would. It always does. It always finds you.

It found me in Chicago, working for Catholic Youth Services, teaching gang kids how to box. It had been nearly two decades since I hung up my priest's collar, and I was drinking pretty heavily by then, and not sleeping very well. The truth is, I was leading the life of a hermit. Thank God I still had that job working with the kids. That job was about the only thing I had going for me. I loved those kids. I always thought that if you could *channel* all that piss and rage, you could actually make a difference in their lives. By teaching them discipline, respect for themselves, respect for each other. I don't want to sound like Pollyanna, but I really did believe that back then, and I guess I still do today.

Anyway . . . that was what I was doing—working thirty hours a week down at the Harrison Street gym—when the beast came back into my life.

Did I mention it was the week between Christmas and New Year? I don't know why, exactly, but there are more suicides during this part of the year than any other.

Probably something to do with the holidays. Or maybe the weather. Or maybe just the weather in Chicago. This particular year, it was especially grim. The sky over my neighborhood was a slate-gray shroud, sending billows and flurries across the urban sprawl. The streets had a tired quality to them, a patina of smog over every brick bungalow. The dominant style here was post-war cinderblock, with plywood Santas and plastic elves in every other yard. And somewhere off to the west, a storm was brewing.

It was enough to drive a man to drink.

And that's exactly what I was doing the night the dark force invited me back into the fold. I was pounding shots of Bushmills at Madigan's pub, getting shit-faced all by my lonesome as usual. I think it was around one in the morning when I finally managed to climb out of my booth, stumble over to the coat rack, pull on my parka and stagger outside.

The night had turned vicious. The snow was spitting in my face, and the wind was shrieking, and you could barely hear the keening of the 'El' two blocks away, sparking its way through the storm. The streets were fairly deserted, and the sidewalks were iced over. I started north, hobbling along like a derelict trying to stay vertical.

I'm not an especially graceful man—even when I'm sober—and that night I was carrying about sixty extra pounds of flab from all that long-term boozing. My once muscular five-foot-ten frame—its fighting weight back at Loyola Seminary about a hundred and seventy-five pounds—had been reduced to a portly fireplug of a body. My ruddy Irish face was now covered with a graying beard, and my arthritis had been flaring up on a regular basis. I was not exactly floating like a butterfly anymore.

The fall came as I was crossing Ridge Avenue, and tried to step up onto the curb at Foster. I didn't see the crust of ice on the edge of the gutter, and my clumsy, drunken foot slipped out from under me. I landed hard on my fat ass, and gasped a little at the impact.

A voice rang out behind me, barely audible over the swirling wind.

'Father—!'

I blinked a little, dazed from the fall. Had I imagined the sound of a voice behind me? I tried to climb to my feet, but my body was not cooperating. Then I heard footsteps approaching, and I was pretty sure I wasn't imagining *that*.

I felt a strong pair of hands on my shoulders, gently but firmly helping me up. I spun around and found myself standing face to face with a handsome man in an expensive Burberry overcoat.

'You all right, Father?' he said.

I stared at him a moment, my head swimming, my cheeks stinging from the cold. *Father?* Good Lord, nobody had called me that in so long. Two decades? I swallowed hard and started to say, 'Who . . .?'

'It's me, Father.' He smiled. 'It's Dodd.'

'Dodd? Dodd?' I was sounding like a parrot now. A connection was sparking in the back of my mind, but the switch hadn't quite tripped yet.

'I used to be an altar boy down at Saint Vincent's,' he said softly, wiping snow from his face.

Then it hit me, like a hook from George Foreman right in the kisser, and I felt emotion welling inside me, and it was so sudden and so unexpected, I had to grit my teeth just to keep from losing my breath.

I stared at him through watery, astonished eyes. 'Jimmy Dodd?'

'How ya doing, Father?'

'I'm . . . I'm just . . .'

What was I going to say? Look at me: Drunk as a reprobate, wallowing in sin. A hell of a long way from

Christ. But here *he* was—standing there like Marley's ghost. Drowning me in a tidal wave of unexpected memories.

Last time I laid eyes on Jimmy Dodd was 1980, one year after my fall from grace. I had been living in a fleabag transient hotel down in Hannibal, Missouri, and the kid had come calling unexpectedly to cheer me up. Dodd had been a skinny little twerp back then, with delicate features and that aristocratic sort of breeding in his manner. His mother was St. Louis socialite Cynthia Kearns-Dodd, so maybe that had something to do with it. But there had also been something stubborn about the young man, something intractable, like a weed that refused to be uprooted. Maybe that was why I always had a soft spot for him then. Dodd had been one of my favorite altar boys back at St. Vinnie's.

But, on that humid summer evening down in Hannibal, that boy and I had talked straight through the night—and well into the dawn—discussing everything from my troubles with the diocese to the nature of good and evil. The boy had been so earnest, so big-hearted, so full of vinegar, it made me wonder whether maybe—just maybe—my short stretch as a Catholic priest had not been in vain.

But that was twenty years ago, and the young kid in that Hannibal hotel bore very little resemblance to the tall drink-of-water now standing in front of me.

'You can't be Jimmy Dodd,' I said finally, grinning and taking another couple of steps toward him. 'Jimmy Dodd was just a skinny kid from Belleville.'

The man in the Burberry overcoat smiled. 'It's good to see you, Father.'

There was another awkward silence, the wind singing through the high-tension wires overhead, and I felt the weight of the years standing on my chest, the tears blurring my eyes. I could see something behind Dodd's gaze, something buried in the wrinkles around his eyes, the lines and creases of time and a career and alcohol and God knows what else. This was the same goofy kid who had filled the chalices before Mass and had fetched the host wafers, and had even befriended me after all the humiliation. That same innocent boy was now standing here in the cold on a street corner in Chicago.

I staggered over to him and gave him a bear hug. Then I stepped back to take a better look at him, sniffing away my tears. 'I can't believe it.'

'It has been a while,' he said.

'Last time I saw you,' I said, still marveling at the grown man, 'you were wearing sneakers to High Mass.'

He grinned again. 'And you were teaching us Muddy Waters songs in the rectory bathroom.'

The memory again washed over me for a moment, and all of a sudden I felt pretty awful about the way my life had turned out. 'That was a long time ago,' I agreed. 'So what's Jimmy Dodd been doing with himself all these years?'

'I got my own law practice up in Baltimore.'

'No kidding? That's great. You heading back to St. Louis for the holidays?'

He smiled sadly at me. 'Nah, not enough time. I'm only in this part of the country for a few days.'

'You oughtta make time for your family, Jimmy.'

He paused, glancing down at the snow. 'Some day, Father.'

I told him then to call me Martin. I told him I'd been plain old 'Martin' for twenty years now.

'Sorry,' he said. 'Old habits.'

'You okay, Jimmy?' A dark shadow had suddenly fallen across the man's face.

He turned, looking as though he had just swallowed something bad. 'I need your help, Father.'

For some reason—which would become clear later—my stomach tightened slightly right then. 'Of course,' I said. 'I mean, I'll do whatever I can.'

'You have to promise me something,' he said, and from his grave tone it was clear that this was not only going to be serious, but was maybe going to even be kind of horrible. 'You have to promise to keep everything I tell you strictly confidential.'

I stared at him for a moment. 'Of course, Jimmy.'

'Good,' he said, the lines around his eyes deepening. It occurred to me right then—even in my drunken state— that these were not the eyes of a man who had taken the world lightly. These were the eyes of a man who had maybe seen just a little more than he had bargained for.

'Tell you what, Jimmy,' I said then. 'My place is just one "El" stop away from here. Why don't we go make a pot of coffee, and you can tell me all about it.'

He looked at me and smiled. 'That sounds excellent.'

2. Haunted

My apartment was never going to appear in *Architectural Digest*, but it was cozy, filled with comforting things, and a bargain at five hundred bucks a month, plus utilities. One of the myriad baby-boom four-flats that lined the streets of Chicago's North Shore, it featured a single cramped living room, a small kitchenette, a bedroom, and a measly little bathroom with one of those old clawfoot bathtubs. There was good light from a front bay window, and the walls were lined with framed photographs of young Latinos and blacks whom I had counseled over the years. Every corner was filled with either one of my guitars or a stack of my blues records—most of them tarted up at the moment with cheap Christmas tinsel.

Over the years, I had seen a fair number of my heroes live on stage. Even during seminary school, I would sneak out on weekends and go across the river to East St. Louis to see BB King or Albert Collins or Sippie Wallace sing in some Godforsaken dive. I picked up the guitar and harmonica in the seventies, after moving to Chicago, and I got pretty good at them. Good enough to sit in with traveling acts at the Checkerboard Lounge and Biddy Mulligan's. I even had the photographs to prove it—a few blurry old snapshots on the wall over my fake fireplace—showing yours truly jamming on stage with Buddy Guy back in '77 at the No-Exit Café.

In fact, Dodd was staring at these very photographs when I came back into the living room from the kitchen with a couple of cups of coffee. I figured Dodd would tell me what kind of help he needed in due time, so I didn't push it. 'Delusions of grandeur,' I said, nodding at the photos before setting one of the cups down on the coffee table next to Dodd's chair.

'I seem to remember you playing a pretty mean harmonica,' he said.

I sat down and sipped my coffee. 'I keep hoping that if I rub elbows with the greats, it'll rub off.'

'Pretty impressive.'

I winked at him. 'Not really.'

He picked up a 45 sleeved in ancient brown paper. 'I remember when you taught this song to the choir,' he said, a twinkle in his eye. 'Put a bug up Cardinal Barclay's butt for a week.'

'Yeah,' I said softly. 'Senses of humor were at a premium back then.'

He picked up a framed photo of me during my middleweight days, and took a closer look. 'You still boxing amateur?'

'Not since my knees blew out.'

'I remember that Haskins fight,' he mused. 'You were a force of nature that night—the Fightin' Father from Fullerton.'

I told him that was ancient history now.

He put the picture back, then looked at me intensely. 'Your last year . . . they never should have treated you like that.'

I shrugged. Right at that moment, I didn't want to talk about it. I didn't want to think about it. Not when I was basking in the warm glow of other memories. I looked at him and said, 'They tend to excommunicate priests who get kids killed, Jimmy.'

'Father, come on, you've gotta stop talking that nonsense.'

'Forget about it.' I waved my hand as though swatting away a swarm of bees.

'That kid was sick to begin with,' Dodd went on. 'It wasn't your fault. You were just trying to help—'

'I got an idea,' I interrupted. 'Why don't we talk about something else, Jimmy. Like how I can help you?'

Dodd turned back to the records for a moment, and I could see there was something burning a hole in his gut. He was turning it over in his mind, chewing on it, and I started feeling a little nervous. I'm not sure exactly why, as I'm not a psychic or anything. I just think this was the turning point, and I knew that whatever he was about to say was not going to be all sunbeams and daisies.

Finally he turned and gave me a hard look. 'Father, I need a favor.'

'Name it, Jimmy.'

'You remember, back at Saint Vincent's, when you used to cleanse houses?'

A little feather of dread brushed the back of my neck. ' "The Blessing of the Domicile." Yeah, of course,' I said. 'Why?'

'I got a client on the East Coast,' he said. 'Old money, blue blood. House needs cleansing.'

Somewhere off in a shadowy corner of my mind, a child was shrieking. 'What's wrong with it?' I asked.

Dodd shrugged. 'I'm not sure. Lady of the house claims the place is just not right.'

'Not right?'

'She used the word "haunted" a couple of times.'

I nodded. 'Uh-huh.'

'I know how it sounds—'

'Jimmy, I didn't even say how it "sounded," one way or the other.'

'I know,' he said, then glanced across the room at the window. The yellow glare of a passing snowplow washed across the glass for a moment. Then it was gone. 'I'm just saying, in this day and age, it sounds a little ridiculous.'

There was an awkward moment of silence then, and I tried to think of something helpful to say. 'Does the lady have a relationship with the Church?'

Dodd looked at me. 'That's the thing . . .'

'Yeah?'

'I was thinking *you* could do it.'

Another stretch of silence, and I said, 'Do what?'

'The cleansing, the exorcism . . . whatever you think is appropriate.'

I knew this was coming. I knew it. But I was still unprepared. I kept sipping my coffee like an idiot. 'Me?'

'They want to keep this very low-key, Father,' Dodd said. I didn't like the extra urgency that was seeping into his voice. I didn't like it one bit. 'They don't want any publicity. They're very clear on that point.'

'I'm a layman now, Jimmy. I don't do this kind of stuff anymore.'

Dodd's eyes lit up with a kind of anxious glow. 'But this is really not that big a deal.'

I looked at him for a moment. 'You don't believe it, do you?'

He looked a little taken aback. 'What—that the house is haunted?' He shrugged. 'Who knows? All I'm saying is, your part would not be that big a deal. I'll fly you out there, you say a few prayers, and we're done.'

I told him things were a little more involved than that.

'Come on, Father. A simple blessing—that's all the family really wants.'

'I'd like to help you out, Jimmy, but I can't.'

He gave me that pleading look. 'What harm could a simple blessing do?'

It was a fair question. What harm *could* a simple blessing do? What harm? I didn't answer right away. Instead, I got up, walked over to the window and looked out at the night. The snow was falling steadily now, a delicate white veil over the street lights. Beyond the rooftops and high-tension wires, I could see a dirty slice of Resurrection Cemetery to the north, the nameless headstones like rotted teeth in the iced-over ground. That was the poor people's section of the cemetery, the potter's field of the North Shore. Little Eric Rivers was buried in a place like that. Paupers' graves.

Right then it occurred to me that I didn't know how to explain to Dodd all the harm just a blessing could do. I just turned to him and said, 'Believe me, Jimmy, if it was anything else, I'd help you in a second. But this—*this* I can't do.'

Dodd looked at me for a moment, then shrugged sadly, turned and strode across the room to the hat rack.

I watched the man put on his coat. I felt mortified. 'Jimmy, what are you doing?'

'It's late,' he muttered. 'Gotta get back to my hotel.' He was buttoning his Burberry overcoat, putting on his hat. He looked grim all of a sudden, like an undertaker going home after a hard day of putting dead bodies in boxes.

'Jimmy, come on.' I was flabbergasted. All these years, and now he was sore at me. 'Don't go off all revved up.'

Dodd didn't answer, just put on his gloves and marched over to the front door.

'Jimmy, please. Come on, it's been twenty-five years.' I started toward the door too. 'Stay for dinner. I'll make some ziti. I'll put some Louis Prima on the stereo.'

Dodd opened the door, paused, then turned back toward me for a second. At first, I thought he was going to punch me in the face. Then he reached into his breast pocket and pulled out a business card.

'You change your mind,' he said, handing it over, 'I'll be staying at the Hotel Nikko until Saturday.'

I started to say something else, but Jimmy Dodd was already out the door.

A moment later, he vanished into the storm.

Of course, at that point, I had no idea just how soon I would be seeing him again.

CHAPTER TWO

Broken Lullaby

1. Night Terrors

Two days later, the other shoe dropped.

Now, being a Catholic, I always seem to be waiting for that darned other shoe to hit the floor. I don't know if it's the Catholic guilt that everybody talks about, or the rich tradition of martyrs skulking around our history, or maybe something else, but I always seem to be bracing for the worst. And, two days after my unexpected meeting with Dodd, that's exactly what happened. To be specific, the Catholic Youth Services people called me up for an emergency meeting, and when I showed up at St. Michael's they told me I was fired.

They had one of their young bureaucrats tell me in his rectory office—remember, this was only a few days after Christmas—and I was not supposed to take it personally, you understand. I was a great boxing coach and I was loved by all the boys. The problem was, one of the CYS board members had been visiting the St. Louis diocese last week and had learned of my past and my dishonorable discharge from the clergy. And the bottom line was, this knowledge scared them. And, since I was currently working with children, the organization could justifiably fire me under the guise of 'protecting the kids.' From what, exactly, they couldn't answer.

There was nothing I could do or say.

That night I didn't go through my usual paces. I didn't tell myself everything was going to be okay. And I didn't remind myself that I had tried everything within my means to help that little boy, that I did what any self-respecting member of the clergy would have done in the same situation. I didn't even try to put it all behind me while I slowly drank myself into a stupor. All I did was the drinking part.

Little did I know I was less than thirty-six hours away from that mansion on the hill, and that damp basement, and that thing behind the door.

I passed out sometime around midnight.

The dream came on like it always did, like a wild animal stalking me, pursuing me. The first part was always the same, and tonight it was no different. I found myself in that squalid corridor down in the Robert Taylor Homes, the nation's largest public housing project, and it was 1978, and I was a young priest, and I was dressed in full vestment. I could even feel a trickle of sweat running down my back.

And I could see the door to the boy's room at the end of the corridor. And, like always, it was a beast—the ugliest door in the world. A huge, scarred monstrosity of a door. Old lacquered oak, cracked and peeling, with a stained porcelain knob that looked like exposed bone, it radiated a kind of unadulterated *badness*. I hated that door, and that door hated me, but the strange thing was, I knew I had to conquer it. I knew I had to go through that damned door. There was a little black boy on the other side, writhing in the grip of an unclean spirit, and I was the only one who could help him.

I had to go through that door.

Of course, this being a dream, I never made it through that door. I got close enough to hear the boy's strangled cries, and smell the piss and misery . . . but I never made it through. I never played out the tragic events. Instead, I found myself someplace else. It happened just like that. It always did. I never questioned it, never felt it strange. After all, this was a dream.

And that was the way dreams worked.

I found myself standing, instead, outside Xavier Baptist Church on a windy spring day twenty years ago. I was standing behind the congregation, trying to see over all the heads. The wind smelled of garbage, and there was a horrible melody drifting on the breeze, a broken music box playing a broken lullaby.

'Wait! It's okay!' I was calling out. 'They fixed his face!'

I was elbowing my way toward the front of the congregation now, toward the small pine casket supported on cinderblocks. I could see little Eric Rivers in that casket, his little navy-blue suit, his delicate little caramel-colored hands folded across his chest.

'But they fixed his face!' I kept hollering, as I fought my way through the crowd.

I finally made it to the front, where the cardinal of my archdiocese at the time—Cardinal Adler—was administering the rites, swinging a brazier of smoking incense and mumbling the litanies, and the boy's mother was sitting nearby on a folding chair, crying softly. She looked up at me, and her ebony face turned ashen-gray, and she started to scream. And I stammered, 'But they fixed it—they fixed his face. I swear they fixed his face!'

Then I looked down at the boy.

His face was a scabrous mess covered with white grease-paint. Somebody had slathered a clown's face over the boy's wounds, and now the little boy's purple, lifeless tongue hung out of his mouth in a horrible burlesque of death. But the worst bit by far—and this was the part of the dream that always cut me to the marrow—was the item wrapped tightly around the dead boy's neck.

It was my own scarlet vestment scarf.

And that was when I woke up in a flurry of sweat and chills, the room spinning, my head pounding.

For a second I couldn't breathe. The darkness seemed to be pressing down on me, and that image of the little boy's face, tumbling around inside my skull, left me gasping. It felt as though my soul was about to split apart.

What happened next I'm not particularly proud of. Although I'd been having the same dream for the past twenty years, it had never affected me this profoundly: I started bawling like a little child.

It's a strange thing when an old codger like me finally lets loose. The sound of your own blubbering makes you cry all the harder. Even when you're alone, it's a strange mixture of release and shame. I hated myself for coming apart like this, and the more I hated myself, the more I wailed. I cried for that little boy in his tenement room, and I cried for my miserable failure of a life.

I have no idea how long I lay there howling, but by the time I was done I felt like a damp rag that had been wrung dry. Snot covered my face, my eyes were burning, and my nasal passages felt filled with concrete. But there was also a weird kind of resolve in the pit of my belly now. Thinking back on it, it's hard to describe—as if a wound inside me had somehow gotten lanced, so that what remained was a new sense of purpose.

It didn't take a rocket scientist to figure out what I must do next.

2. Making the Call

The phone had rung three times when my heart started flip-flopping in my chest.

I can't remember it ever beating that hard, and when you've been on this planet for fifty years—and I'm talking fifty years of Italian sausage consumption—you take irregular heartbeats seriously. It felt as though my chest was splitting open, but I kept gripping that sweaty receiver, staring at that pale strip of street light leaking under my window shade, hoping, *praying*, that he would answer.

The click sounded on the fourth ring.

'Hello?' His voice sounded groggy and slow.

'It's your friendly neighborhood exorcist,' I said softly into the phone.

'Father?'

'Sorry to wake you, Jimmy.'

'No, no, it's okay. What's going on?'

I swallowed hard, the top of my scalp tingling. I had an idea I was about to make a big mistake. How big, I wasn't sure. Looking back on it, I don't think I ever could have dreamed how deep a hole I was about to jump into. 'I've decided to do your cleansing,' I said finally.

There was a slight pause, during which I thought I heard Dodd letting out a sigh of relief. 'That's fantastic,' he said.

'How difficult could it be?' I said.

'Absolutely.'

'It's like riding a bike,' I said. 'You don't forget.'

Another pause, then his voice returned. 'There is one thing.'

I asked him what that was.

'I don't know any easy way to say this,' he said.

'Then just say it, Jimmy.'

I heard him sigh, and then: 'You'll watch the drinking?'

I told him it was no problem; I reminded him I was a Jesuit once, and that's practically being a monk.

He said he believed me.

I asked him when he wanted us to leave.

'Eight a.m. sharp. Midway Airport.'

'I'll be there,' I promised.

After another pause, Dodd's voice returned with an extra edge to it. 'Father, there is one more thing. Something I neglected to mention about this particular cleansing . . .'

'I'm listening.'

Dodd's voice continued: 'There are going to be a few conditions . . . conditions that might seem odd.'

'I'm all ears, Jimmy.'

There was a long stretch of silence, then Dodd started explaining the ground rules.

CHAPTER THREE

Flying Blind

1. Drawn to the Darkness

Had I known what I was getting into I think I would have packed more stuff. I probably would have brought along a few extra ampullae of holy water too, maybe revised my Roman Rituals a little harder. Hell, had I known what was waiting for me in the basement of that old house, I'm not sure I would have gone at all. But then again, maybe something like this has always been on the cards for me.

From my earliest days in the seminary, I was drawn to the dark corners of the world. I gravitated toward the disenfranchised, the prostitutes, the welfare mothers and the drug addicts. I always figured that the middle-class suburbanites could take care of themselves. But there was something else that drew me to the grittier side of life. There was a constant current of darkness running underneath these people's lives, a constant temptation, a constant torment that I still find hard to explain. But I know it's there. The Devil is a dirty fighter. He goes after the weak and the downtrodden, and he hits below the belt.

Maybe that's why I had gotten involved with the Rivers family. They were from Chicago, that big city up north, a place that I was slowly but surely being drawn to. I had been taking periodic trips up there to work with gang kids as part of my Catholic missionary work, and I had stumbled upon this poor child almost by accident. Of course, there *are* no accidents, are there? But this child seemed like a soul I could actually save. The boy was way beyond the scope of Western medicine: He wasn't a schizophrenic, he wasn't sick. He was under the influence of a more powerful force, and I thought I could help free him through spiritual means, through ritual. But the Church refused to clear it for me. Was it because the boy was black? Because he was poor? I still don't know. But I went ahead and traveled north, and did the exorcism anyway. And it went *south* on me. It went wrong. It went about as badly as they can go. And the little boy died.

And I lost my first title fight to the other side.

The next day, back in St. Louis, they gave me the ax in Archbishop Merriweather's inner sanctum, in the rear of the parish offices. Father Henschull was there, his pale, wrinkled face downturned through most of the proceedings. I remember how the silvery light shining into the office was diffused by the stained-glass skylight overhead, and how it made everything kind of sad and solemn. I sat front-center in a stiff-backed rectory chair as the excommunication was read to me: . . . *You are forbidden to have any participation in the Eucharistic Sacrifice or in any other ceremonies whatever of public worship; and you are forbidden to celebrate the sacraments, or discharge any ecclesiastical offices, ministries or functions whatsoever . . .*

In fact, those same words were bouncing around in the back of my mind some twenty-odd years later, as I sat waiting in that desolate airport on that wintry morning.

. . . *you are forbidden to discharge any ecclesiastical offices, ministries or functions whatsoever . . .*

Who did I think I was, going off on some half-baked ghost hunt?

'Father?'

A voice behind me.

'Father?'

I blinked, looking up through the commotion and noise flowing through the airport-terminal corridor.

It took me a few moments to remember where I was: Sitting on a plastic contour bench at Midway Airport, awaiting a rendezvous with Dodd. It was a Friday morning at the end of December, yet the airport was business-as-usual with holidaymakers, the walkways echoing with shuffling travelers and public-address announcements, the gray winter light streaming through the endless plate glass. I was huddled near a snack bar, bundled up in my parka, boots and jeans, still holding a paper cup full of Starbuck's coffee that had gone cold long ago. My overstuffed duffel bag sat on the floor next to me, my lower back throbbing with a dull ache, my stomach fluttering at the prospect of flying. I was not exactly a good flier under the best of circumstances, and this morning my flight was promising to be off-the-scale bizarre.

I rose to my feet with a tepid smile. 'Hiya, Jimmy.'

Dodd approached, lugging a hardshell attaché. 'You ready, Father?'

'Always ready, Jimmy. You know me.' I grabbed my duffel.

Dodd glanced at his watch. 'Looks like we got a few minutes yet. You want to get some breakfast?'

'I had a bagel in the cab on the way down.'

'You want to get something else before we go?'

'No . . . no thanks, Jimmy, I'm fine. I'm just . . . wondering . . .'

'You're wondering about the blindfold, right?'

I shrugged. The night before, Dodd had told me about the blindfold, but that still wasn't sitting right. 'Seems a little paranoid,' I said.

'It's like I told you last night, Father; this particular client is what you would call *obsessed* with anonymity.'

'Do we put it on now? Or do we put it on when we get there?'

'We'll do it on the plane.'

I reminded him that I was going to have to see the house in order to cleanse it.

'Don't worry about that, Father. Once we're inside the place, we'll take your blindfold off.'

I nodded. 'That's all well and good, Jimmy . . . but there are other considerations.'

'Such as?'

'It's helpful to know the history of their home. Stuff like that.'

'Short of identifying the house's owner,' he replied, 'I'll give you all the background you need on the plane.'

I took a deep breath, then finally said, 'Smoke 'em if you got 'em.'

Dodd nodded. 'Let's go.'

Then he started toward an unmarked door, but I grabbed his arm. He paused and looked back at me. 'What's the matter, Father?'

'The gates are this way, Jimmy.'

He shook his head. 'We're not taking a commercial flight this time, Father. Not on this trip.'

2. White Knuckles

It was a small yet luxurious corporate jet, which took off in a sudden flurry, leaping off the tarmac, hellbent into the gathering storm. Like I said, I wasn't much of a flier, and the abruptness of this take-off rattled me. It felt as though we were sitting in a toy plane whose molded-plastic parts creaked each time we banked, a fist turning in my belly. I could hear muffled radio voices sizzling in the cockpit a few feet in front, and I could smell coffee brewing a few feet behind me.

I took several deep breaths and reassured myself this was a Godly mission. I chewed Tums incessantly. But nothing worked.

There were a dozen empty leather swivel-seats along either side of the plane's center aisle, and the walls were richly appointed with brass and wood inlay. I was sitting four rows back, with Dodd in the seat across the aisle. For nearly fifteen minutes, neither of us said a word. Dodd was consumed by his laptop, madly tapping away at the tiny keyboard, while I gazed out the portal to my right, wondering where in God's name we were headed.

The wall of clouds revealed nothing.

Finally Dodd looked up and said, 'How you doing, Father? You need anything?'

'I'm fine, Jimmy, thanks.'

'Can I get you some water? Coffee?'

I told him no thanks again, then I said: 'Actually, there *is* something you can do for me.'

'Name it.'

'Call me Martin,' I reminded him.

Dodd smiled. 'That's a hard habit to break. I apologize.'

I told him not to worry about it, and tried to ignore the dizziness washing over me with every lurch. I felt like a faulty gyroscope, my sense of balance going haywire with every new squall of winter winds beneath the plane. Dodd had said we were heading east, and that the flight would take about two and a half hours. But how far would that get us? Nova Scotia? No, somewhere south. The Carolinas? I started going through all the big eastern cities in my mind, the ones that might be two and a half hours distant by air. New York City? Philadelphia? Boston? Was it Dodd's current home city, Baltimore? Was that where we were going? Probably. And then, for some reason, I found myself wondering what the weather would be like there. I had brought along a week's worth of clothes, my shaving kit, a couple of harmonicas, a book I was reading on the life of Cardinal Bernardin, and a hundred dollars in traveler's checks. There was also a small, worn, black-vinyl satchel full of ritual hocus-pocus.

The satchel contained my old liturgical tools, still tucked into their respective sleeves and pockets like sacred rounds of ammunition. There were silver medallions, various crucifixes, caffeine pills, cones of incense, a flashlight, rosary beads, a small tape recorder, a lighter, and small brass cruets of holy water taken from St. Michael's Cathedral, blessed by a Franciscan friend whom I knew from St. Louis. There were also a couple of tattered leather Roman ritual books and my old concordance Bible.

The tools of an esoteric, forgotten trade.

'Can't you tell me anything more about the family itself?' I said at last, still gripping the arms of my seat as the plane dipped and shuddered.

'Excuse me?' Dodd looked up from his laptop.

'The family. What can you tell me about them?'

'I'm afraid I can't tell you all that much,' he said. 'They've only lived in the place for about eleven months and, like I said, they're very private.'

I asked him about the house itself.

'It's pretty old by American standards,' he said above the steady drone of the engine. 'Built around 1800, I think. The architect was a man named James Hoban, a pretty well-known builder at the time. He designed a number of homes for wealthy planters along the eastern seaboard.'

I asked him what the house looked like.

'Its design was a bastardized version of what they called the Dublin style,' he explained. 'That was used in a lot of plantation homes. With big Palladian façades, hooded windows, all that kind of stuff. Much of the building was constructed in stone, which was more popular than brick among rich Southerners at the time. Took a couple of years to complete it, and several hundred black slaves were employed in the construction.'

I tensed yet again as the plane shuddered convulsively. 'Sounds like quite a place,' I said finally.

'It really is,' he said. 'Sits in about eighteen wooded acres, and it's a real landmark.'

I looked at him. 'Anything special about its history?'

'Whattya mean? In terms of the house itself?'

'Yeah, anything out of the ordinary?'

'Well, it's an old house,' he said, 'so lots of water under the bridge. I understand a fire nearly destroyed it shortly after it was built, and much of it had to be restored. Lots of renovations over the years . . .'

'For instance?'

Dodd was consulting his notes now. 'Let's see . . . balconies and porticos were added in the mid-1800s. In 1927 the third floor was expanded in a major way from being just storage to living space. In 1950 the owners completely gutted the interior and assembled a steel frame inside the load-bearing walls.'

Another pause.

'Is that it?' I asked.

Dodd shrugged: 'Yeah . . . pretty much. Are renovations important?'

I told him I didn't know, then enquired about the interior.

'I can tell you this much,' Dodd said, 'that the interior is fairly—what's the word?—eclectic, I guess. The shapes of the rooms are unusual, a lot of bay windows, cathedral ceilings, greenhouse sections, archways, rounded corners. The decor is . . . well, it's eclectic. A lot of Beaux Arts,

French Provincial, Oriental, Mission, the whole range. A lot of hardwoods, walnut, teak, including a lot of inlay.'

There was a pause, and I said, 'You're sure there's nothing else you can tell me about the residents?'

After another tense pause, Dodd finally replied: 'What do you want to know?'

I asked if there were any children.

He said there was an only child, a girl.

I asked how old.

'She's . . . twenty, I think. A freshman at Yale.' Then he stopped. 'Is that important?'

I told him I had no idea as yet. I told him I didn't know what might be important yet.

I just wanted to survive this flight.

A few minutes later, I excused myself and went back to the lavatory.

It was a cramped but lavish bathroom: Walnut panels and metal fixtures and fancy soap in the soap dish. The air smelled of disinfectant, and the noise was tremendous, the rush of the engines sounding louder in there. My hands shook so badly I could barely dig the small metal flask out of my back pocket. I finally got the cap off and took a long swig of the cheap blended whiskey it contained, letting it burn my throat, bring tears to my eyes and warm my innards. I needed courage right now. I needed it from on high, and I needed it from the bottle.

I stared at myself in the mirror. 'You can do this,' I told my reflection. 'You can do it.'

The man staring back at me—his eyes drawn and haunted—didn't seem convinced.

3. A Hole in the Air

The blindfold they used on me was actually *two* blindfolds, one of them made of soft fleece to block out the light, the other made of flexible plastic to hold the first one in place. It was a serious rig, devised by serious people, intent on keeping me from seeing a God-blessed thing.

Dodd asked me to put it on as soon as the plane started its descent through the cloud layers.

The next fifteen minutes passed in a dark blur against my eyelids. I tried to keep talking in a feeble attempt to ignore the lurching of my stomach. 'What else can you tell me about the disturbances?'

I heard Dodd thumbing through his notes as we descended through various pockets of wind. 'Lemme see,' he said. 'It all started with the standard stuff: The strange noises, footsteps creaking down empty hallways, shifting sounds like furniture being moved around in rooms. Then there were the running faucets.'

'Plumbing problems?'

'Not exactly,' he replied. 'The daughter noticed it first. Apparently, she'd be doing her homework when the faucets in nearby rooms would spontaneously come on.'

I asked him if there was a chance somebody could have left them on by mistake.

'Not a chance. We're talking about *every single faucet* on the same floor. And all of them going full-blast. This went on regularly for a couple of months, and then the electric lights got in on the act.'

'The lights?'

'They'd come in at night sometimes to find every single light on the same floor was lit . . . along with every water faucet turned full on.'

'Okay,' I said, gripping my armrests. There were white

smudges on the backs of my eyelids, which would flare and flash each time the plane lurched. I was having trouble breathing, and bile burned the back of my throat.

I heard Dodd's voice: 'At first these were just annoyances. I mean, the family realized something odd was going on, but were prepared to live with it—like a leaky roof or something. But then things started to go missing, like articles of clothing, dishes, books. Weird stains would appear on the walls, weird scratch marks—'

'Scratch marks?' I asked.

'Yeah. They'd hear noises in the closets and the hallways, sometimes under the very armchairs they were sitting in— scratching noises—and they'd take a look and find these weird marks all over the floorboards or the backs of doors. Almost like claw marks.'

'I see.'

'And, of course, the strange odor.'

'Go on.'

'The odor is something that all the family have commented on at one point or another, and it defies description. I smelled it myself once—unbelievable. I was there late at night, sitting in the library, when I noticed it emanating from behind a desk. Just comes out of nowhere, the worst smell you could ever imagine. I'm really serious when I say it's hard to describe. It's like . . . burned meat—but not really. It's like . . . I don't know. It's impossible to describe.'

'Try, Jimmy. Try to describe the smell.'

Another pause. 'Well . . . it's like . . . if the color black had a smell, this would be it.'

Chills rippled down my spine, and faint images of ancient texts flashed across my blind eyes, mostly because I knew the smell Dodd was talking about. After a moment, I managed to say, 'What else, Jimmy?'

'That's sort of when things went from bad to worse.'

'You mean with the smell?'

35

'No, no—the house, the place itself. Worse in the sense that it started getting difficult to be there. Maybe even dangerous. Small fires would break out for no reason: Toasters blowing up, TVs, other appliances. Inexplicable seepage of liquid from electrical outlets. One night, the lady of the house was nearly electrocuted when she turned on a light switch to check on some running faucets. And once, when she entered an area of the house being refurbished, she found an inch of water on the floor—with live power saws still plugged into the wall sockets.'

The plane shuddered, the engine whining as it plunged downward at thousands of feet a minute. I gripped my armrest, the blindfold making my eyes itch unmercifully.

I finally managed to say, 'Is this when they called you in, Jimmy?'

There was a pause, the recycled air humming loudly above us, and finally Dodd said, 'No, actually, they called me in later—shortly after the sightings started.'

'The sightings?'

There was another pause as I waited for him to continue, my stomach seizing up with something like nausea. I knew exactly what was coming next. I knew it like a terrible fable that I could recite from memory, an all-too-familiar story that all the years and the booze and the numbing loneliness could not erase. And I sat there in that lurching aircraft, listening to the young attorney's voice as he raised it to be heard above the rush of forced air.

'There's something there in the house, Father. We've had dozens of separate statements from family and servants. They are each convinced they saw something, and they corroborate each other. Each time, the thing would appear after the stench had grown to unbearable levels. One time at the end of the third-floor corridor, another time in the library, and again on a staircase off the kitchen, which is used almost solely by domestic staff.'

I asked him how the various witnesses described this apparition.

'You know, that's the convincing thing,' he said. 'They all described it in a similar way. It wasn't anything like a stereotypical ghost or whatever. Each insisted it was nothing like you see in the movies. They each said it was more—'

I finished the sentence for him: 'Like a hole in the air?'

A pregnant beat of silence. Then Dodd's voice: 'That's exactly right, Father, but how . . . how the hell did you know?'

'I *didn't* know,' I replied. 'Not for sure. But I think I've encountered something like this before.'

'Seriously?'

I nodded, but said nothing further.

Finally Dodd said, 'Any chance you might be able to get rid of this thing for us, Father?'

I told him I would give it my very best try.

And we didn't say anything else until we were securely on the ground.

Which was fine by me, since by then I didn't feel much like talking anyway.

CHAPTER FOUR

The Shrieking Room

1. Death Row

The plane eventually touched down in a cyclone of noise, the wheels yelping against the tarmac. I tried to ignore the dots of light streaking my blank field of vision. The blindfold was driving me nuts, and I found myself wondering whether blind people experience these teeming, glowing images in their mind's eye.

Once the plane had stopped taxiing I felt a hand on my arm as Dodd murmured: 'Let's go, Padre.'

I was shuffled out the exit hatch, down a series of iced-over aluminum steps, and out into the billowing winds. I could feel the snow on my face and I could smell the storm. That wretched blindfold just added to the harshness of it all. I could barely hear the racket of other jet engines above the wind and the amplified voices of runway controllers.

I felt Dodd's grip on my arm tightening, and a moment later I was ushered into an echoing, empty space like a warehouse, at which point I heard a series of clicks and metallic clangs, and then an engine starting. Before I knew what was happening, I was guided into a car which smelled of stale cigars and air-freshener.

The vehicle pulled out of the warehouse and into the

raging elements. It fishtailed around a series of tight turns and ramps, then made its way presumably into the outbound lane of the terminal's access road. I could now hear muffled traffic noises against the beating of the windshield-wiper blades and the rush of heat on my face from the heaters. Judging from the number of times we jiggered to a stop, then started up again, I guessed the roads were getting pretty bad. My eyes were still itching like crazy, and I rubbed at them through the sweat-damp fabric of the blindfold.

Speaking of blindfolds, it was amazing how much peripheral information I could glean from my other four senses. By touch I could tell that I was traveling in some big expensive luxury sedan—a Cadillac or a Lincoln maybe. The seats were buttery leather, the suspension smooth, the engine strong and potent beneath us. From the chaotic street noises—or what I could hear of them—we were driving through some large transport network, and were very likely city-bound. From the severe weather conditions I was starting to think Boston. Even the odors seeping through the window seals were damn provocative—a mixture of crisp air, pine needles and something else that I couldn't place. Was that a lake out there? A large bay? Or even the ocean?

But mostly I was thinking about confronting that black hole in the air.

At some point in the car ride—maybe half an hour had elapsed, but I had lost all track of time—we got caught in a traffic jam probably caused by the build-up of snow. I listened closely to the horns honking, the muffled sound of snowplow blades scraping through ice, an occasional snow-blower's engine whining. I was straining to hear some additional clue to our present whereabouts. But there was merely a jumble of wintry urban noises that could come from any city. I again started feeling nauseous and jittery.

My nerves were so raw that I found myself jumping at sudden sounds.

'Will they be waiting for us there?' I finally asked.

'Who?' Dodd sounded as though his mind had been wandering as well.

'The owners of the house, the family.'

After a long pause he said, 'Not exactly.'

'What does that mean . . . "not exactly"?'

There was another awkward pause while I could almost hear Dodd's mental wheels turning. Finally he said, 'This is a very delicate situation, Father. Very tricky. I can't even tell you all the politics involved.'

'Stop dissembling, Jimmy.'

The sound of Dodd sighing. 'Okay, look. Here's the deal. The lady of the house came to me first, asked for help. I understand the daughter's also involved.'

'What's the problem?'

'The problem is the man of the house. He's not exactly . . .' Dodd's voice trailed off.

'So the father's a skeptic,' I said, finishing the thought for him.

'That's putting it lightly,' Dodd said. 'The father is adamant, completely adamant. He wants no more talk of spirits or infestations.'

'That makes this all a little harder, Jimmy.'

'I know,' he said.

I asked him if this was why we were sneaking in furtively.

'That's right—the father's away on urgent business today,' Dodd said. 'Mother and daughter will keep a low profile while you're there. The housekeeper will let us in . . . and there'll be a few service personnel. That's about it.'

I thought about that for a moment. 'You know, Jimmy, it might take us a while . . . to complete the blessing.'

'I know, Father. Don't worry about it. I don't expect you

to come in like the Lone Ranger and fix the problem in one fell swoop.'

Then we drove on in silence for several miles.

Eventually the car made its way out of the piled-up traffic, and whisked around a series of tight curves. I figured we were entering a residential area, or had maybe even reached the outskirts of town. I could hear the telltale noise of the wheels crunching on deeper snow and we came to a full stop several times—probably at country crossroads—then continued mysteriously through a series of turns. At one point I thought I felt the car rumble over a speed-bump.

Finally the large vehicle slowed to a crawl, and it became real quiet, so I figured we must be inside a garage now.

The car glided to a stop, and all I could hear in the silence were dripping noises, and the engine ticking as it cooled.

'Wait here for a second, Father, I'll be right back.' Then Dodd was opening his door and climbing out.

I sat there in the stillness for a while, my ears ringing.

A moment later, Dodd was back. 'Okay, we're all set,' he said, his voice close to my ear, suggesting that he was leaning into the car. All of a sudden his hands were on my shoulder, gently urging me out of the vehicle.

'We're gonna go in the back way. You can leave your stuff in the car for now. We'll just go in and get the lay of the land first.'

We shuffled across a hard cement floor, then passed through a doorway and were outside again. I could feel snow on my face again, harsher than before, its flakes as sharp as broken diamonds. The wind had picked up further, and we were obviously in for a doozy of a blizzard. I thought I could hear distant voices, maybe the faint drone of a highway, but at this point I wasn't sure. Besides, I was too busy trying to keep up with Dodd, who was ushering me over the icy surface at a fast clip.

We reached a sidewalk, a crust of ice crackling beneath our feet.

'Okay, slow down now, Padre.' Dodd squeezed my arm again. 'There's a flight of stone steps, about a dozen, right in front of you. They haven't been shoveled yet, so they're kind of icy.'

I felt my way gingerly up them.

'That's good, good,' Dodd was saying. 'Okay, now we're gonna turn to the right, and our friend is going to let us in through the service entrance.'

The door creaked open and I stepped inside.

'Okay, that's great, great. Let's pause here for just a second,' Dodd continued, holding me steady.

All of a sudden, powerful feelings began bombarding me, and it started with the air itself. It was warm and seemed to weigh a ton, laden with must and layers of old furniture wax. It was a rich, timeworn smell, like in the back room of a museum, and it had a patina of oily resin over it that reminded me of ancient treasures that have been well cared for. It was the smell of 'old money.' The floor beneath me was hard and cold—probably antique parquet—and the sound of footsteps was fading away down some nearby passage. There was static sizzling across the darkness of my mind's eye, like a shortwave radio barely receiving regiments of distress calls.

A lot of dramatic things had occurred in this house. And I could feel them.

'What's happening?' I whispered at last.

'Everything's fine, just fine,' Dodd muttered. 'Just give me a second, Father.'

I waited on the cool parquet, listening to Dodd's footsteps heading off down an adjacent corridor, then pausing, then heading back toward me. 'What's going on, Jimmy?' I said.

'Almost ready,' he whispered.

'I'm dying here, Jimmy. Can I lose the blindfold?'

'Gotta get you into the room itself first.'

'What room?'

'The library.'

'Why the library?'

'That's where most of the disturbances have occurred.'

'All right . . . lead the way,' I whispered, the back of my neck prickling.

We shuffled slowly along, our wet boots squeaking on the hardwood.

It took almost five minutes to negotiate the narrow turns and the staircases. There felt something vaguely grim about this place, like we were walking along the corridor on death row, and each footstep raised new hackles along my spine. It was as though the very air were vibrating with rancid energy. And the dark, blank screen of my mind started to flash with odd shapes and dream images—hazy but powerful, and all making me dizzy as hell.

At last I felt Dodd's hand tighten on my elbow.

'We're now outside the library door,' he murmured. 'Once we're inside, you can take off the blindfold.'

'Ready, Jimmy . . . I'm ready to get to work.'

The door creaked open, and we stepped inside a room reeking of ancient bindings and yellowing paper. I heard the door click shut behind me. 'Okay, Padre,' Dodd's voice said, 'let there be light.'

He peeled away my blindfold.

And for just an instant it was like the whole room was shrieking at me.

2. The Opposite of Human

The room was calling out to me. That's the only way I can explain it. It was calling out to me in some inhuman tongue. And I was blinking and squinting, my eyes watering, struggling to see through the bone-white light. I almost collapsed right then from the dizziness, but Dodd steadied me by grasping me by the shoulders.

I remember wiping my eyes, trying to take in the whole room.

On the surface it wasn't much more than a gentleman's study, decorated in conservative French Provincial style. Nice, tidy, but nothing extravagant. The wainscoted walls were painted white, with crown moldings all around, and shelves brimming with old volumes: Reference books and classics. There was a jeweled chandelier overhead, and a round mahogany table placed in the center of a colorful Persian rug. There were also fresh flowers in expensive vases: Carnations and lilies in bright salmon pinks and yellows. It was all very tasteful, staid, rich . . . very old-money.

But I knew immediately there was another dimension to this room, a dimension just beneath the surface. I had felt this kind of presence before—in the Robert Taylor Homes, and also on a trip I took to Auschwitz with the Catholic missionaries. It was like an imperfection in a camera lens pointed towards the sun. It was the opposite of sound, the opposite of light. Like I said, the opposite of human. It was like a silent black depth-charge erupting in my brain, calling out in waves, crashing against my soul—

HATE!

I doubled over suddenly, as though punched in the gut, but Dodd steadied me.

'Are you okay? Father?'

'Dear God, dear God . . .' That was about all I could muster at that point.

'What is it?' Dodd was asking me.

'I have to leave this place,' I managed to utter.

'What are you talking about?'

'I have to leave . . .'

'What is it, Father?' Dodd sounded irritated. 'What's going on?'

I tried to explain to him but, before I could get any more words out, another silent blast struck me—like a hard jab to the ribs—and I reeled backward. And then, as I gazed up at the tasteful colonial decor, I swear to the Lord I saw the surfaces of the room peeling away like black photographic negatives curling under intense heat. In my mind's eye the walls were wavering in and out of focus. And I knew what was happening. I knew. I knew precisely what was going on.

The true nature of that room was revealing itself, like the skin of a snake peeling away, and underneath was a cancer, like a sediment of human suffering distilled into rotting, diseased parchment.

'Father, talk to me,' Dodd was saying, his voice coming from a million light years away. 'What is it? What's wrong?'

'I have to—'

Then the odor struck me, choking the words out of my throat. I fell to my knees, flailing at the air like I was sparring with the Devil, but my gestures were futile. The smell permeated everything, and it was that old familiar odor that I could never forget as long as I lived. The odor of bestiality, of sickness, of death—but this time stronger than ever before. It's like I could smell it with my nerve endings, with my pores, with my eyes, and with my ears—

HATE!-HATE!-HATE!-HATE!-HATE!

'Father! What are you doing?'

Before I knew what was happening, I was crawling

toward the door. I was murmuring litanies, ' "God of heaven, God of earth, God of angels, God of archangels—" '

'Father, wait!'

Somehow I told him I had to get out of there, I had to leave this place.

I reached the door and clawed at the knob, my sweat-slick fingers fumbling with it. Something was coalescing behind me, something from the shadows, something huge and malignant and very angry. But before it could reach out for me, I got the door open and careened out into the corridor. There I collapsed onto the hardwood floor.

'Father, wait a second—the blindfold!' Dodd was rushing toward me.

I rose up on my knees and vomited.

It roared out of me and spattered across an Oriental carpet-runner and a length of varnished baseboard. Dodd appeared behind me, reached down and tried to help me up, but I was heaving with involuntary spasms now. It was pretty awful. The bile was acid-hot in my throat, and I nearly choked on it.

Eventually I vomited out the last of my stomach acids, and I collapsed onto my side. Dodd knelt down beside me, patting my back, whispering, 'You okay, Padre?'

I think I uttered something like, 'Peachy,' and wiped my mouth, getting my bearings. I heard footsteps coming down a corridor fast and furious, rushing toward us.

'We gotta get moving,' Dodd said grimly.

At that point I looked up and saw the girl.

She had come suddenly around the corner, a skinny little waif in a black leather jacket, torn leggings and big black army boots, like some pint-sized stormtrooper. Approaching cautiously, she seemed to take in the entire scene all at once with her big intelligent doe eyes, but she didn't say anything at first. Just stood there with hands on hips—suspicious, wired. She wore a Public Enemy T-shirt underneath her jacket, and her bottle-blonde hair was buzz-cut along one side, a streak of lime green down one tendril on the other.

I blinked. Even in the throes of my nausea and fear, I felt something strange as I made eye-contact with this girl. An odd connection. Did I know her from somewhere? She looked so familiar; was she famous?

The girl took another step toward us. 'Who puked?' she said, pointing toward the rug.

'Melissa, please,' Dodd said urgently, 'go back to your room.'

The girl put her hands back on her hips. 'Fuck you too, James. You guys have really bad timing.'

Dodd stared at her. 'What's the matter?'

'Burke is on his way.'

'Burke?' Dodd seemed frozen at the mention of the name.

'He somehow found out about your little visit,' the girl went on. 'He's on his way right now with a couple of goons from the SS.'

Dodd wrestled me to my feet. 'The blindfold, Padre, quick. Please put the blindfold on.'

The girl said: 'You can still beat 'em if you take the south drive.'

'Come on, Father!' Dodd fumbled with the blindfold, pulling it back over my eyes. I was still reeling from my violent retching, and now I was blind again.

And then we were moving again, faster than before. I felt myself being hurtled back down the corridor, back toward the shadows from which we had come. I could hear Dodd's anxious breathing right next to me, and my own heartbeat pulsing noisily in my ears . . . and the girl's voice, receding into the corridor behind us.

'Better hurry, guys, the brownshirts are coming.'

3. Dark Heart

Despite my grogginess, it took us less than four minutes to make it back through a labyrinth of hallways, stairwells and anterooms. We would have made it even faster, but I tripped a couple of times, then Dodd managed to take a wrong turn at the end of the central corridor.

Eventually we were scuttling along that familiar parquet hall again, heading toward the service door.

'Quick, Father, turn immediate right here. NOW!'

I stumbled out through the door.

The sudden wet wind on my face sent starbursts across my blinded vision, and shivers up my spine. Though this was bracing, dizziness still hobbled me and my joints felt like ground glass. I started to stagger down the icy steps, Dodd's vice-like grip on my elbow pulling me along.

'Hold it!' A voice pierced the silence behind us like a pistol shot. Presumably some security guard hollering at us from about a hundred yards away. He sounded more surprised than hostile.

'Keep moving, Father. Keep moving!' Dodd was urging me onwards as fast as he could manage.

Another voice: 'Dodd, hold on a second! Burke wants to see you!'

Then I heard Dodd's voice right beside me: 'Can't talk right now, boys. Family emergency!'

We had now reached the garage—or whatever it was—and I careened through the door, tripping on the threshold. We shuffled frantically across the cement floor, our huffing-puffing breaths echoing loudly, till finally we reached the vehicle we had arrived in. Dodd tore open the front passenger door and quickly shoved me inside. I banged my head against the door jamb, knocking my blindfold out of kilter. Now I could partially see through one eye—albeit blearily—as Dodd hopped behind the steering wheel and fired up the engine.

All sorts of things began registering in my one light-stricken eye. We were indeed in a garage, and it was drenched with fluorescent light and filled with similar cars, some of them unmarked cop cars maybe, and several black limousines, and the door at the far end was rising up, letting in a dull glow of overcast daylight. I blinked, wrestling with the blindfold.

Finally I tore it off, just as Dodd was pulling out through the exit.

My senses were bombarded by the gale of snow lashing at the windshield. It made my eyes ache. I tried to focus on the stretch of icy road surface ahead of us, but now things were happening very quickly. Dodd was pushing the car as fast as it would go in such conditions, and veils of snow were obscuring nearly everything. I saw vague outlines of buildings in the middle distance, and figures emerging from the trees on either side of the road ahead. They were dressed in identical dark parkas, wearing headsets and with automatic weapons cradled in their arms. By now Dodd was cursing loudly, pedal right to the floor, and the Cadillac was swerving and sliding toward a huge wrought-iron gate. And everything was starting to look vaguely familiar . . .

And all at once I realized why—and why Dodd had been so secretive, and why there had been such a production number just to get me inside this place, and why we were now surrounded by men in identical parkas. The answer was right there—rising as large as life behind us.

Viewed through the rear window—and through a haze of wind-blown snow—the building maybe lost some of its majesty. But it was still an awesome edifice and, apart from other buildings clustered nearby, it would have looked just like any other opulent plantation house you would see dotting the Virginia pastures in the nineteenth century.

As our car skidded across the icy macadam toward the gates, the north portico came clearly into view behind us: Its breathtaking Doric columns rising three stories high, dominating a façade familiar from countless American tourist artifacts and from the twenty-dollar bill.

There loomed one of the most famous buildings in the world.

And deep down inside it a dark heart was festering.

CHAPTER FIVE

The Black Door

1. Out of Control

Held in the grip of that terrible moment, our car sliding toward the eight-foot-high gates, the snow relentlessly strafing our windshield, I still had no idea of all the different kinds of trouble we were getting ourselves into. I had no idea what kind of breach of security Dodd had visited upon his employer's headquarters, or how many government agencies were at this precise moment putting us on their highest-priority lists, or even the depth and variety of security measures surrounding us at that very instant. As our car careered across that icy stretch on the edge of the White House lawn, trundling toward the south-east exit, I was even ignorant of the fact that we were being tracked by the most sophisticated home-security system in the world.

As I found out later, there are eight entrances to the White House grounds: Two on Pennsylvania Avenue, three on Seventeenth Street and three on Fifteenth Street—none of which are open to the public. Gone are the days of balloon salesmen and bucolic sight-seeing strolls across the edge of the north lawn, or the days of Easter-egg hunts and solemn suffragettes protesting outside Warren G. Harding's bedroom window. We live in an era under siege—with dime-store assault rifles and Prozac-fueled gunmen aiming their single-engine Cessnas at the President's balcony. The White House had become a fortress.

Take the guard-post buildings, for instance. There were eight of them—one at each exit—complete with bulletproof glass windows and a minimum of two White House policemen in each. There were a dozen roving guards on patrol that day—each of them packing semi-automatic weapons—sweeping the grounds on regular shifts. There was also a couple of police dogs sniffing for bombs and weapons and suspicious-looking intruders. There were also fence sensors spanning the entire eighteen-acre lot, and vibration sensors buried at regular intervals just beneath the surface of the lawn. There was even a microwave Doppler-radar unit aimed at the airspace above the house, along with two anti-aircraft bazookas armed with heat-seeking stingers on the roof of the west wing.

But none of that seemed to matter to Dodd as we skidded sideways toward those imposing iron gates. Not the guards with their assault rifles, or the dogs charging toward us through the snow, or the sounds of secret-service agents signaling to each other above the howling winds, across the edge of the front portico. None of that mattered, because right at that moment Dodd had lost control of the Cadillac.

And the wrought-iron fence was looming.

2. Trapped Inside its Secrets

The car slammed into the fence, its impact loud and jarring, rattling the Cadillac down to its chassis. It whiplashed me sideways, and I smashed into the window, my teeth clicking in my skull. The big vehicle came to a stop at an angle to the fence. And for a moment I was so stunned I didn't realize what was happening. I just sat there, my ears ringing, the wind and snow swirling around the car. The Caddy's horn was beeping rhythmically; its anti-theft system had evidently been rattled awake.

I tried to move, but Dodd's hand pressed down on my shoulder. 'Let me do the talking,' he muttered, craning his neck to see over one shoulder.

There were three figures trudging shin-deep across the snow-covered south lawn. Two of them were security guards—I could tell from their uniforms—and the third was a tall young black man wearing an overcoat and headset. I guessed he was secret service. The guards held their rifles at the ready—not aimed exactly, but at the ready. The rest of the security circus—the dogs and the patrolmen—were already standing down and returning to their posts.

I started to say something, but Dodd shushed me. The black man was now approaching the driver's door.

Dodd reached inside his breast pocket, pulled out a laminate ID card, then opened his door to get out.

'Put the goddamn pass away, Dodd, I know who you are,' the young agent said with disgust.

At that point, a gust of frigid wind whistled through the open door, and I had trouble hearing exactly what they were saying. I was cold and I was bruised from the collision and my heart was doing the mambo in my chest, but I focused as best I could on their conversation. Here's what I think they were saying:

'This thing was supposed to be under the radar,' Dodd began explaining.

'Excuse me!' the black guy was barking at him.

'I'm trying to tell you—'

'Excuse me!'

'I'm trying—'

'Excuse me, please! Burke has warned you about this kind of thing.'

'Redding, listen to me, just listen,' Dodd was saying. 'This whole thing comes straight from the third floor.'

'I don't care if it came from the goddamn Eagle!' the man named Redding replied. I found out later that 'the Eagle' was the security moniker given by the secret service to the President himself. 'The Raven' was the First Lady, and 'the Swan' was their daughter.

'But, wait, wait, Redding. Give me a chance—'

'No, that's not—'

'I'm trying to tell you, the lady asked me to keep this under the radar.'

'Did she also tell you to cause a breach in the whole fucking security system?' Redding was working hard to control his anger, but, even obscured by gusting snow, it was clear that he was livid. Framed by the upturned collar of his London Fog, he had a square jaw and a perfect chocolate egg-cream complexion; he looked like a male model. 'Burke is going to be very unhappy about this business,' he added.

'She was very specific,' Dodd insisted.

'I know all about the Raven,' Redding snapped back at him. 'The old lady's an eccentric, so what? She's got strange ideas about the house—'

'She wanted me to handle this thing.'

'You handled it, all right.'

'Wait, wait just a second. I'm trying to explain something to you.' Dodd was getting upset now. 'I'm trying to tell you, I was acting on the lady's orders. I'm trying to tell you, this was supposed to be a private matter.'

'Bullshit, nothing's a private matter,' the black man shot back.

'Okay, okay, look, here's the thing: This guy in the car, he's a priest—'

'I don't care—'

'I know, I know, I know you don't care, but just hear

me out. He's a priest, and the lady requested I slip him inside without making a big deal about it.'

'Yeah, well—'

'I know, I know, I screwed up. I panicked. Things didn't turn out the way I planned. But here's the thing: He's here now, so why don't we—?'

'Why don't we what? Ignore every procedure in the book?' Redding asked angrily.

Dodd was looking around the lawn. 'I'm just saying, before things get too public—'

'The priest thing is your problem, amigo. You deal with it yourself.'

'I'm telling you, Redding, in about one minute this thing is going to break. I'm just asking you to give me some slack, that's all.'

There was a windy pause, and Redding glanced across the south lawn, and I noticed there were more vehicles coming our way down an adjacent street. There were blue-and-yellow emergency flashers, barely visible in the storm. I didn't know it then, but the street—South Executive Avenue—was closed to the public. These were D.C. police, probably summoned automatically when the system was tripped by Dodd's wild retreat. In the hazy distance, beyond the east wing, out by Pennsylvania Avenue, there were other vehicles, unmarked vans. One of them had a satellite dish on top; more than likely the media. Probably the last thing Dodd or Redding—or anybody affiliated with the White House, for that matter—wanted right then.

'What I'm saying is,' Dodd went on, 'let me bring the priest back in.'

'Whoa!'

'I'm just saying, let me bring the priest back in before this thing ends up in the *Post*.'

'Why? What are you doing, Dodd? What are you doing with this priest?'

Dodd licked his lips nervously, and the wind howled on.

Through the Cadillac's rear window, in the distance, the mansion was barely visible in the white mist. It rose up into the featureless sky, white-on-white, with its Roman columns and soaring balconies. It was so strange looking at it from this angle. It looked strangely shrunken, like a three-quarter-scale model. But there was also something horrible about the house, something that radiated out from it. And I was receiving it loud and clear. It was a bad dream come to life. I had never even been to Washington, D.C. before, and now I was trapped inside its darkest secret.

Beyond the Presidential mansion the unmarked vans were making their way down Executive Avenue, while I was trapped inside that idling Caddy, shivering, listening to the winds wail. I felt like I was being buried by the weight of snow and cold, like that Cadillac was a tomb. The snow now covered the windows. How could Dodd have deceived me like that? And who the hell was he anyway? He sure as hell was no small-time lawyer from Baltimore . . .

'He's here to do a blessing, Redding, that's all,' Dodd was saying. 'At the special request of the First Lady.'

There was another long pause in their dialogue.

Through the open door I could see police cruisers approaching, pulling up behind Redding. The snow made everything seem surreal and gauzy, as though glimpsed through a veil. I could see the police getting out of their cars, talking to the guards while gesturing toward us. Some of them were keeping careful tabs on the gates, making sure no casual onlooker wandered into this unauthorized space.

In the middle distance, the media vans were approaching. They were like sharks smelling blood in the water. And if it weren't for the poor conditions, they would have been here already. I was guessing they would arrive in about sixty seconds.

Finally Redding turned to Dodd and said, 'All right, get him inside quickly, before this thing gets any worse.'

Dodd leaned down and looked inside the car. 'Come on, Father, let's go.'

I couldn't speak. There were so many contrary emotions brewing in me.

'Father, what's the matter? Let's go, come on. We gotta move.'

The media vans were getting closer, shimmying and fishtailing on the snow. Evidently the D.C. police had allowed a couple of them through the cordons. They were going to be all over us in about forty-five seconds.

Finally I managed to say, 'How could you hold out on me like this, Jimmy?'

'What? Oh, Jesus. Okay, look, I was just trying to do my job.'

'I don't like being lied to,' I said, looking him square in the eyes.

'Father, I'm sorry, I'm sorry,' he said. 'You have every right to want to punch me in the face, but if you'd just come inside—'

'I'm not going anywhere,' I said.

He glanced nervously over his shoulder, then back at me. 'Father, now is not the time—'

'Yes, Jimmy, now *is* the time. Now is *exactly* the time. You're gonna give me some answers.'

'What do you want to know?' he replied quickly.

'For starters, who the hell are you—really?'

He licked his lips. 'My official title is Special Counsel to the President of the United States.'

I stared at him, the words sinking in—the horrible surreal truth sinking in.

At last I said, 'I can't go back inside, Jimmy.'

'Why not?'

I began to explain it was because I was no longer an ordained priest.

Dodd burned his gaze into me. 'Father, please, this is not the time.'

I insisted that he needed an ordained priest for something as important as a cleansing in the White House.

Dodd said, 'Father, listen to me. I'm putting my ass way out on the line here.' He glanced over his shoulder at the vans coming slowly through the curtain of white. Another thirty seconds or so and they would be there.

I looked at him and said, 'Jimmy, you lied to me. You blindfolded me and brought me along on a wild-goose chase. I'm too old for this kind of crap.'

'What are you talking about—*too old*? You could beat the shit outta me. Come on, Father, I'm asking you as a friend. For old times' sake. But we gotta get inside now.'

All of a sudden my anger evaporated and I found myself feeling sorry for earnest young James Dodd. So I looked at him and said, 'Jimmy, the truth is, I'm not the man you think I am.'

'Father, please—'

'No, listen to me. I haven't worn the vestments for over twenty years. Sure, I used to carry out blessings of the domicile. I've even done a few blessings off the books over the past few years. But this—Jimmy, this is out of my league.'

He looked at me then for a long, tense moment. Behind him, the vans were looming. Fifteen seconds and they'd be on us.

Finally Jimmy looked deep into my eyes and said, 'You're scared, aren't you?'

'You're damn right I'm scared,' I started to say. 'And you ought to—' I clammed up suddenly, stunned speechless.

I had caught something out of the corner of my eye, in the misty middle distance.

And I just couldn't believe what I was seeing.

3. Invitation to the Dance

At first I thought I was hallucinating. I figured it was all the excitement, all the adrenaline playing tricks on me. But the more I stared at it, the more the thing stubbornly stayed in focus, like a tiny malignant dot on a canvas of white. I wiped the snow from my brow and peered harder, but it would not go away.

Up on the third floor of the mansion, barely visible in the storm, a darker shape nestled among the row of frosted Palladian windows, like a rotten tooth in the center of a smile, occasionally obscured behind clouds of gusting snow. It was a huge, scarred, black oak door, leading straight into the third-floor level, way off the ground. It was the ugliest door in the world. The door from my nightmares.

The door to little Eric Rivers' bedroom.

Then I blinked, and the door wasn't there anymore.

And now I knew what was happening. I was sure of it. Whatever was in that house had acknowledged me personally, so I realized I probably never really had any choice in the first place. It was that same dark fate again, and I knew I couldn't run away anymore. I had to go back inside that building.

I had to.

'All right,' I heard myself say to Dodd.

'All right, what?' he said.

I told him I would go back inside.

'Great,' he said. 'Come on—'

I grabbed his arm. 'You gotta promise me something, Jimmy,' I said.

'What's that?'

'You gotta promise me you'll follow my instructions totally.'

'Yeah, of course.'

I squeezed his arm for emphasis. 'I mean *to the letter*, Jimmy.'

He looked back at me. 'You got it.'

I nodded, then struggled out of the car and into the icy winds.

We were accompanied back inside the White House by Redding and three of his patrol guards.

The newshounds never even got the chance to plug in their cameras.

Part II

THE MANSION

And I saw, issuing from the mouth of the dragon and from the mouth of the beast and from the mouth of the false prophet, three foul spirits like frogs; for they are demonic spirits, performing signs, who go abroad to the kings of the whole world, to assemble them for battle on the great day of God the Almighty. And they assembled them at a place which is called in Hebrew Armageddon.

Revelation 12:13

CHAPTER SIX

Storm Front

1. Through the Doorway

They continued to make sure I didn't see much of anything.

They took me around to the service entrance on the rear side of the east wing, where the snow was battering the masonry before clinging to the sides of the building. Redding had to blow snow out of the inside of the key-card terminal just to get it unlocked. They finally got the door open, and ushered me inside.

There was a metal sign standing on the threshold that said: *No Tours Today.*

I found out later that the east wing was the public entrance to the White House from which the tour guides embarked on their circuits. Built in 1902, it was connected to the main mansion via an elaborate, vaulted walkway running along at ground level. This corridor was kept in pristine shape, with antique portraits on the walls, gleaming tile floors, and the smell of lemon wax in the air. That day there were tasteful Christmas decorations everywhere: Enormous poinsettias in pots ranged along each side, fresh greenery wrapped around the chandeliers, as well as count- less red-velvet ribbons everywhere. But I took in very little of this as I was ushered through the east wing, catching only glimpses as I was hurried along between Dodd and Redding—almost like a prisoner—and escorted through an emergency door toward the main residence.

One thing I did notice, though: The whole east wing felt as dead and cold as a mounted fish. Again, that's not some sophisticated psychic reaction—I could just feel it. And whatever darkness dwelled in this huge place, it lived further inside, through the arched doorway ahead.

In the main house itself.

As they moved me along quickly, nobody spoke, and the wind sounded just like a freight train outside the windows, rattling the glass and whistling through any cracks and crannies in the old building. My scalp was prickling furiously now, as increasingly the house turned its attention on me. That seems the best way to explain it. Once in a while, back when I was regularly doing the blessings, I would experience exactly the same sort of sensation, and always when entering a house possessed by something otherworldy. It was like walking into the lair of a sleeping animal: You could sense it coming awake.

Its eyelids opening.

They ushered me past a men's washroom and up a small curving flight of stairs, then through a marble anteroom that smelled of sulfur powders and old paint. The portraits on the walls were watching me intently. Abe Lincoln glared, and Millard Fillmore stared, and Ulysses Grant leered at me through deep-set eyes. For a moment, I thought of those old horror flicks where the eyes of paintings track the characters' movements, but I quickly pushed that notion from my mind.

I had read about this kind of thing back in seminary school, before having any experience of it, and remembered obscure texts by a French Jesuit, Pierre Teilhard de Chardin, reporting 'hysterical nausea brought on by two spiritual polarities in a charged setting.' Even the great

Father Lankester Merrin had written about 'a soul falling ill' at the prospect of evil. In all my subsequent experience of cleansing parishioners' homes, I had only felt this a couple of times—and then just fleetingly. But the nausea I felt that afternoon, as I stepped over the threshold into the main residence, was unlike anything I'd ever known.

It started deep in my bowels, like heat worming upward, searing and acrid. And with every new step it resonated inside me like the pluck of a bowstring; rising up and causing my throat to tighten, filling my mouth with a smoldering nausea. At one point I had to stop and clutch onto the edge of a door for support. When Dodd asked if I was okay, I assured him I was feeling just fine, though secretly I was starting to wonder whether I could tough this thing out.

It was all too clear that the house did not want me inside it.

We ended up in a claustrophobic little closet room adjacent to the library.

'Sit here for a second, Father,' Dodd said, indicating a metal stool shoved under a workman's bench.

The room couldn't have been more than a couple of hundred square feet, with a scarred hardwood floor and walls of unfinished timber. There were boxes of cleaning supplies stacked to the ceiling along one wall. The other side of the room was cluttered with electronic surveillance gear, and rows of black-and-white monitors revealing camera shots of various empty rooms. I sat down on the bench and unzipped my parka, taking deep breaths in order to quell my nausea and nerves.

'We'll be right back,' Dodd assured me before they both walked out and locked the door on me from the outside.

At first, it felt rather good to be left alone to catch my breath and to recover my bearings. The silence was even welcome. I wiped moisture from my beard and glanced around the room. In the corner stood a bucket holding a mop and a broom, and a long pole with a hook on it for removing high-up light bulbs. On the workbench was a small plastic radio spattered with old paint.

I turned from it to examine the surveillance equipment . . .

. . . and my heart practically skipped a beat.

2. Empty Rooms

Dead faces were watching me—from every screen. After-images of a ghostly corpse, superimposed over the black-and-white angles of deserted rooms, watched me with feverish interest. Wanting to devour me.

Then I realized this was probably my heightened imagination because the faces had already vanished, like the dying embers of a camera strobe.

I took a deep breath and contained the urge to vomit. I said a couple of Hail Marys and a quick Anima Christi, then I gripped the side of the stool until my nausea settled. Eventually I was calm enough again to think.

I looked back up at the screens.

From this vantage point, the entire White House was laid out before me like a cubist puzzle. The dozens of six-inch video monitors—which were mounted to a pegboard panel—showed flickering wide-angle vistas of historic rooms; rooms I had only read about in school books. But even with my limited knowledge of the White House, I recognized some of them: The old Victorian rosewood furniture of the Lincoln bedroom up on the third floor; the oval blue room on the second floor; and the richly appointed library at ground level—the place where I had first encountered the dark force.

A faint chill slithered up the back of my neck. That library was not right. There was something full of hate in that room, and I was about to go into battle with it, and I was starting to wonder whether I was up to the task. Of course, I still had no real idea how powerful it was. And thank God I didn't.

Sitting there in that tiny closet room, the silence was starting to bother me. There should be people about: This was the White House, for God's sake. Where was everybody? There should have been staff in evidence, and aides and advisors and guards, and even the First Family itself. What was going on here? Staring up at the bank of screens, I now noticed that a few of the monitors were dark, some being labeled 'PRIVATE QUARTERS' and 'WEST WING.' So I realized that most of the normal denizens of the place could be in those rooms. But, still, wouldn't there be just a little more activity?

Finally I got so unnerved by the silence, I turned to the bench next to me and flipped on the radio. It was tuned to an all-news station, and within a couple of minutes the weather forecast came on.

And I then found out why the White House was so deserted that day.

3. Black Ice

'. . . Accuweather predicts that we're in for a long hard night, folks, as D.C. braces itself for one of the worst winter storms seen in quite a while. Stay tuned for emergency road and school closings in and around metro Washington, Arlington, Alexandria and outlying areas. Frigid cold tonight, with gale-force winds up to seventy miles an hour, and subzero temperatures driving the wind-chill factor down to dangerous levels. A low near minus-five is expected tomorrow, with wind-chill as low as forty to forty-five below zero. The D.C. Department of Transportation has issued a travel advisory until further

*notice, with black ice and drifting snow making driving
extremely hazardous. If you're traveling by air either tonight
or tomorrow, you'd be wise to call ahead: Washington
National and Dulles are both reporting cancellations across
the board, and area emergency teams are bracing for a tough
go on the ground. Mayor Williams has issued a city-wide
alert for all emergency crews and snow-removal teams, and
local law-enforcement officials are asking that all public
events be postponed, at least for the duration of the storm . . .'*

At that point, the announcer moved onto a traffic report,
and I switched the radio off.

I had heard enough. I didn't care about Georgetown
traffic, or all the major arteries now crippled by the storm,
or all the alternative routes a citizen might try in order to
make it home that night. At that moment all I cared about—
alone in that cramped and airless security closet—was how
I would manage to face whatever was creeping around the
shadows of that huge house. And was I at all prepared for
what I might find?

Right then I heard a faint voice crackling out of the
wall somewhere.

I glanced around the room, looking for a speaker in the
wall, or maybe some vent or a duct which might be
the source of the voice. Or was it a disembodied voice?
Was it something from the house itself trying to communi-
cate with me? I stood up on wobbly legs and scanned the
room. The voice kept sizzling softly somewhere nearby. No,
wait, I got that wrong. It was a couple of voices.

They were originating from the bank of surveillance
monitors.

I drew closer to the screens and searched through each
of the rooms in turn. Finally I spotted something on the
monitor in the bottom row at the far end. Its label indicated
'GND FLR KITCHEN,' and it gave an unobstructed view of
about half a large, tiled service kitchen. There were huge

stainless-steel counters running down the middle, with racks of gleaming butcher's knives, and industrial-sized pots and pans hanging from the ceiling. At the edge of the screen something was moving.

It was part of a man's shoulder, and I recognized it immediately. The collar of a fancy Burberry overcoat.

Below the screen was a row of rotary dials. I reached over and turned the first one, and the sound of Dodd's voice came squawking through the tiny speaker. I couldn't believe my ears. In all the excitement, these men seemed to have forgotten where they had deposited me. I was in the one place where I could hear everything they had to say about me.

I turned up the volume further and listened carefully.

CHAPTER SEVEN

Ghost Stories

1. Dialog in a Dark Kitchen

'I'm trying to explain to you, we have to let him finish what he started.'

Through the surveillance speaker, Dodd's voice was insistent, but strained. I could see him fidgeting and his body language—what I could register—was full of repressed emotion. He was definitely holding back his anger, because no doubt the mysterious person he was talking to was his superior.

'And I'm trying to tell you, you stepped way over the line,' the other man said, and I could tell this guy radiated authority. He had that kind of deep, patient state-trooper's voice. The kind of voice that asked to see your license, registration and proof-of-insurance . . . then requested you to please step out of your car.

Dodd's reply: 'The lady really wants this thing done, Jerry. What else can I tell ya?'

A pause, and then the other voice. 'The lady swims in the same ocean we all do.'

'Meaning what?'

'There are rules.'

'I understand, but—'

'No, I don't think you do understand.'

After a long pause, Dodd said, 'Go ahead, explain it to me.'

At that point, the two men shifted positions—Dodd fidgeting to one side, and at last the other man coming into view as he paced around the kitchen.

He was tall, thin, athletic looking, in a navy-blue suit. He had dark hair, razor-cut marine style, and was holding a rolled-up sheaf of documents which he waved about to punctuate his points. He had that kind of confident intensity you see in former military officers. I guessed that this was the Burke fellow that Redding had referred to earlier, and I guessed further that he was the head of the White House secret service.

It later turned out I was right on both counts.

'First of all, there are channels,' Burke said. 'I mean correct ways of doing things. We've been through this before, Jim. You should have advised the lady of that, then you could have come up with some excuse and discussed it with me first. Then maybe we could have accommodated you—'

'Come on, Jerry, gimme a break. You think I could have come to you with this?'

'I've been stationed here for three administrations,' Burke said. 'Nothing surprises me anymore.'

'Come on,' Dodd said incredulously. 'What was I supposed to say? "Hey, everybody, I've got an old friend of mine here. And, oh, by the way, he's a defrocked priest."'

'I'm trying to explain something to you,' Burke said sharply. 'There are ways of handling things. You say the lady wants somebody to come do some hocus-pocus on the house—do a blessing, whatever. Okay, fine. But she orders you to do it on the sly. Bring him in during a down day. Bring him in for an hour tops, right? Well, guess what: You're just drawing attention to yourselves by doing it behind our backs. We're gonna find out, Jim. It's what we do. People don't pass wind around here without me knowing about it.'

'Okay, all right, we've established the fact that I screwed up.' Dodd was now partially hidden behind a pot rack. 'But don't you think we ought to let the man finish what he came here for?'

'Far as I'm concerned, he's finished.'

'An hour, Jerry, that's all I'm asking for,' Dodd said.

'We've been through this a million times. You want this guy going to the press?'

Dodd assured the security chief that I would not go to the press, then he continued, 'Besides, he already knows where he is; so what do we have to lose?'

'Yeah,' Burke said, 'that's the problem, isn't it?'

'Look,' Dodd said. 'Bottom line: This guy's a devout former priest.'

Burke looked at him. 'Is that supposed to impress me?'

'He's got ethics,' Dodd went on. 'He's discreet.'

'Yeah, right.'

'It's like attorney–client privilege with them.'

There was a pause as Burke chewed on this. On the tiny screen, I could just see him smirking as he slowly shook his head. Finally he said, 'You realize what the Old Man would do if he found out about this?'

'That's why we're doing it *now*,' Dodd said.

I wondered what he meant by that. I figured the Old Man must be the President himself, but where was the Old Man today? Why was *today* any different?

Burke paced back over to where Dodd was standing, and now both of them were obscured by the pot rack. All I could see was Dodd's shoulder, then half of Burke's face as he leaned in closer for a confidential exchange.

I leaned across and turned the volume up.

'What happened in there, Jim?' Burke was saying.

'Where? The library?'

Burke nodded.

Dodd shrugged. 'I really don't know. But I trust Martin Delaney. I really do.'

Now there was a long pause, and I saw Burke staring at the floor, wiping his mouth with a handkerchief, thinking hard. And I got the feeling that maybe Burke had seen some things here himself over the years while walking the halls and corridors late at night. And maybe that's why, after much deliberation, he looked back at Dodd and said, 'There's a major storm blowing in tonight. I want you to finish your business as soon as possible, then get this guy out of here. Or it's gonna be *my* ass.'

Dodd nodded, and they both turned and walked off-screen.

I turned the monitor down, then felt another shiver flutter down my spine.

2. Private Business

Shortly after that, Dodd returned to the room I was in, with Burke this time.

Introductions were made, and I tried to get a fix on this guy Burke. He had an easy, confident manner and, considering all that I had just heard, he seemed fairly relaxed . . . but there was also an edgy glint in his eyes. He had the eyes of a drill instructor, a man who saw everything. Back in seminary, I had known Jesuits like Burke, and I had never gotten along with them too well. I guess I had always been a little too bohemian for their tastes. But with this guy, I could tell he didn't like me from the very beginning. Or maybe it was just the loose end of having a defrocked priest in his house. One thing was clear, though—it was definitely his house. In his eyes, it was not the President's. Not the First Lady's. Not even the country's. But *his* house.

And I was invading his privacy.

We stood there in awkward silence for a moment, my boots forming a puddle beneath me. I felt dizzy again, and needed some Pepto Bismol. But my bags were still outside in the damaged Cadillac, and for some reason I was reluctant to make any demands just now. There was too much tension already in this crowded room. I could see Burke's eyes scanning the surveillance monitors, and I could see his expression tightening. He looked at me and our eyes locked. And I realized he knew—he knew that I had been eavesdropping on their conversation in the kitchen. A range of emotions crossed his face, and he turned to Dodd, but didn't have to say anything.

You could tell he thought Dodd was an idiot to leave me here in the surveillance room.

Finally I told them I needed my bag, and the tension was broken.

Burke took charge of the situation and sent Redding off to the garage to collect it—the Cadillac had now been stashed safely out of sight. Then Burke and Dodd led me along the ground-floor corridor. As we walked, I continued marveling at how deserted the place was. This definitely did not seem the nation's nerve center I had imagined. The corridor, with its vaulted ceiling and marble walls, resembled a grand museum lobby after hours. There was hardly any sound other than our muffled footsteps on the plush red carpet, and the faint murmur of a steam radiator sputtering somewhere nearby . . . and of course the wind outside.

As we passed a few open doorways I caught glimpses, amid Christmas decorations, of familiar furniture and decor seen in a thousand news programs. Bronze busts of dead presidents stood in the window recesses. Patterned wallpaper commemorated scenes from the War of Independence. A faded presidential seal was emblazoned across a carpet. The footprints of famous diplomats, the invisible stains from countless receptions, the past was hanging in the air . . . weighing down on me, suffocating me.

At last we entered a kitchen—the same one where Dodd and Burke's conversation had taken place—and it looked a lot bigger than it did through a tiny surveillance camera. In fact it was huge: A great bright maze of stainless steel and fluorescent light. And, as I was being led across this big room, I finally got sight of some ordinary White House staff; a couple of domestics emerged through a swinging door way off to my left. Both were black and looked like they had worked here since the days before electricity. And both were wide-eyed with alarm. The heavy-set woman was dressed in white with an apron; the man was a beanpole in a sort of modified butler's uniform.

'Mr. Burke!' the butler called out, moving across the kitchen on his brittle old legs.

'Hold on a second, Father,' Dodd murmured in my ear.

Burke turned to the old-timers. 'What's up, Henry?' he said.

The woman waddled over too, wringing her hands. The man named Henry swallowed hard before speaking. 'Mr. Burke, it's young Miss Melissa,' he said, his tired old eyes jumping with nervous tension in a face like old brown leather. There was just a stubble of gray hair on his head and he looked like a kindly soul who had seen it all.

'It's what?' Burke said, his right hand rising to his ear. He frowned, touching his earpiece, as if listening for something that wasn't there.

'It's young Miss Melissa, sir,' the butler repeated, his Adam's apple bobbing. 'She done locked herself in her room again.'

'She what?' Burke said, and then, before Henry could answer, he turned his wrist toward his mouth. 'Twenty-three, you there? Zorn? Forty-one? Redding?' Burke's frown deepened, and I could now tell something was definitely wrong, not only with the girl named Melissa locking herself in her room, but with the agents' communication system. Burke turned back to the old man. 'What are you talking about, Henry?'

'Mrs. Fallon, sir, she up there right now. She trying to get that door open.'

'Miss Melissa's bedroom?' Burke asked.

The old butler nodded.

And right at that very moment—and it's hard to explain—I heard the house whisper something to me. That's really the only way I can explain it. I knew nobody else was aware of it, because nobody showed any sign. They just went on with their anxious exchange. But I practically fell over when it happened. It was like an echo of a sound without the sound itself: A soft, deep, breathy whisper in my mind. Like the last reverberation you hear upon waking up in a darkened room when someone has just said something right next to you.

But before I could mention it, Burke was moving toward the door.

'You two stay put!' he said, pointing at Dodd and me.

'Wait!' I called after him. He was almost out the door already.

'Not now, Father,' Dodd muttered next to me, clearly not wanting to rankle Burke any further.

Burke paused in the doorway, glancing over his shoulder. 'I need you both to stay *here*,' he said with very little equivocation.

'But I think I might be able to help you,' I told him.

'Father, please . . .' Dodd murmured.

'Private business,' Burke insisted, drilling me with an angry glare. 'And that's the end of this discussion.'

Then he vanished through the doorway.

3. State of Shock

What could I say? How was I supposed to tell that gung-ho military operative that 'his' house was reacting to my presence, whispering messages in my mind? For that matter, how was I supposed to explain it to Dodd without sounding like I was a couple of tacos short of a combination plate? Hell, maybe I *was* losing my mind. I was definitely bug-house loony to stay in that place, what with the storm increasing and all the unmistakable portents. Of course, it wasn't until much later, when I learned just exactly what had happened to Melissa—and what those whispered words had meant—that I realized just how nuts I really was at the time.

For the moment, though, I tried to keep my heart and my mind open for the task at hand.

At least I was in a kitchen. After the earlier nausea my stomach was starting to rumble, and I needed to get something into it as soon as possible. The elderly black woman—she was introduced as Mrs. Whittaker—offered to make whatever I wanted, so I told her that I would have whatever came easiest, just so long as it was relatively bland. I took off my coat and grabbed a seat at the staff table in the rear of the big room. Mrs. Whittaker meanwhile made me a traditional Southern belly-warmer of grits, red-eye gravy, biscuits and honey; and she served it on White House china with a cloth napkin embroidered with the presidential seal. And, for the first time since I had arrived, the surreal quality of this place began to sink in. All the little details—the edible flower on the edge of the plate, the surveillance camera in the corner, even the weather reports on a transistor radio across the room—only added to my sense of dislocation.

And my lingering state of shock.

Dodd sat on my right, sipping strong black coffee, while Henry hovered just off to my left, nervously rubbing gnarled black hands. I wish I could say the food tasted good, but I was feeling too unhinged to enjoy it. It was like scooping moist Styrofoam into my mouth. All I could think about was that weird after-echo that had recently appeared unbidden in my head. That single phrase, clipped like a shorted-out circuit—something to do with the kid, Melissa. But I still couldn't figure out what it meant. The only thing I was sure of was that it was happening right now in some other part of this house. And it was happening to Melissa herself . . .

'I really feel awful about how this all came down,' Dodd started to say.

I looked up at him, then over at Henry, and noticed something glimmering in the old man's hound-dog eyes. Maybe it was sadness, maybe fear, I couldn't tell which. Was he in on this cleansing business, too?

Dodd must have noticed me studying the old butler, because he said, 'Henry's okay, Father. He's one of the people who came forward to report a sighting.'

I looked at the old man. 'Like a hole in the air?' I asked him softly.

The butler nodded. 'Yessir.'

I nodded, then shoveled another spoonful of warm grits into my mouth, though suddenly I could hardly swallow. I turned to Dodd again and said, 'I wish I could say how proud I am of you, Jimmy, getting to work here at the White House, but I'm too damned alarmed by all this.'

'I don't blame you, Father,' he muttered.

I asked him how in God's name he had ever thought he could to pull this exorcism stunt off.

He gave me a kind of lost look. 'To be real honest, Father, I couldn't think of anything else to try.'

I shook my head. 'I'm almost afraid to ask,' I said then, 'but how does the President fit into all this?'

Dodd and Henry exchanged a glance. 'The President is overseas, attending an emergency European summit,' Dodd said finally. 'He's likely to be gone until early next week. Which is precisely why we brought you in at this particular time.'

I had suspected as much. I said to him, 'So you're telling me the President really doesn't know anything at all about this?'

Dodd licked his lips nervously. 'Put it this way,' he said. 'You can only squeeze so many different types of problems into the President's head. Daniel Fallon's a pragmatist and a realist, and he just doesn't have time for something as obscure as . . . a spiritual cleansing in the White House.'

I nodded. Although I wasn't much on politics, I knew enough about President Fallon to understand what Dodd was talking about. The first true libertarian to occupy his office, Daniel Fallon had been elected in a whirlwind of controversy stemming from several campaign promises to 'get the government out of the bedroom.' Fallon had himself been the target of a sleazy exposé exploring his own marital infidelities, and now he was on a mission to clean up what he called 'First Amendment tyranny.' A lot of folks saw this stance as self-serving crap, but enough people had voted for him in November to get him elected by a nose-hair. But then, during his first few weeks in office, came a series of angry speeches calling for a complete overhaul of the media and the campaign process. He droned on and on about how his personal life had no bearing on his ability to do his job—and, of course, this just made life more difficult than ever for his handlers. Call it the Gary Hart syndrome: Either out of pique or because the gauntlet had been thrown down, the press began to apply more scrutiny than ever to Fallon's personal life. So far, they had come up empty-handed. But what if they now learned about a bizarre Catholic ritual being performed in the White House itself— by an excommunicated priest, no less—in order to cleanse the place of evil spirits? What kind of fun would they have with that?

'Burke's right about one thing,' I said flatly.

'What's that?' Dodd said.

I stared at him. 'We definitely need to get this thing over with as soon as possible.'

Right then, Redding came back into the kitchen, hauling my worn canvas duffel bag. I already felt better just having it at my side, especially that leather satchel inside, full of vestments and icons. Redding told us to stay put for another few minutes, because everything was fine upstairs with Melissa and the First Lady, and Burke would be back in a matter of minutes. And then he hurried back out again.

At that point I realized just how very silent the big kitchen had become. All I could hear was the wind again: A low whistling that seemed to surround us. Mrs. Whittaker was gone—she must have slipped out at some point during our conversation with Redding. The huge exhaust fans over the ranges had powered down, and now I could hear a ticking noise like either a clock or a dripping faucet. Whatever it was, it was bothering me. I pushed my plate away and just sat there trying to keep my cool.

Eventually I turned to Dodd. 'So when am I gonna be able to finish what I started?'

'As soon as we get the all-clear from Burke,' he said. 'But before we do anything else, there's somebody I want you to meet.'

'Who's that?'

'Somebody who knows a lot more about this house than I do.'

I didn't ask who that might be, too occupied with my racing thoughts to even care much. I took a deep breath and stifled a belch. It felt as though the food had got lodged halfway down my gullet, and I was freezing now. My khaki pants were still half-soaked from the snow, and even my sweater seemed bone-chillingly cold. But what was bothering me most was the whispery voice in my head.

It would not stop reverberating inside my mind, like some horrible jingle you've heard once and cannot forget. The stakes had been raised. I was no longer standing outside the cage, looking in at the beast; I was connected to it in some way now—connected directly to this house. Whatever was festering there had gotten right into my head, delivering a message meant for my ears only. I was fairly sure the message had something to do with the girl named Melissa, but as yet I had no idea how important it was about to become.

That voice in my head, whispering: *Tonight, tonight, tonight . . .*

CHAPTER EIGHT

Black Snow

1. The Tour

'You're looking at the bumps.'

It was one of the first things that came out of the little man's mouth as we began our secret tour of the White House, an itinerary that would never appear in any guidebook or brochure. This particular tour guide was a little troll in a Savile Row suit, named Henry Tooms. Barrel shaped, with a liver-spotted bald pate and tiny round eyeglasses, Tooms was a professor of Colonial History at Georgetown University. He was also—as Dodd politely explained when making his introductions—the official White House curator. I have to confess, I hated the little bastard the moment I laid eyes on him. I realize that's not very Christian of me, but I couldn't get around the fact that this little pipsqueak was so full of himself. From his birdlike movements to his annoying habit of pursing his lips when others were talking, he always seemed just a bit too superior. But I had the feeling that he wasn't too wild about me, either.

He had met us outside the usher's office off the main entrance hall on the north side, a grand foyer full of chandeliers, marble columns and Victorian doodads. There was a gigantic fake Christmas tree in one corner, but otherwise the emptiness of the place resembled a showroom at a funeral home. Clearly the oncoming storm had driven most of the staff off homewards, so there was now just me, Dodd and this snooty little Tooms character. He was obviously keeping a close eye on me, while I kept an eye on the house.

'Pardon me?' I replied, looking up at him. I was dressed in a fresh sweater, my belly full of antacids, clutching my worn leather satchel like a doctor making a house call. Dodd hovered beside me in his shirtsleeves. I had been staring at a small lump about the size of an egg in the parquet floor, buckling up through a seam between two wooden tiles.

'Those bumps in the flooring—' the professor sniffed, '—they occur elsewhere throughout the house.'

I asked what might have caused them.

'Water damage,' he replied. 'Very unfortunate but, alas, she's a very old building, and the water table is particularly high in this area.' He turned on his heel like a little Nazi. 'If you'll step this way.'

We started across the foyer. The wind was lashing furiously at the vaulted windows behind me, yet I thought I could hear whispers stirring beneath the noise of it, but that was probably just my imagination. Or maybe it was indeed the residual shreds of tormented lives once spent in this place. I found myself remembering how often presidents would enter this building in sound health, but four years later depart as wasted old men: Their hair turned gray, their faces shrunken, their eyes sallow and haunted. You didn't need to be an exorcist to sense the dark forces working on the residents of this place.

'Millions of visitors tromp through this place each year,' Tooms was saying, sounding as though appalled by the idea.

'Tracking mud over two-hundred-year-old Vermont marble, smearing fingerprints over priceless works of art—'

'Professor, we don't have a lot of time,' Dodd interrupted. 'Let's cut to the chase.'

'Forgive me, I apologize,' Tooms said. 'The design is classic Beaux Arts.' He gestured at the high ceiling. 'Four main floors, besides two basements. A hundred and thirty-two rooms. Also thirty-two bathrooms, three elevators, seven staircases . . .'

'And the private quarters are where?' I asked, trying to keep my wits about me while keeping in a prayerful frame of mind. In the old days, I would plan a 'cleansing' like a big prizefight, trying to get a feel for my opponent. Was the dark spirit in my face? Was it a dancer hiding in the shadows, waiting me out on the ropes?

'Living quarters are on the second and third floors,' Tooms replied. 'The ground and the state floors constitute the main public areas, and the second and third floors are more private.'

I asked him if the Lincoln bedroom was on the second or third floor.

'Second,' he said. 'The second floor contains the more formal bedrooms, the Rose suite for instance, and the Monroe room. The third floor was created in 1927 as a more private area for the First Family.'

I asked how many people worked in the place on a normal day.

'Usually over a hundred, but not today.'

'How many today?' I asked.

'I believe we're down to about twelve or thirteen right now.'

'That includes security?'

'That's everybody,' he said. 'And tonight there'll be even less.' He paused for an instant. 'Forecast is predicting one of the worst storms ever seen here.'

Dodd spoke up: 'And that's why we want to keep this business moving along as quickly as possible.'

I told him I would work as fast as I could. Then I remembered something I had been meaning to ask from the moment I had overheard Dodd and Burke's cryptic conversation. I turned to Dodd and said, 'After all the workers go home at night, how many of the staff are live-in?'

There was no reply. Dodd just glanced uneasily at Tooms, and Tooms looked away and continued across the foyer.

'It's not a trick question, Jimmy,' I said, following them across the parquet, feeling every one of my fifty years. My satchel felt as though it weighed a hundred pounds, and my knees were complaining unmercifully, like I had gravel in my joints. The scar tissue from my boxing days had calcified over the years and every once in a while it flared up in my knees.

We reached the east end of the central corridor.

At that point I stopped waiting for an answer, because I found myself staring down along another elegant, carpeted hallway done up in rich tones of red and brown, and it set off all kinds of associations in my mind. I discovered later that it led to the formal and public area of the house, as immortalized in films and news broadcasts: A place of banquets, balls and ceremonies. The six main reception rooms were all visible through the open doorways around me. As I gazed around at them, I felt compelled to say a quick Lord's Prayer.

I reached into my satchel for my crucifix and, as I pulled it out, I saw those doors spontaneously move . . .

One after another, they all slammed shut.

I jumped, and I'm sure Dodd and Tooms jumped as well. There was a moment of tense silence, and it felt as though the air around us had frozen, as though the passage of time had momentarily halted. None of us drew a breath for a full ten seconds, and I noticed that Dodd and Tooms were gazing at each other again with that hard, almost doomed expression.

I glanced along the corridor again, and all those tightly shut doors reminded me of a face concealed by a mask.

I turned to my guides. 'You fellas all right?'

Tooms looked at Dodd and said, 'Do you want to tell him, or shall I?'

2. A Sickness in the Beams

Tooms proceeded to do most of the talking, and I can't say I was shocked by what he had to say; me standing in that cold corridor listening to the wind, holding my bag like a little kid clutching a security blanket. I was certainly not surprised by any of it, after what I had felt previously in the library, or what I had heard whispered in my mind. But still, it was pretty strange to hear it talked of aloud, referring to the Executive Mansion of one's own beloved country.

Bombshell number one: No First Family had spent a single night in the White House since the Truman administration of the late 1940s.

The way Tooms explained it, this had to be one of the most closely guarded secrets—'conspiracies' might be a better word—perpetrated on the American people throughout this country's long and sordid history. The Executive Mansion had become more or less a façade: A sort of decaying ceremonial palace within which the President entertained his guests, held diplomatic functions, and appeared to reside. But for reasons which were becoming painfully obvious to me, the First Family never ever slept overnight in the main residence.

The way it worked was simple. Back in the early fifties—

at the outset of the Cold War—Harry Truman had a series of sub-basements and bomb shelters built under 1600 Pennsylvania Avenue. These were joined by a knot of tunnels, designed to provide the First Family with quick and easy escape in the event of an air raid or incoming missile. One of these tunnels led to Blair House, a venerable old residential building situated diagonally to the White House, just across Lafayette Park.

And the First Family always slept in Blair House.

Always.

Because the White House was rotten. Or, as Calvin Coolidge put it in one of his diaries, 'The place is as sour as a barren cow.'

Which leads me to bombshell number two: The White House had been 'wrong' from the get-go.

It went all the way back to 1798, before the paint was even dry. In their diaries, John and Abigail Adams wrote of putrid smells and knocking sounds, and a phantom wandering the halls at night. And, through the years, this presence must have taken on more and more power, because Dolly Madison wrote of night terrors and 'floors as cold as a tomb.' President Van Buren wrote about deathly sounds that kept him awake at night, coming from *above* the top floor. James Polk's wife Sarah suffered stigmata-like wounds in her sleep, claiming they were the bite marks inflicted by an apparition. Abraham Lincoln was plagued by violent dreams—visions of his own death. His son, Willy Lincoln, died a mysterious death in his sleep in one of the private rooms, and Lincoln wrote of his son's 'terrified expression frozen into his dead angelic face.' Mary Todd Lincoln eventually lost her mind from grief and fear, raving about the pictorial wallpaper coming to life and cursing her in foreign tongues.

The modern era brought no relief; in fact the trouble seemed to be escalating. Grover Cleveland's wife Frances was tormented by the 'black dread' settling over her every night, and secretly called in spirit mediums to identify the presence—remember this was the turn of the century, at the height of spiritualism's popularity—but the tampering only made things worse. Teddy Roosevelt was among the modern presidents who allowed his family to occasionally sleep off-premises at night. Although TR refused to buy into the troubles, he grew tired of hearing his family's complaints of ghostly voices in the walls. Finally Eleanor Roosevelt wrote in her journals of a 'sickness' in the beams and the flooring, as profound as a 'human body racked with consumption.'

The turning point was August 6th, 1945—the day we dropped the Big One on Hiroshima. According to presidential diaries, Harry Truman awoke that night to the sound of voices coming from his personal bathroom. But, when he investigated, he stumbled upon something he couldn't even manage to describe in his diaries. Something really horrible. Psychologists later convinced him it was a delusion compounded by the trauma of ending the war in Japan, but, from that point on, Truman no longer slept in the mansion.

Nor did anyone in his family.

Nor did any member of any other First Family.

The dance had begun.

'But how did all this stay under wraps?' I asked finally, standing there with my knuckles clenched white around the handle of my satchel. We were still alone in that elaborate hallway on the state floor of the White House, and we hadn't come across another single soul since we had emerged on this level. 'What about overnight guests?' I said. 'I mean, you read about people sleeping in the Lincoln bedroom all the time.'

Tooms made a prissy little gesture, wiping his brow with the back of his hand. 'The occasional overnight guest is heavily guarded, and the First Family always plays along right up until bedtime, but they never stay here themselves, never.'

I told him I still couldn't believe this had stayed secret all these years.

Tooms shrugged. 'The fact is, it hasn't stayed completely under wraps.'

I told him I didn't understand.

Dodd spoke up: 'Father, look. We realize this is not common knowledge, that the First Families are sleeping somewhere other than inside the White House. But there are bits and pieces of the problem—if you can call it that—floating around all the time.'

'I still don't follow, Jimmy.'

'Ever heard about Nixon talking to the portraits of dead presidents?'

I gave him a sidelong glance. 'You're not telling me . . .?'

'Mrs. Reagan consulting psychics?' Tooms offered, his brow furrowed.

'Happens a lot,' Dodd said, 'stuff like that seeping out. I could tell you other stories you wouldn't believe.'

At first I thought he was joking, but his face told me everything I needed to know. I stood there for a moment, listening to the wind mewling through a distant window-pane, a spider of chills crawling up my legs. Cramps were starting to knife through my gut. Was that due to Mrs. Whittaker's red-eye gravy?

'But now Mrs. Fallon wants to break with this unpub-licized tradition,' Dodd said.

'To say the least,' Tooms added with a roll of the eyes.

'Meaning?' I asked.

Dodd looked at me. 'It's because she believes something can be done about this thing . . . that's why you're here. She's adamant about it. She wants to see this thing through, and so does her daughter.'

I told him I still wasn't following.

Dodd sighed. 'For the first time in fifty-some years, members of the First Family are staying overnight in this place.'

I stared at him a long moment, hearing that whispered warning in my mind's ear.

. . . tonight . . .

3. Trapped

It took about an hour to tour the rest of the mansion. We started with the public rooms on the first two floors. Then came the service areas underneath—the kitchens, the rest rooms, the maintenance rooms—and finally the private quarters on the third floor. I tried to stay focused on prayer, paying close attention to those places suffering from the most frequent disturbances.

Tooms called them 'trouble areas,' and Dodd called them 'hot-spots,' and I understand the First Lady referred to them as 'bad places.' The East Room was one such: A huge, drafty Victorian ballroom on the first floor, a place of pomp and circumstance—and so much pain. During the Civil War, dying soldiers had breathed their last in that room. And, later, Abraham Lincoln had lain in state there, under walls and ceiling draped in black bunting. The air was so thick with the past—with trauma and emotion—it almost crackled as we passed through it. The hundred-year-old parquet floor was ravaged with water damage. I counted half a dozen more of those strange lumps in its oak surface.

And, as we moved from room to room, I laid the ground-work of my cleansing. In the map room where Ida McKinley once wrote of the 'horrendous odor of death,' I recited a Hail Mary and genuflected in each direction. In the state dining room on the second floor, where Warren G. Harding reported 'infernal black stains' that would reappear 'regard-less of the cleaning method employed,' I did a Pater Noster and sprinkled holy water. In the private dining pantry, where LBJ's butler wrote of bare light bulbs 'exploding like fire crackers,' I recited three Glorias and a Salve Regina. And in the library, the place in which that dark entity had first called out to me in waves of hate, leaving me puking my guts out, I offered my best Anima Christi.

But the further I got in the process, the more my guts screamed for relief. It started deep in my intestines as cramps, and by the time we got to the private quarters on the top floor I was walking with a limp, hunched over, clasping my belly with my free hand as though my innards were about to spill out.

Dodd finally noticed my discomfort. 'You all right, Father?' He was standing outside the Lincoln bedroom, nervously fiddling with his beeper. Tooms was standing beside him, wiping his nose with a monogrammed hankie, his eyes shifting nervously. I could hear the storm outside intensifying.

'Yeah, I'm fine,' I told him. 'I just don't think those grits could have agreed with me.'

Tooms was eyeing his Rolex. 'I wonder if we might finish things up soon?'

Dodd shot him an angry glance. 'You'll be on your way shortly, Professor. Don't worry about it.'

I turned toward the bedroom doorway, reaching into my satchel for my hymnal and crucifix. And a sudden increasing pain tore through my midsection.

I gasped and staggered backward. I didn't realize it then, but the cramps were reacting to my prayers, my vestments, the slightest contact between my fingertip and the Bible page. The house was reacting to me like white blood cells attacking a virus.

'Oh boy,' I grunted. And I must have looked pretty

awful then because Dodd and Tooms came over to me immediately.

Dodd tried to steady me. 'Father, what is it?'

'I need to . . . I mean . . . can you show me the nearest . . .?'

'Restroom?' Dodd enquired, practically holding me upright by then.

I managed to nod.

'This way, this way.' He ushered me past the Lincoln bedroom, down the hall, past another doorway, and into a smaller bedroom. There was a small bathroom at the corner of the room. I grunted a thank-you and slipped inside.

It was a modest little john with beige tiles and French Provincial fixtures, though to be honest I didn't really notice the decor. I was too busy with the pressure working through my bowels, and I felt as if I was about to erupt. I slammed the door shut and stumbled over to the commode, pulling my pants down and dropping my satchel. I made it in the nick of time.

Now, I don't mean to make anybody sick—nobody wants an elaborate narrative of somebody else's bowel movements—but I think this was another turning point. Bloody bile roared out of me from both ends. I've never experienced anything like it. For several moments I vomited and shat uncontrollably, like a pressure cooker finally boiling over. And, good Lord, the pain—the pain was beyond anything I had ever endured.

I don't know how much time passed before I could finally breathe normally again. Then I cleaned myself up and just sat there like a limp rag, my stomach scoured out, my lower regions still throbbing.

And that's when I started getting steamed up. It was as though the house had thrown the first punch, and it was way below the belt—literally! And that touched off some wellspring of anger in me. I kicked the wall and I cursed under my breath—yes, priests swear like everybody else; especially ex-priests—and I thought about just walking out. I thought about telling that drafty old pit of a house to go to hell, and I thought about telling Dodd to stick the cleansing up his ass. I reached down and angrily yanked open my satchel and found that dented flask tucked underneath the vestments.

Holding my breath, I guzzled the cheap Irish firewater. The warmth coated my sore stomach for a moment, and I let out a mad hiss between my clenched teeth. I tucked the flask back into the satchel. Rage was boiling in me. I felt like driving a fist through the tile wall. A cold sweat had popped across my forehead, and I could smell myself all over the porcelain. And there was something else bothering me all of a sudden, something urgent jolting through my brain, something vague but powerful.

Something was happening.

I looked up at the window—a small decorative porthole above the toilet-paper dispenser—which must look out over the north lawn. It was of dimpled glass, and let in only a faint glow of diffuse light, but that light was slowly but surely being swallowed up. I managed to stand and peer through the window. The outside was barely visible due to the snow clinging to the window, and the last of the light was definitely dwindling.

Outside, something suddenly brushed past the window, as faint as a whisper. It left a tiny streak across the fogged glass. Then another one, leaving another streak. The wind surged, and the bathroom grew dark, and I finally realized what was happening. Picking up my satchel, I heard again those whispery words in the back of my head (. . . *tonight, tonight, tonight* . . .) and I stared again at the window. The marks across the glass were forming a familiar shape. Five parallel streaks: A handprint. As though someone outside was clawing at the glass.

But then I realized this handprint was forming on the inside of the pane.

On the inside?

'Okay, I get it!' I said, glancing around the bathroom, addressing the house as though it was waiting for a reply. 'I'm ready, you son of a bitch! Bring it on! I'm waiting! Get on with it!'

A muffled gust of wind buffeted the window.

I stood there, breathing hard, staring at it. It looked as though some invisible hand was struggling to get out. Outside, even the snow was turning black, and soon there was nothing but pitch darkness in that little bathroom.

Finally I tore myself away, threw open the door and rushed out into the bedroom.

Dodd stood there looking worried. When I came bounding out, I nearly crashed into his arms. 'What? *What?*' he said. 'What is it?'

My heart was beating like a tympani drum. I clenched my fists, huffing and puffing like a fighter waiting for the bell.

'Jimmy, listen. I've gotta meet the mother and the daughter as soon as possible. I don't want them spending the night in this place. I want them out of here.'

Dodd glanced at Tooms, then looked back at me. He shrugged. 'Good luck, then,' he said.

He led me out of the bedroom and down the hall.

CHAPTER NINE

The Perfumed Corpse

1. Hollowed-out Eyes

At first glance, the second floor of the White House seems like an old Victorian hotel. The corridors look a little run-down, the rich carpet runners have seen better days, and the decorations—the antique vases and hundred-year-old portraits—have all congealed in their places like fossilized butterflies pinned to a plaque. The air smells of ancient paint sediment and cleaning fluid, and the lighting in the corridor is lower and more subdued than in the public areas.

It was here that I met the First Lady of the United States of America.

Suzanne Fallon stood smoking nervously at the west end of the corridor, just outside a sitting room. Burke was standing nearby, his hands clasped behind his back, his eyes constantly scanning the passage. There were strands of Christmas garland draped from the crown molding, and a tasteful little string of tiny white lights around the doorway. Mrs. Fallon was a stick-figure of a woman, as thin as a razor, dressed in a severe blue skirt and white brocaded top. As I approached—with Dodd and Tooms on either side of me—her eyes rose from the floor and met mine, and something painful was exchanged. That's the best way I can describe it.

'Suzanne, I'd like you to meet a dear friend of mine,' Dodd said as we approached. 'Martin Delaney.'

I extended my hand, and she grasped it weakly. Her hand was cold. Her spindly little fingers felt like a dead bird in my grasp.

'It's a pleasure and an honor,' I said finally, feeling strangely humbled by her presence.

'Don't be silly,' she said in a taut, hoarse voice. At this proximity, I got a better view of her face, and I didn't like what I saw. The elegant fashion-model looks had dried up and cracked around the edges. Her once magnificent cheekbones were now skeletal. Her once lustrous straw-berry-blonde hair was now the color of spiderwebs, pulled back into a tight French braid. And her eyes . . . her eyes were tragic. Once full of sparkle and courage and intelli-gence—the subject of countless magazine covers—they were now like hollowed-out cinders. 'I'm the one who should be honored,' she said.

'I don't think so,' I said.

She took a nervous drag off her cigarette, leaving a dark lipstick stain. 'Sorry about the blindfold routine,' she continued. 'We're grasping at straws around here.' I could tell she was sizing me up.

'I don't blame you,' I said.

'I understand they gave you the full tour?'

'Yes, ma'am.'

'And what do you think?'

I told her I thought there was something nasty in this building.

'That's an understatement,' she said softly, then glanced at Burke.

He made a sound like he was clearing his throat, and I could tell we were verging on forbidden territory here:

Letting a civilian like me inside this bizarre conspiracy; letting an outsider see the First Family at its most vulnerable. But then again, I supposed they did not teach secret-service agents how to deal with evil incarnate. A few feet away, Professor Tooms looked like he wanted to crawl into a hole and die.

I tried to smile. 'I promise you, Mrs. Fallon, I will do everything in my power.'

'Call me Suzanne, please.'

I said, 'Okay . . . Suzanne.'

She puffed at her cigarette again and looked away for a moment. I got the feeling there was something else she wanted to tell me. Finally she looked at me and said, 'You realize we're not Catholic?'

I told her that was no problem, and the blessings I performed were equal-opportunity.

'We don't even go to church anymore,' she said bitterly. 'Not seriously anyway. We only show up when the media's around—'

'Suzanne—?'

'—which is par for the course around here,' she went on, flicking ash on the floor. 'Everything's just a big charade for the cameras.'

I could see she was near the end of her tether, and it was not a pretty sight. This was the same woman who had risen from an impoverished childhood in rural Illinois, earning her law degree from Harvard before she was twenty-five, and becoming a shrewd political advisor to her paramour Daniel Fallon by the time she was thirty. The same woman who had bravely appeared on *Good Morning America* the day after her husband's latest affair had broken in all the tabloids, defending him to the end. This same woman seemed now a brittle shell about to crack.

I told her I didn't think it was at all a good idea for her to stay in the White House that night.

She looked at me like I had just thrown cold water on her. She took another nervous drag and said, 'I'm *not* going to let it chase me out of here tonight.'

'I understand how you feel, but it might be better—'

'Don't tell me *you're* going to start heavying me about this,' she said. 'It seems nobody wants me to sleep in my own bed.'

'It's not that . . .' I started to say, and then stopped short. I thought I had heard something strange off to my left—like a cracking sound. Not like glass cracking exactly, but something under pressure.

Burke was looking around too, his eyes sharp and wide. 'What was that?'

I listened intently, but the sound had already faded away, and now only the wind could be heard clawing at the windows. I looked at my watch, and saw that it was edging toward five p.m. It was already well into dusk, and there was no telling how bad this storm was going to get.

Burke was murmuring orders into the tiny transmitter fitted inside his cuff.

I turned to Mrs. Fallon. 'Suzanne, I wonder if I might meet your daughter.'

There was an awkward silence. Burke glanced at Dodd, and Dodd looked at Suzanne, then Suzanne emitted a terse, painful sigh. 'My daughter's ill,' she said at last.

'Is she still here in the house?'

'Yes, upstairs in our private quarters.'

'She's alone?'

'Redding is with her. Why do you ask?'

'When you say she's ill, what exactly do you mean? Is she running a temperature?'

Suzanne looked at Burke, who was getting more fidgety with each passing moment. Another cracking noise echoed through the shadows behind us, this time from the other end of the corridor. I wondered if it was a windowpane cracking from the cold.

Then there was silence.

'It's probably just exhaustion,' Suzanne finally said. 'My daughter's a little highly strung.'

'I'd really like to meet her.'

Suzanne stared at me. 'I didn't want her to get involved in this. I begged her to stay at Blair House tonight. I begged her. Have you ever seen a parent beg her child, Mr. Delaney? It's not a pretty sight.'

I managed a smile, then asked her to call me Martin.

'She's a stubborn girl, Martin. She's like her father.'

'Do you think I could see her?' I repeated.

Suzanne Fallon shrugged. 'Why not?'

She nodded at Burke, and Burke led us across the sitting room to an elevator in the corner. Its doors were already open and waiting.

We rode up in silence, except for the whirr of the lift. I could feel tension like a fog in this enclosed space. Especially from Tooms. I could tell he simply wanted to get out of the place; pearls of sweat glistened on his bald pate, and his hands were trembling. If he had only known the source of those cracking noises, he probably would have jumped out of the nearest window right then and there.

2. An Ancient Hand

Up until the late twenties, the third floor of the Executive Mansion had been used mostly for storage, and the moths and the ants—and the occasional rat—reigned up there in the damp cubicles and unfinished corridors. For generations, the shelves strained under junk from past residents: Trunks of nineteenth-century baby clothing, some of them cast-offs from tragic infant deaths; cartons of speech drafts, war declarations, carbon copies of sympathy letters to the mothers of dead soldiers; even forgotten heirlooms left behind by exhausted tenants, worn down by the stress of the job and the dark gravity of the building itself.

Then, in 1927, Calvin Coolidge commissioned a major renovation. Brand spanking new facilities were installed on the third floor. The hallway was cleared and redecorated; the storage rooms were turned into luxury bedroom suites; and a gorgeous new solarium was constructed, providing First Families with a warm, private setting for morning brunches and afternoon teas far away from the public glare. They even built a fancy sun-porch above the south portico. They called it the 'Sky Parlor,' and it became a favorite haunt of the younger residents. Margaret Truman played ping-pong with her mother up here, and Luci and Lynda Johnson entertained their high-school pals there.

It seemed as though they had successfully swept away all the sadness and grief.

But things were never as they seemed in this place.

Which is exactly what I was learning as the elevator doors opened onto a narrow hallway in the north-west corner of the third floor.

'Melissa's room is on the other side of the penthouse,' Suzanne was saying in her terse, nerve-racked way as we stepped out of the elevator. She was already digging in her cigarette case for another Marlboro Light. She carried the tiny corduroy-covered case in one hand with a wadded Kleenex gripped around it, her bony knuckles so white they looked almost translucent.

We proceeded—Suzanne Fallon, Dodd, Burke, Tooms, and yours truly, still lugging my satchel—down a narrow passage that reminded me of a Motel 6, and then into the main corridor. The atmosphere was completely different up here: More like a suburban home, with paneled walls and Berber carpet. There were personal photographs here and there, and small piles of domestic clutter: Magazines and shopping bags still full of recent purchases. The air smelled of toasted-cheese sandwiches, and muffled music was coming from one of the rooms, the pistol-shot drumbeats of a hip-hop tune; all of which normality only added to the depressing sense of dread hanging in the air. The dark spirit was just as strong up here, maybe even stronger, and this happy-go-lucky sense of family simply drew keener attention to it. It was like somebody had sprayed perfume on a corpse.

We discovered the music was coming from the last bedroom suite on the right—I presumed this must be Melissa's room.

Redding was standing outside the door, like a royal guard in a Brooks Brothers suit, his hands clasped formally behind his back. You could see the tension on his handsome brown face. The house had been working on him, too.

'She give you any more trouble?' Suzanne asked him, as we approached.

'No, ma'am,' Redding said. He had a flat, Eastern-educated accent, with just a hint of street underneath it. I could tell he had worked hard to get rid of his 'black' patois—and that bothered me. There was something about this guy I didn't like. Something about his face.

Burke asked if the girl had tried locking herself in again.

Redding shook his head. 'I disabled the deadbolt. She's just been sitting in there, listening to music.'

Suzanne knocked on the door. 'Honey, it's me. We've got the priest with us.' Then she carefully opened the door, and led us inside the First Daughter's room.

The first things that struck me were the CDs. They were everywhere—stacked in cheap plywood cases crowding three of the walls, crammed into shoeboxes on the dresser and along the window sills. It was a typical college kid's lair, with particle-board furniture and posters of Henry

Miller and Beck. There were a few 'girly' items, like a large bureau and a couple of stuffed animals. But mostly there were the CDs, and a huge sound-system blasting Rage Against the Machine in our faces. And of course, the First Daughter herself, Melissa Fallon, in the corner, staring at us through haunted, dark-shadowed eyes.

'Everything all right, honey?' Suzanne asked loudly, so as to be heard above the music as we cautiously approached.

Melissa was reclining on her bed with her army boots still on, and holding a damp cloth over her head. She looked almost simian to me at that instant, like an exotic animal trapped in a cage, made sick by some horrible parasite. The feisty punker I had seen earlier outside the library was now reduced to a shell of a girl. Her Public Enemy T-shirt was damp, and her face was flushed, and her eyes were either puffy from crying or creased from some horrible internal pain. But when she saw me she lightened up a little bit, propping herself up against the headboard.

Dodd went over to the stereo. 'You mind if I turn this down, Melissa?' he said, reaching for the volume. She didn't say anything as he turned it down.

Suzanne Fallon sat down on the edge of her daughter's bed and reached over to stroke the girl's forehead. 'You feeling all right now, honey?'

Melissa shrugged. 'I haven't decided yet.' She looked up at me with a tepid smile. 'So you're, like, this famous Catholic ghostbuster, huh?'

I moved closer to her bed. 'More like a freelance Bible thumper.'

'That's cool,' she said, again with that wan but cynical smile. 'There's been a spiritual void around here lately.'

I smiled at that one, too. I have to admit I found myself taking to this girl immediately, and I'm pretty sure she had already made up her mind that I was okay myself. She seemed to have one of those quicksilver minds characteristic of a gifted, slightly neurotic twenty-year-old. But it was more than just personal chemistry. There was some other connection firing between us; but at that point I just couldn't tell what. At that point I was too focused on looking for signs of the 'process,' looking for evidence of the oldest struggle in the world.

I had started to say something else when the ceiling creaked suddenly, followed by the muffled runaway-train sound of wind lashing at the building. We were closer to the storm up here, and conditions were obviously reaching the critical point.

'Your mom tells me you're feeling under the weather,' I said to her finally.

'My mom tends to exaggerate,' she said.

I enquired what was wrong with her.

'Nothing much,' she said with a shrug. 'Just a dizzy spell—you know, the usual.'

I asked her to tell me about it.

She sighed. 'It's like I get these headaches, and I start smelling these heinous kinda smells, and then it's like I'm suddenly punched in the face.'

'Do you see things? Visions? Hallucinations?'

She looked at me. 'Yeah, I guess. They're not real distinct. I mean, they're kinda vague.'

I nodded and looked around the room. I could feel the dark force pressuring on the back of my neck like clammy fingers. The heat was building back up in my belly again. I glanced at the girl and saw her left eye was twitching. I'm pretty sure I was the only one who noticed it, and I'm positive I was the only one who recognized the symptom: A sudden cloudiness in one pupil, like a wisp of cream swirling through a cup of coffee, or a milky imperfection in a gemstone. And then it was gone—and it merely looked as though the girl was batting away an insect.

'You okay?' I said, kneeling down next to her bed to take a closer look at her.

'Yeah, I'm cool, I'm totally cool,' she said, laying her hand back on the bed. But her fingers—with their stubby nails painted black—started twitching in tiny little spasms, and curling inward. And for a moment her hand looked ancient.

In all my years, I've never felt goosebumps like the ones that washed over me at that point.

Above us, the wind roared, the cracking sounds echoing out in the corridor.

I looked up at Dodd. 'We gotta get her out of here.'

3. Behind the Walls

'What's wrong, Father? What exactly's the problem?' Dodd said, glancing over at Suzanne Fallon, then glancing back at me, then back at Suzanne again. I could tell he was getting upset. I was starting to frighten the woman, and thus making the secret-service agents skittish, and time was running out.

I turned back to the girl. 'You've heard sounds, here in your bedroom?'

She did not answer at first—just stared at me with those raccoon eyes. Then she said, 'Sure. Doesn't everybody?'

'Under your bed? Behind the walls?'

'I guess, yeah.'

'Like an animal scratching?'

She just chewed her lip some more. The continuing twitches were fairly subtle, like tiny puppet strings were attached to certain muscles at the corner of her mouth, at the corner of one eye. I had to study her closely to observe the symptoms, so I was probably making her fairly nervous. But I wanted to be sure. I wanted to be absolutely sure. Finally she looked back at me and said, 'Did Dodd tell you about the scratching noises? How did you know?'

I confessed that Dodd had told me.

Suzanne reached over and stroked the girl's cheek, then she said, 'Show him your ankles.'

'Mom, can you, like, for once in your life let me speak for myself?'

Suzanne raised her hands in surrender. And right then I realized something important about these two women. On the surface it seemed their relationship was strained, forced, awkward. But I could tell they loved each other—a lot. Emotionally they clung to each other. In fact, I could now tell this hard-shell punker reclining on her bed, spouting her cynical wisecracks, was actually a softy deep down inside. Maybe that's why I liked her so much. She reminded me of my favorite Golden Glove kids, all bark and very little bite.

I looked at Melissa intently. 'Something up with your ankles?'

She rolled her eyes. 'Oh God, this is getting like . . . show and tell.' She sighed dramatically, then reached down to lift the cuffs of her jeans and undo her boots. Then she pulled off her socks and showed me her bare ankles.

I had seen marks like these a couple of times before. Once back in my seminary years, on a trip to the Sudan with the Franciscan missionaries as part of my postgraduate work. While observing a ritual in one of the villages, I saw the same kind of marks all over a young boy's back. The second time was later, in Chicago, during one of my unauthorized 'house calls' on the south side. I saw them on the belly of a sick prostitute at the St. Regis transient hotel. They looked like big egg-shaped welts, the edges deeper and serrated.

Like teeth marks.

'I'm not sure how they happened,' the girl was saying,

staring at the phantom bite marks. 'I felt something suddenly while I was in the shower, like a cold wind round my ankles, and then I looked down and there they were.'

I suppose I must have grunted something or said 'uh-huh' or something.

'Whattya think, Doc?' she said. 'Give it to me straight. I can take it.'

I smiled my best nonchalant smile, trying not to alarm her as she put her socks and boots back on. But, on the inside, I was starting to panic. I was starting to hear again those whispered words in my brain, and starting to feel the night closing in, and time running out. And still those faint cracking noises out in the corridor, just barely audible above the wind—what in God's name was making those noises? I was trying to block all this out of my mind. Of course, the girl probably saw right through me. This kid was too sharp to miss a trick. Trying to change gears, I finally turned toward a shelf of CDs.

'Don't tell me,' I said, spying one of my favorite old records. 'You're a Parliament/Funkadelic fan?'

She cocked her head at me. 'What?'

'Best funk band ever,' I said, and it was the gospel truth, as far as I was concerned. Back in the late seventies, when I had picked up the blues harp and started jamming with bar bands—much to the chagrin of my Jesuit teachers—I started listening to all kinds of black music: R&B, soul, funk . . . James Brown, Herbie Hancock and the Head-hunters, Booker T and the MGs. I'm sure I still have the largest collection of seven-inch Grandmaster Flash records anywhere in the world. 'Nobody could touch George Clinton and Parliament,' I went on, thumbing through her extensive disc collection. 'With the possible exception of Bootsy Collins.'

Melissa was starting to look at me like I had just told

her I was an extraterrestrial. 'A Catholic priest?' she marveled aloud. 'Down with seventies funk?'

'Hey, priests are people too,' I said.

'In a manner of speaking,' she said.

I winked at her. 'We're all *One Nation Under A Groove*, right?'

It was the title of my favorite Funkadelic album.

At that point the girl stared at me silently for a while as I continued thumbing through her collection. I could feel her eyes on the back of my neck, and I could tell she was trying to make up her mind about me. Was I feeding her a bunch of bull, or was I on the level?

At last she said, '*The Clones Of Doctor Funkenstein* is a way better record.'

I smiled and kept thumbing through the discs. 'Been having any nightmares lately?'

After a slight pause, she said, 'Yeah, you could say that.'

'Pretty bad ones?'

Another pause, then she said, 'Oh, you know . . . your standard blood-and-guts, axe-murderers-on-parade kind of thing.'

I pretended to concentrate on the CDs. 'How about things moving?'

Suzanne jumped into the conversation then: 'Tell him about the handprints, honey.'

I turned towards the girl. 'Handprints?'

She nodded.

Outside, in the hallway, another delicate cracking sound could just be heard.

CHAPTER TEN

Disintegration

1. The Haunted House Syndrome

Her story only took a minute or two to tell, but had an edge like a machete.

It had started with the scratching noises, sometimes violent tearing sounds behind the walls, like an animal struggling to escape. Then Melissa began encountering them wherever she went, under tables, behind domestic appliances. Until, finally, one evening she was taking a hot shower before her nightly secret departure for Blair House—she preferred the water pressure in the Executive Mansion—when she heard the sounds beginning behind the tiled walls of the shower stall. Horrible, abrupt noises like huge claws tearing at sheet-rock. But when she jumped away from them, nearly slipping on the soapy floor, the sounds started moving too.

They slithered along behind the wall to her rear, then around to her left, then back around to her right whatever way she turned. And although she was terrified, she couldn't make herself get out of that shower. She felt paralyzed. And that's when she realized something was moving across the shower stall's sliding door.

She spun toward it and saw something brush across the

steam-fogged glass. At first she reassured herself that it was merely a large drop of condensation . . . but it seemed much too regular for that, and it was moving at a sideways angle. Then followed another, and another, and another . . . and soon there were dozens of handprints appearing spontaneously in the condensation. And they were all now moving: Long adult fingers outstretched and hungry. Hungry, desperate fingers.

And at that moment, naked, and shivering despite the steam rising around her, she felt certain that those hands wanted her.

Only her.

'And that's when you started talking about these experiences with your mom?' I asked her softly. By that point, the other men had moved closer to us, as though gathering around a campfire, and Melissa's messy room had taken on a sort of surreal quality in the feeble light. Only a single lamp was burning on the bedside table.

She nodded. 'Yeah, that was when I found out about the whole haunted house syndrome.'

Next to her daughter, Suzanne swallowed hard. 'And that's when I finally realized something had to be done about it.'

I started to reply when I noticed something else about the girl that hadn't struck me before. It's kind of difficult to describe: I saw her hand dangling over the edge of the bed, and I saw those same inexplicable tremors in her fingers. Almost like a flower reacting to some poisonous gas, its petals curling inward in jerky spasms. Again, I'm pretty sure I was the only one in the room who noticed it— as I said, it was subtle—but this time, something else caught my eye. A few minutes ago I had set my satchel down on the floor next to the bed . . . and her hand was dangling a hair's breadth away from it. Her hand was *reacting* to the contents of my satchel.

I stood up very suddenly.

'What is it, Father?' Dodd was staring at me, as were the others.

I didn't know what to say. That terrible night was now engulfing the whole mansion like a shroud. The freight-train winds, the musty smells, the bizarre cracking noises—all of it was making me crazy with anger at myself. How in the hell did I end up in the middle of this? One little guy from Chicago with bad knees and gastro-intestinal problems! How did this happen? Dodd had no idea what it was that he was asking me to do. I felt like Alice at the Mad Hatter's tea party.

I wanted to scream in frustration.

'Father . . .?' Dodd was getting exceedingly nervous.

I turned to him. 'Jimmy, let's talk outside in the hall for a second.'

2. Catechism

The corridor felt even colder than it had done earlier. Before I was able to get a single word out, Dodd grabbed me and said, 'Father, what are you doing? You're making matters even worse in there.'

'Hold on a second, Jimmy—'

'We need to get moving on this thing.'

'I understand that, but—'

'I'm telling you, Father, we need to finish this thing before the storm gets any worse.'

'Damn it, Jimmy, slow down! Come here,' I said, grabbing his elbow and ushering him away from the half-open door. I didn't want the others to hear us. I didn't want to make the girl any more skittish than she already was. Or make Suzanne Fallon any more nervous either. Or give Burke any more reasons to mistrust me. I led Dodd over to the other side of the corridor, next to a Louis XIV love seat, directly under a skylight. The sky had turned deep indigo blue and it put a deathly pallor on Dodd's tense expression.

'What is it?' he said, staring at me. 'What's going on?'

'I'm gonna insist that the girl leaves this house immediately, Jimmy,' I said flatly.

He shook his head. 'I've tried, Father, believe me. It's no use.'

'No, Jimmy, you don't understand. This is very important. That girl should not spend even another second in this house.'

He looked at me for a long time as the wind howled right above us, lashing the skylight. I could feel the night closing in around us, and could barely hear that delicate, intermittent cracking noise from a nearby room.

Dodd sighed. 'Look, there's one thing I can tell you for sure: That girl is not gonna do anything she doesn't want to do.'

'Jimmy, I'm trying to tell you, she's in real danger. I've seen it before.'

He gave me a searching look, like he was trying to see through me. 'I understand why you're nervous about this, Father,' he said finally. 'I don't blame you a bit.'

'Jimmy, you got it all wrong. It's not because—'

'I know what you've been through,' he said, a glint of sadness in his eyes. 'All these years, carrying that guilt around on your back.'

'Jimmy, trust me, that's not it. I'm trying to tell you, this girl here is in the early stages of possession.'

He gave me a sidelong glance at that. 'She's what?'

'It's real, Jimmy. It's a bona-fide condition recognized by the National Institute of Mental Health—'

'Father, come on—'

'I'm telling you this is real. The Catholic Church has

ways of authenticating the condition. Bottom line, it's all the same: The gradual disintegration of the will—'

'Wait a minute, hold on a second.' Dodd glanced over his shoulder nervously. This was leading to places he didn't want to go. 'I can understand, you know, certain things happening in an old house. Energies—whatever you want to call it. This place is as bad as they come. B-but . . . what you're talking about—'

'Jimmy, I'm not saying—'

'What you're talking about here is—what?—demonic possession?'

I took a deep breath, trying to control my frustration. 'Jimmy, what did I say earlier about you following my lead?'

'I understand, but—'

'You promised me you would follow my instructions to the letter.'

'I know—'

'You agreed—'

'I know, I know,' he said, wiping his mouth awkwardly. 'Just tell me, are we talking about demonic possession?'

I sighed painfully. 'The honest truth is, I don't know what the source is yet. But sometimes you see things—'

'Things?'

'Things that are familiar; signs, symptoms . . .'

'Okay, okay.' Dodd raised his hands in surrender, looking like a cornered animal all of a sudden. 'I'm gonna trust you on this,' he said at last. 'But this storm's getting worse. And time's ticking away. And I think we should get this thing going—this cleansing or exorcism or whatever it is we have to do.'

I heard raised voices coming from Melissa's room, then I saw Redding and Tooms emerge. The little professor, wringing his hands, began heading toward the elevator. I figured he must have finally convinced Burke to let him out of this place. I grabbed Dodd by the arm.

'Jimmy, come here.' I led him along the hallway, deeper into the shadows, further away from Melissa's room. 'I don't think you realize what you're asking me to do,' I finally said when we were out of earshot.

'Whattya mean? I'm asking you to perform an exorcism.'

I looked at him. 'You're asking me to perform an exorcism on a *place*?'

'Okay, yeah, so what?'

'Think back to catechism classes, Jimmy.'

'I'm not following.'

I explained to him that the rite of exorcism consists of two parts. 'First part,' I said, 'you summon the spirit. You *summon* it, Jimmy.'

'So?'

I couldn't believe he wasn't following me. 'Don't you realize what we're flirting with here, by doing the ritual in this house? Maybe the most important building in the free world?'

His eyes locked onto mine, and he said, 'What kind of risk are we talking about?'

I glanced around the corridor for a moment. We weren't alone. There was a presence in that corridor with us. But even now it's hard for me to articulate exactly what it was. 'When you summon a demon, you open a doorway,' I told him. 'Second part is, you drive it out. But it ain't foolproof, Jimmy. Only God is foolproof, and He ain't talking right now.'

He gave me that hard look of his. 'What are you saying exactly?'

I wiped my brow, still moist with beads of sweat. I needed a drink. Dear Lord, how I needed a drink. I could feel the thirst at the back of my tongue, at the base of my spine, in my belly like a hot branding iron. Just a jigger, just a taste of Bushmills to get me through this thing. I spoke in a low tone: 'Most times, Jimmy, a possession—a haunting—is an isolated battle in a continual, ongoing war. A battle over a single human soul, or a single place.'

He looked at me. 'But . . .?'

'But this, *this* is what I would consider unprecedented,' I said. 'I think this place has a war going on in it. And if we screw up—if *I* screw this thing up—the negative energy here can make things happen in a place. *Physical* things.'

Dodd thought about this for a long moment. Finally he said, 'It's like this, Father. I don't know if I understand all this metaphysical stuff, but I told you I would follow your instructions to the letter, and I meant it. You just tell me what you want me to do.'

It was my turn to think things over.

I could feel the worm turning in me, as sure as the darkness outside had swallowed up the mansion. The wind sounded like an insane person, howling just outside the house's skin. The epicenter of the storm was upon us. I could hear icy snow—by this point, flying almost horizontally—crash against the stone façades and marble columns outside, and it was only fueling my inner anger. I wanted to fight that house so badly. It had been taunting me all along, daring me to step into the ring, and I had had enough. No piece-of-shit house was going to scare me off with cheap hallucinations such as handprints on windows, or visions of ugly black doors from my nightmares.

I turned to Dodd and said, 'I'll do the ritual—and I'm talking a full-blown exorcism—on one condition.'

Dodd nodded. 'Anything, Father.'

I burned my gaze into him. 'Evacuate the entire house. Get everybody out of the place.'

He gaped at me. 'Father, are you sure you want—?'

He stopped abruptly at the sound of footsteps approaching noisily along the hallway.

It was Redding, and he was moving quickly, obviously all bent out of shape. His eyes were wide and hot and shifting around the corridor as though trying to detect a leak in the hull of a ship. He spotted us standing in the shadows and pointed a long slender finger. 'You two stay put!' he called out, then he rushed into Melissa's room.

As Dodd and I glanced at each other, something unspoken passed between us—I don't know what it was exactly.

A moment later Burke came out of the girl's room, a tiny cellular pressed to his ear. From the expression on his face, clearly something was wrong. We hurried over towards him. Mrs. Fallon and Redding were standing by the bedroom doorway, looking worried as hell. Inside the room itself, Melissa was sitting up on the edge of her bed. Burke was shaking the cellular, while yelling into it: 'Answer it, Zorn, goddamnit!'

'What's the matter?' Dodd asked him.

Burke snapped the phone shut, stuffed it back into his pocket. 'South gate isn't answering.' He looked at me and Dodd. 'You two, stay up here until we get back.' He turned to Redding. 'You stay with Mrs. Fallon and Melissa.' Then he started toward the elevator.

Dodd grabbed his arm, held him back. 'Wait a minute, Jerry. Wait! What's going on?'

Burke nervously glanced around the corridor, then explained, 'Redding was escorting Tooms out through the north exit when—'

Another series of delicate cracking noises, like icicles breaking, suddenly interrupted him, and he turned and glanced again down toward the far end of the corridor. The noise seemed to be moving along one wall. Burke's eyes narrowed as he murmured something under his breath. I'm not sure, but it was something like, 'You gotta be fucking kidding me.'

'What is it, Jerry?' Dodd said. 'What's wrong? What's wrong?'

Burke didn't answer him, but instead started down the narrow corridor toward the cracking noises.

And we all followed him silently.

And when we got to the French doors opening out onto the sun porch, we at last discovered the source of those cracking noises.

Suzanne Fallon's hand fluttered to her mouth like a wounded butterfly. Her voice was barely a whisper now.

'Oh my God in heaven . . .'

CHAPTER ELEVEN

Nightfall

1. Dead Line

'It's just the cold—that's what it is. It's the cold, that's what's doing it,' Dodd was mumbling, backing away from the doors, blinking hard as though he was dreaming and trying to wake up. The rest of us were gaping at those three large arched doors in disbelief.

They were fairly new, part of the Reagan renovations of the third floor. Triple-pane, bulletproof glass, wired for security, Palladian reproductions. The storm had almost completely iced them over, frosting them with ripples of wind-blown rhinestone. Through this layer of ice we could see snow outside billowing in great ghostly blankets. Night had fallen, its arrival announced by the increasing frenzy of winds. But here, at last, was the source of the cracking noises: Down at the base of the French doors, where there was a metal release for opening them.

The doors were spontaneously sealing themselves.

'Give it another try!' Burke ordered.

'It's no use.' Redding was already crouching down, digging his fingers under one vinyl-coated handle. He strained and grunted, the veins in his powerful brown neck bulging, his eyes slammed shut. Then he gave up. 'Damn thing's totally jammed.'

'Oh my God.' Suzanne started backing away from the French doors, her eyes wide.

Dodd touched her arm. 'Stay calm, Suzanne, it's just the cold—'

'That's right,' Burke said. 'Everybody just take it easy. This is just a glitch.'

'Try the windows.' Dodd pointed.

I watched as Redding hurried over to the bay windows. Dodd was still trying to keep Suzanne calm. Then, out of the corner of my eye, I saw Melissa. She was standing there in her boots, a few feet away from Burke, her arms folded defiantly across her breast, her eyes feverish. She seemed outwardly a tough cookie, this kid, but I could tell she was scared. Scared of this big house. Scared of what was churning inside her. Scared of the drama unfolding there in the hall.

Redding was still struggling to push the window up, when the very air seemed to crackle all around him. He reared backward, as though shocked by static electricity. The cracking noises continued from the base of the French doors, with hairline fractures spreading across the icy rind coating the glass. And the window right in front of Redding seemed to press downward against his efforts, tighter than before. It was as if some invisible ratchet was sealing it shut, locking us off from the outside. And all at once I realized that those other cracking sounds we had been hearing off and on during the afternoon were the other doors and windows of the house gradually sealing themselves too.

'Damn it.' Redding frowned.

'What in God's name is happening?' Suzanne moaned.

'Let's not jump to conclusions,' Burke said, pulling out his cellular phone.

I didn't know it at the time, but Burke's cellular was actually a closed-circuit walkie-talkie tuned to a special frequency. A single push-button could bridge him over to the secret-service headquarters a block away, and to the White House police dispatcher, as well as emergency services, army special forces, and a chopper pilot on twenty-four-hour call. But on this particular night his phone was not working. All Burke could hear now was a totally dead line.

He glanced up at Redding, shaking his head.

Suzanne Fallon finally wriggled away from Dodd and said, 'Talk to us, Burke. What's going on?'

Dodd started to say, 'Suzanne—'

'Okay, it's nothing we can't deal with,' Burke interrupted him.

'Let me try,' I said and went over to the window, adrenaline pumping, anger stewing inside me. I dug my fingers under the sill and started furiously rattling the window. It was as solid as pig-iron. 'The trick is not to be afraid!' I grunted, rattling the window futilely. 'It wants us afraid!'

Redding was watching me. 'What the hell are you talking about?'

'It feeds off fear!' I grunted, still angrily jarring the stubborn window. My fingers were already numb and aching.

'Father—' Dodd started to say.

'Never back down!'

'Father—'

I started to say something else, when a soft voice murmured behind me.

'It wants me.'

The voice sounded so low and measured, I didn't even recognize it at first. But we all instantly clammed up and turned toward Melissa, who was standing gazing at the shadows cloaking the far end of the corridor.

'What did you say, Melissa?' Suzanne asked.

The girl gazed at her mother, then looked around at all of us in turn. She had a strange kind of dreamy expression that worried me. Not exactly frightened—more brooding than that. 'It wants *me*,' she muttered again. 'Whatever it is, I can feel it. It wants *me*.'

I walked over and put my hand gently on her shoulder, and looked straight into her eyes. I was still breathing hard from my efforts with the window. 'I promise you, kiddo,' I said softly, 'we're not gonna let it get to you.'

She didn't say anything, just looked at me sadly. Outside, the wind shrieked eerily.

Suzanne moved over and put an arm around the girl. 'It's okay, honey,' she said. Then she turned to Burke. 'I'm starting to re-think my brilliant idea about staying here tonight.'

2. The Black Box

We made history in more ways than one that night. In the last two hundred-plus years, the White House had only lain empty twice. The first time was in 1814, when citizens of the new presidential city saw the fires of British aggression gobble up the surrounding countryside, taking the Executive Mansion with it. Only a shell remained, and it took years to make it habitable again. The other occasion was in the late forties, when Harry Truman had the whole place gutted and rebuilt from the ground up. But on this hellish night, as Burke and Redding raced up and down the corridors, and we braced ourselves for the worst, we got it down to six only. Six people left in the whole huge building.

Burke, Redding, Suzanne, Melissa, Dodd and myself.

I found out later that the rest of the remaining staff had gotten out before the doors had completely sealed themselves. Half of them—including Henry the head butler and Mrs. Whittaker the cook—had got out through the service entrance at the rear of the ground-floor kitchen. The rest of them—an appointment secretary, a couple of White House police, a maintenance man and three housekeepers—had managed to escape via the east-wing breezeway. Thank Christ Mrs. Whittaker had had the kindness and foresight to leave out some provisions for us, instead of locking everything up and going off with the keys.

Evidently the old gal had been witnessing strange phenomena here for decades, so when she saw the windows and doors sealing themselves tightly shut she had acted quickly. She made sure there was sufficient unfrozen meat in the walk-in fridge downstairs, and plenty of fresh food on the shelves for quick and easy meals. She also left care packages in the guest rooms upstairs. On each bedside table was a small wicker basket filled with essential items such as fresh batteries, a small flashlight, drinking water, a butane lighter, a small first-aid kit, a writing tablet, extra pens, granola bars, fresh fruit and even chewing gum. In mine she had added a small Gideon's Bible and a gold cross on a chain. Of course, it would take hours yet before I would understand exactly why she had done this. At the time, I thought it was a decent gesture nonetheless. Like leaving a life-preserver for people caught on a storm-tossed ship.

And speaking of storms, the one outside had reached some kind of crescendo. I watched it through a spiderwebbing of cracked glass in one of the arched windows flanking the ground-floor south vestibule. It needed only a quick glance to realize what was happening outside. The wind seemed like a pack of rabid dogs chewing at the portico, lashing the façade and battering the whole structure until every joist seemed to creak over our heads. The blizzard had gotten even angrier since the last time I checked, swirling wildly out there in the darkness, assaulting the spindly groves of boxwood trees and naked sugar maples. I could barely see the dark crater of the south fountain, frozen over and inactive, or the tennis court a few hundred yards to the right. Executive Avenue was gone. The city beyond it was gone. And, in that one quick glance, I think it finally hit me: We were about as isolated then as a scientific expedition camped at the South Pole.

'. . . should get something to force it open!' Redding was hollering next to me.

I turned to see the two secret-service agents wrestling with the huge brass deadbolt securing the south entrance doors. The doors themselves dwarfed us like doors from a fairy tale: Huge, burnished hardwood items, arched at the top and inlaid with teak and walnut and cherry. But right now they were totally jammed in place, the lock frozen.

'You've got to be kidding me,' Suzanne was saying. She stood behind Burke, her eyes glimmering with fear, her arm around Melissa protectively. Melissa herself was in a daze, watching the chaos around her. I was standing off to one side with Dodd, trying to plan my impending ritual, trying to keep a game face on. This vestibule was modest by the standards of the rest of the mansion; two hundred square feet of parquet floor and plaster walls, it echoed flatly and had that cold stony smell of winter.

'Try the utility closet!' Burke was saying. 'Should be a pry-bar or jimmy or something in there—'

'You mean the dip-rec room?' Redding was backing toward the inner stairway that led up to the diplomatic reception room—or 'dip-rec room' in the vernacular of the secret service.

'Yeah, go, go!' Burke yelled at him, then he tried his cellular again. But it was no use: The phone was dead—which, by the way, was another historic event. Like I said, it was a specially designed digital phone linked to a ground transformer one block away. It was technically failsafe, absolutely failsafe. But not that night, and not in that house.

'Try another window,' Suzanne was saying. 'We'll go out through a window, for Chrissake.'

Burke was shaking his head. 'Already tried that. They're all stuck.'

'Well, break the goddamn glass!' she barked.

'It's bulletproof safety glass,' Burke explained. 'Almost impossible to shatter, and even if you did, it'd be a bitch to climb through. Very jagged, very nasty, specially designed to keep intruders out.'

Dodd spoke up. 'How'd the others get out, then?'

Burke shook his head again. 'Service exit in the kitchen, but it jammed itself shut only minutes after they got away.' Burke put a finger to his earpiece, then tried the tiny microphone attached to his cuff. 'Twenty-three? Twenty-seven? Respond!'

'Who's still here then?' Dodd asked.

Again Burke shook his head. 'Zorn was supposed to check in before he left the west wing, but I don't think his radio was working.' He fiddled with the cuff-mike again, but I realized it was futile. I didn't have to hear the static crackling in his earpiece, or see the delicate hairline fractures forming in the windows, or hear the creaking of door jambs and window frames as they pressed down against their sills with thousands of foot-pounds of pressure. I didn't even have to see the storm outside smothering us.

'Isn't there some kind of emergency communication system?' Dodd asked.

Burke was trying to pry the faceplate off the deadbolt, his eyes feverish. 'The landlines are down, the cellulars won't work. The back-up system is in the west wing— basically a shortwave—but we can't reach anybody on it. We can't lock onto anything.'

'You're kidding me,' Dodd marveled. 'Goddamn executive mansion of the world's top superpower, and we can't even call fucking nine-one-one!'

'Shut up, Jim.'

'Don't tell me to shut up!'

I stepped into it then. 'Enough with the bickering!' I shouted, though my throat was raw. 'That crap's not getting us anywhere!'

Dodd stood there panting for a moment. 'Look, I'm sorry. I'm just saying this isn't right. It's not right. There's this box. I got briefed about it. A black box, works on microwave frequencies or something like that. Immediately summons the guys at HQ, Langley, the White House police, the secret service—'

Burke's angry voice cut him off. 'It's in Prague, for Chrissake!'

3. One Way Out

There was a tense silence for a few moments as we all absorbed the information. Even I knew what he was talking about. The emergency communication device—the black box—was with the President himself. Overseas. At the European summit. Five thousand miles away. In fact, it was always with the President, wherever he went. And there we were, alone in this two-hundred-year-old ghost house, and all the lines dead.

Right then, Redding returned with a piece of metal about the size of a yardstick. 'It's all I could find,' he said. 'It's from the coat rack—'

'Come on, quick,' Burke said.

The two agents tried to pry the door open, but all they succeeded in doing was bending the piece of metal.

'Get back!' Burke yelled, tossing it to the floor, then

reaching down to his ankle holster. He kept a semi-automatic in there, made of black steel and distinctly blocky. I don't know much about guns, but it looked like the kind of weapon you see ATF agents carrying.

'What in God's name are you doing, Jerry?' Suzanne cried out.

'Get back, all of you!' He took a handkerchief out of his pocket and draped it over the deadbolt. 'Turn your heads away.' He aimed his gun at the latch. 'Now!'

We did as instructed.

The three blasts lit up the vestibule, and made us all jump in unison.

My ears were ringing as I turned back to see the handkerchief smoldering. Burke tossed it to the floor and tried kicking the door open. But that was no use: The perforated deadbolt held tight, the door squeaking stubbornly at each clump of Burke's wingtip shoe. The hot, peppery smell of cordite hung in the air. I saw the tendons throbbing in Burke's neck and could sense the house feeding off our growing panic.

Melissa's voice came from somewhere behind me. 'Ghosts can't hurt you, right?' I spun around and saw her standing there, chewing on her black fingernails. She looked at me with a nervous smile. 'I mean, they're just, like, disembodied spirits, right? They can't hurt you. Even these marks on my body—I, like, gave them to myself, right?'

'That's right, kiddo,' I said, though I wanted to say so much more. I wanted to say it was time to circle our wagons, time to open the Bible and call the presence out. But I didn't—not right then. All I did was wink at my young pal, and hope that the girl's innate courage would protect her.

'Come on, everybody.' Burke started toward the flight of stairs.

Suddenly a noise made us all freeze.

It came from all directions—above us, along every corridor, from beneath us in the bowels of the basement—and it sounded like fireworks erupting, like some crazy festival bursting forth inside the house, the strings of M-80s and firecrackers going off in random sequence, the screams and cries of revelers rising up and bouncing off the walls. Then I realized what it was—I think we all did at the same time—and a fist squeezed at my heart.

It was the sound of four hundred and twelve doors slamming shut in unison.

The silence that followed was charged with menace, like the silence of a mortuary.

Finally Burke's voice snapped us out of our paralysis. 'Suzanne, Melissa, listen to me!' He took hold of the First Lady's arm with a firm grasp.

She jumped in surprise. 'Jesus—'

'Listen to me, Suzanne. Listen to me.' He was now urging her toward the stairs. 'You too, Melissa. Come on, come on.' He beckoned to the girl. 'We're gonna go through the map room, then down the passage to the service elevator—'

'Where are you taking them, Jerry?' Dodd demanded, following.

'To the service elevator,' Burke said. 'Redding will escort them—'

'But where, Jerry? Where?'

Burke paused by the bottom of the stairs, his eyes flashing with anger and more than a little bit of panic. In that instant—as he stared back at us—I had no idea what was going through his mind, but I could tell by his eyes that he was now taking this place seriously. He turned to Dodd and said, 'The only way out of here, Jim . . . down!'

CHAPTER TWELVE

A Scream in the Dark

1. Flight

We split into three groups. Redding, Suzanne and Melissa headed for the basement, where Harry Truman's civil-defense tunnel lay waiting in the shadows, allowing access off the property for anyone brave enough to walk its length. Agent Redding walked a couple of paces ahead of the two women—I found out later he was packing a military-issue Glock that fired eight rounds faster than any other over-the-counter firearm available in this country—and he carried this weapon in the upward-ready stance, his eyes shifting nervously from shadow to shadow. What he was expecting to encounter, I'm not real sure about. Burke went off alone to check the passageway leading into the west wing. Meanwhile Dodd and I were told to begin whatever it was we were planning on doing that night.

But something was changing all around us—in the grain of the wood, inside the walls, I could feel it down to my toes—and the worst part was, I was doubting myself, and doubt is deadly for an exorcist. The most important thing about performing exorcisms—or any cleansing ritual, for that matter—is to stay in a prayerful frame of mind, to keep that wavelength to God open and hot. Down through history, it's a fact, the most successful exorcists have been skinny, sickly men—in physical terms, at least. Father Francis Dyer, Teilhard de Chardin, Father Merrin. I could have knocked any one of them out in the first round with one hand tied behind my back. But spiritually they were Mohammed Ali: They were forces of nature. Their faith could topple mountains, and that's exactly how they fought the dark side—with *faith*. But as I stood there in that empty mansion, listening to the wind clawing at the windows, I felt like I wanted to tear the place apart with my bare hands. What kind of a priest was I, with all that anger stored up inside me?

I glanced across the hall toward the library, the room where I had first encountered the presence, the room that had given me a glimpse at the dark underbelly of this place. Its door was closed tight—one of the many that had slammed shut. And now it seemed to be taunting me. Daring me to go inside. *Tonight, tonight, tonight . . .*

'I want to do another pass of the library,' I said quickly, motioning at the door.

'Yeah, okay,' Dodd said. He went over and opened the door.

I paused on the threshold, fishing in my satchel for one of my ampullae of holy water, my hands shaking like a schoolgirl's on her first date. I had brought along six of them, each filled with about two ounces of water from the font at St. Mikey's, but now I was wishing I had brought along a whole Sparkletts jug full of the stuff. I said an Ave Maria and tossed a few drops toward each of the four walls. Then I braced myself and waited for the room to call out to me. I waited for a silent black depth-charge to erupt in my brain. I waited for my stomach to ignite.

Nothing happened.

The room just sat there in all its elegant French Provincial decor, silent and empty. No ghostly emanations from the wainscoted walls or the molded ceiling. No horrible smells wafting out of the crowded bookshelves or from the jeweled chandelier. No demonic energy leaping up from the expensive Persian carpet. Whatever had been in that same room earlier seemed no longer there.

I turned to Dodd and angrily said, 'The son of a bitch is playing possum.'

Right then a noise from above caught my attention, and I glanced up at the ceiling. It was unlike anything I had yet heard in that place. A rhythmic creaking sound moving in fits and jerks across the floor of the room directly above us. It sent a cascade of gooseflesh down my back, because it sounded so distinctly human, like footsteps. And when I glanced at Dodd, I could tell he was thinking the same thing I was. His eyes were wide.

'Is that Burke up there?'

Dodd shook his head. 'No, Burke's in the west wing right now.'

I nodded.

'That's the East Room above,' Dodd uttered, still staring up at the ceiling, his voice almost a whisper.

A tense pause.

'We better get up there, Jimmy,' I said, and closed my satchel.

We took the stairs up to the state floor, and made a quick left into the east ballroom. Again, the door was shut tight. When I opened it, I half expected some dark presence to leap up at me, like it had in the library earlier, but no such luck. The room was cold and silent. The massive windows groaned and rattled against the winds, and the burnished wood of the parquet floor gleamed in the dim light. The ballroom lay empty most of the year, used only when some grand reception or banquet was scheduled. And now that very emptiness gave it an extra layer of melancholy.

As I opened my satchel and took out the crucifix, I

noticed something strange about the floor. The water damage was still visible in the dim light, at least half a dozen warped spots in the parquet tiles, about the size of grapefruit halves. Three of these were clustered under one window, probably from a leaking radiator. There was another one in the corner, under the grand piano. And there was a couple along the baseboard of one internal wall. We had noticed some bumps earlier, but the more I stared at them, the more certain I was that they had moved.

I turned to Dodd. 'Jimmy, you remember seeing that lump in the floor by the piano?'

He told me he did.

I looked at him. 'Wasn't it closer to the wall when we were in here before?'

He had started to answer when the sound of footsteps returned, louder than before and directly above us.

There's nothing as distinctive as the sound of someone walking across an old wooden floor. I remember, while growing up in an old Victorian house in St. Louis, I could never sneak in at night without waking up my mother as I went up the stairs. There's nothing else quite like the sound of old wood groaning, and that's exactly what we were hearing right now. We both simultaneously looked up. The footsteps were creaking their way across the ceiling toward a far corner. Then they stopped. Then came another sound: A heavy thump, followed by a settling sound.

Then a rhythmic squeak, over and over.

'What room is that up there?' I said.

'Um . . . that would be the Lincoln bedroom,' Dodd replied, looking a bit nauseous.

'Come on, then,' I said and headed for the corridor.

It took us a couple of minutes to negotiate the stairs leading up to the second floor. The staircase itself was roped off by velvet cordons and a metal sign saying 'PRIVATE', and we had to weave between the stanchions in order to get up the marble steps. By the time we reached the landing at the top, my heart was racing and my mouth was dry.

An empty hallway stretched before us.

A sudden tide of emotion was rising in me as I stared down the length of that well-worn Victorian corridor. All the doors were shut on either side, the air filled with unseen tension. This was *it*. This was the confrontation I had been bracing myself for. The muffled creaking emerged from one of the guest rooms at the far end, perhaps the Monroe room, maybe one of the others. I wasn't familiar enough with the place yet to identify each room. I turned to Dodd.

'Stay here, Jimmy.'

'No way,' he said. 'I'm with you all the way, Father—just like the old days.'

I tried to smile. 'A dutiful altar boy to the bitter end.'

'You got it.'

'It's probably some stray housekeeper,' I said, as I started slowly along the hallway.

'Exactly,' said Dodd, walking beside me, but not sounding very convinced.

We made it to the threshold of the room in which I had first met Suzanne Fallon. The noise was louder here. It squeaked and creaked percussively behind one of the closed doors nearby. For a moment it sounded like people were fornicating on tired old bedsprings. Most of the corridor lights were turned off, so the only illumination came from some small brass table lamps.

Dodd touched my shoulder. 'Father,' he uttered softly, as though afraid of scaring the source of the noise away. He pointed to one of the closed doors. 'The Lincoln bedroom.'

The Lincoln bedroom.

I reached into my satchel for my large, gold-plated crucifix. Then I went over to the door and listened to the rhythmic squeaking and creaking from within. Dodd stood behind me, holding the satchel for me as I reached down and turned the doorknob.

A voice blurted out something garbled and inaudible in my head as I opened the door.

In the corner of the room, a rocking chair was swinging back and forth.

'Jesus!' Dodd's voice rang out behind me, and I heard the satchel fall to the floor as I gaped in at the antique wallpaper and the mahogany furniture and the grand old bed . . .

And the antique rocker near the window rocking under its own power.

' "In the Name of God! In the Name of Jesus Christ!" ' I was trying to stand steady, raise the crucifix and address the spirit, just like I had learned in those cryptic, extra-curricular classes at the Jesuit retreat outside Kansas City. But I was rusty, and distracted by that damned rocking chair swinging wildly all by itself. The same rocking chair— I found out later—that Abraham Lincoln had sat in at Ford's theater the night he was assassinated.

'Look out!'

The chair seemed to lurch toward us as though tugged by a powerful magnet and we both jerked backward. I raised the crucifix higher, my arm feeling weak. I cried out: ' "In the Name of Jesus Christ!" '

The chair toppled forward, like a puppet yanked by invisible strings, and the sheer violent sureness of it sent a chill across the back of my skull.

And then, just like a light being switched off, the room fell silent, emptied of all energy. It happened that quickly. Dodd and I just stood there for a frozen moment, tensed like springs, staring at the fallen chair. It looked like the skeleton of some dead animal. But we didn't have much time to ponder it, because the voice came next.

'Did you hear that?' Dodd cocked his head toward the doorway.

I had to admit I had heard something in the back of my consciousness, like a distant high-pitched scream muffled by layers of floor and ceiling, seeping through the heating ducts maybe. I wasn't quite sure, but started to reply, 'It sounded like—'

Then the noise came again, louder, through an air-duct over in the corner.

Down in the basement, someone was shrieking.

2. Descent

We rode the elevator down in tense silence. Instead we just listened for the shrieking. It had sounded like a woman— maybe Suzanne or Melissa? My heart was pounding as Dodd fidgeted, poking the 'Down' button again and again. I could see perspiration marks under the arms of his sports coat. We could hear some sound drifting up through the elevator shaft, but couldn't identify for sure what it was. It was the longest elevator ride I had ever experienced. It seemed to take us for ever to reach the service basement.

When the lift finally jerked to a stop, my heart leapt into my mouth.

I could hear Melissa's voice clearly then, echoing through empty storage rooms.

The doors slid open to reveal yet another lobby, with simple chairs and a coffee table stacked with old magazines. The floor was carpeted with a worn blue fabric decorated with the presidential seal, and all the walls had historic photographs on them. In the wall opposite was a metal door that seemed to lead into storage areas.

We raced across the room, shoved open the same door and entered a dingy passageway lined with exposed plumbing and furnace ducts. Bare bulbs in wire cages hung from the ceiling and filled the tunnel with a harsh light. The air seemed damp and heavy and old and full of rot. This was the mansion's underbelly, with its dark energy pressing down on us. We could hear the girl's voice more clearly now, echoing through the gloom somewhere nearby. It seemed to suggest anger more than anything else, but it was also just one step away from hysteria.

We found them gathered around a desk cluttered with greasy forms and various cleaning products—Melissa and Suzanne, Burke and Redding. The floor was concrete, the ceiling above them a tangle of filthy pipes and ducts, looking as if some of them dated back hundreds of years. Redding and Suzanne were already wrapped up in down-lined parkas, ready to move, but Melissa had not yet put on hers.

'No!' she screamed, backing away from her mother, who was holding out to her the extra parka. 'I said no! No! NO!'

Suzanne was looking furious as she tried to get the girl to put on her coat. 'Melissa, I'm not going to ask—'

Melissa yelled: 'Why is that so fucking hard to understand? JESUS CHRIST!'

Then Burke intervened. 'Melissa, listen to me!'

'I said *no*!'

Her scream was piercing, full of pent-up rage, and I stood there transfixed, not understanding what the hell was going on. This girl was obviously almost out of control. But what in God's name had happened here? I glanced around the grubby cellar and noticed there was a huge oval hatchway just a few feet away from where we were standing. Made of iron, it looked like the entrance to a submarine.

Then it hit me: This was Harry Truman's tunnel. The last possible way out of this house. Beyond the entrance, a passage stretched away into shadow, with grimy fluorescent tubes shining down occasionally on leprous cement walls.

'What the hell's the problem?' Dodd yelled, taking a few steps toward Melissa. I noticed he was trembling.

'Goddamnit, stay out of this, James!' Melissa snapped at him.

'She won't come with us,' Suzanne informed us, her eyes bright with panic.

Dodd looked at Melissa. 'You're kidding me?'

'This does *not* concern you!' Melissa yelled at Dodd. 'Stay out of it!'

Burke broke in: 'Melissa, come on. Whatever point you're trying to make, it's useless staying here.'

'He's right, Melissa,' Suzanne added nervously. 'The staff's all gone, everybody's gone home.'

'And the tunnel is open,' Burke continued. 'But we don't know how long it'll stay open, so I suggest you get out of here while you can.'

Dodd put his hand on the girl's arm. 'Come on, Melissa. Don't make matters worse.'

She shoved him away, shrieking: 'Goddamnit, leave me alone!'

'Melissa!' Suzanne yelled. 'You stop this nonsense right now!'

The girl looked at her mother with contempt. 'Why am I being treated like a child all of a sudden?'

'Because you're acting like one,' Suzanne retorted.

Melissa rubbed her eyes and muttered, 'Did anybody think of asking me just why I don't want to go through there?'

Her mother looked at her impatiently. 'Okay, why not?'

'Because I think I can help by staying here. I think I can help with the cleansing.'

There was an awkward silence as everybody exchanged glances, not knowing what to say.

I stepped forward. 'Okay, time out. Time out, everybody.'

I went over to the girl, waving the others away. 'Just give us a minute, folks.'

I quickly escorted her over to the far side of the cellar, where a huge industrial furnace rumbled softly, sending warm air up through a gigantic Medusa-snake of metal ductwork into the basement's ceiling. It was covered with fifty years of filth, and the air around it smelled of moldering dust.

I looked into the girl's eyes. 'You okay, sport?'

'I'm fine, really. I'm totally fine,' she muttered, her eyes wide with fear. Behind her, the others were nervously glancing along the escape route, listening to the house creaking and ticking upstairs. I could tell everybody had a sense that time was running out.

I asked Melissa if I could look at her hands for a second. She showed me her small, black-tipped fingers, their well-chewed nails. She was trembling worse than I was, and right then I felt my affection for this unkempt little girl strengthen further.

'Another nail-biter,' I said finally.

'Excuse me?'

'I can spot one a mile away,' I said, and I showed her my own hands. My fingernails, too, were bitten down to the nubs, and they had been that way for years. I had been a compulsive nail-biter myself ever since I was booted out of the priesthood. 'A kindred spirit,' I added, managing a tepid smile.

She studied my fingers for a moment, then looked into my eyes. 'I think I *can* help you if you'll let me stay,' she said softly.

I told her I couldn't allow that.

She gave me a desperate look. 'Whatever's haunting this place, it's after *me*.'

'And that's why we gotta get you out of here,' I said.

'But what I'm saying is, I can, like, help you identify it.'

I looked into her frantic brown eyes for a moment, and I saw past the body-piercings and gothic make-up and punk attitude, right down to the vulnerable little girl. Smart as a razor, tough as a tenpenny nail . . . yet vulnerable too. I glanced over my shoulder at the others for a moment. One by one, they were losing their composure, waiting impatiently for us to make a decision, wired out of their minds with dread—understandably so. There were new noises emanating from somewhere above us. Something shifting faintly in the house's infrastructure. I turned back to the girl. 'Listen to me, sport. Whatever's in this house, you don't want it getting its claws into you.'

She sighed, looking away. And then, right at that moment, I'm pretty sure I saw that flaw in her eye again. Just a faint dapple of white passing through the pupil like a sun spot. She flinched slightly, and rubbed her eye as though she felt dizzy.

I gently touched her shoulder. 'You sure you're all right?'

'Yeah, yeah—I'm cool,' she muttered, blinking away her daze. 'I'm just . . . I gotta . . .'

That's when her eyes rolled back into her head and she collapsed.

Thank God I caught her, because otherwise she would have toppled to the concrete floor and cracked her skull. Instead she swooned into my arms, and her lightness surprised me. She couldn't have weighed more than ninety pounds, and she felt hot to the touch, as if feverish. I heard her mother call out, and I yelled, 'Jimmy, gimme a hand!'

Dodd and the others rushed across, and he helped me carry the girl across the cellar to the large desk. There was a cluster of folding chairs leaning against it—probably used by maintenance crews during their lunch breaks—and we shoved several of them side by side to create a makeshift cot. We carefully laid Melissa on the chairs, and Suzanne stroked her damp forehead, murmuring softly to her.

The girl seemed delirious by that point, muttering, 'Let me out . . .'

'What did she say?' Dodd asked.

'Give her some air!' I cried, kneeling down next to the girl.

'This is not good,' Burke was saying to Redding grimly. The two agents glanced back and forth from the girl to the tunnel entrance.

'I'll carry her out of here if I have to,' Redding replied.

Suzanne was murmuring, 'It's okay, honey.'

And the girl was moaning: '. . . can't breathe . . . can't breathe . . . can't breathe!'

'Get back!' I waved them away, feeling that awful goose-flesh creeping up my back again. I *knew* what was happening. I just hadn't expected it so quickly.

Then came the noise.

It sounded like the floor was unzipping. The sound traveled across the cement in fits and starts. I glanced down and saw a crack spreading in the concrete, like a faultline. The racket was tremendous.

I rose to my feet. 'Get back, everybody!'

At that point the ceiling started trembling, the dust sifting down, a sound like an enormous harp-string being plucked. And the vibrations were indescribable. They resonated down through all the plumbing, into the cellar, and for a moment it seemed as though my very eyeballs would vibrate out of their sockets.

As suddenly as it had started, the commotion promptly ceased.

It happened that quickly, the noise just stopping as though someone had flipped a switch, and we stood dumbstruck for one awkward instant, not knowing what to do next—not knowing whether to turn and high-tail it along that inviting escape tunnel, stay here and say our prayers, or simply bend over and kiss our asses goodbye.

Without warning, the girl sat up with a jerk.

We all jumped—it was so abrupt, as though she was yanked forward by invisible hands, like a ventriloquist's dummy. Sitting bolt upright on those hard chairs, she smiled at us.

'You will all die in this place,' she said in someone else's voice.

And right at that instant—somewhere in the back of my brain—I heard the after-echo of another whispered word, barely audible . . .

. . . *now* . . .

CHAPTER THIRTEEN

Unclean Spirit

1. A Flood of Words

There are moments in a person's life—car accidents, muggings, home break-ins and the like—where the passage of time seems to get all fouled up. It's not as if time passes more slowly during these moments, nor more quickly either. It's something else altogether. It's as though time is removed from the equation. That's the best way I can describe it. It's as though the passage of time is irrelevant, and the incident is occurring in some dreamlike limbo, where every sight and sound and sensation is absorbed in some crazy heightened state.

That's exactly how it was that night, when the girl Melissa fell into the grip of the spirit.

Immediately I heard things shifting above us. I glanced up and saw the hot-water pipes seething and contracting like huge gray tendons straining in the dark cavities of the ceiling, and the sheer impossibility of it took us all by surprise—even me. I instinctively jerked away from the girl, my hands raised, my body all clenched up.

But there wasn't a thing any of us could do except gape at all this spontaneous movement. When I glanced back at the girl, she was looking straight at me. I swear to the Lord

Almighty, those diamond-hard eyes burned into me, and I heard a sound come out of her like a giggle, except there was no mirth in it, no humor, only that terrible glassy stare, and that giggly sound in the base of her throat, rising up like the laughter of a madwoman—half amusement, half tormented howl—and I saw her mother starting to make a move toward her again.

'Stay back!' I yelled at Suzanne.

'It's a power spike,' Burke muttered, staring up at the undulating pipes, grasping for an explanation. Redding, meanwhile, had pulled his gun.

'What's wrong with her?' Suzanne cried, clutching herself with those skinny arms.

'Suzanne—' Dodd started.

'Back off, everybody!' I yelled, waving them all back—never taking my eyes off that poor kid.

She was leering at me. 'All of you will die,' the voice from inside her informed us again, just in case we missed it the first time.

Next to Dodd, the massive desk suddenly slid across the floor and slammed into the furnace with a crash, scaring the bejesus out of Suzanne Fallon and nearly crushing the toes of Dodd's designer loafers. Black dust rained down from the phalanx of pipes above the furnace as we all jerked away—again moving reflexively and again shielding our faces. Redding aimed his gun at the desk, probably a trained reaction, and my mouth dried up almost instantly as I studied for a brief instant the scrape-marks on the floor. That desk must have weighed three hundred pounds.

'It's—what? It's a magnetic field,' Redding muttered under his breath, keeping his gun trained on the desk.

I was trying to stay focused, digging in my satchel, my hand shaking so badly it looked as though I had contracted cerebral palsy. I managed to grasp my crucifix again just as the girl snapped her face toward me and hissed, 'Now!'

Renewed fear crawled over me as I heard all kinds of things in that strange voice coming out of that girl. It was deep, male, faintly European, and I could hear pain and rage and, most of all, hate. There was sheer hatred stitched through that voice, probably the same raw hate that had assaulted me earlier in the library. And right then it was being directed at me.

Somehow I managed to raise the crucifix and take a step closer.

For an insane moment, I thought I smelled a strong body odor wafting off her. It was a musky smell, like the spoor of an animal in distress, and there were traces of other smells: Mold, rot, something decaying. I was starting to speak, when her face seemed to fall suddenly. Her whole expression slackened as though someone had cut the current inside her, and her head lolled forward.

I genuflected once with the crucifix, and I recited a Pater Noster under my breath.

'What's wrong with her?' Suzanne Fallon screamed behind me, making me jump.

The girl's head lolled suddenly to the left, and a deep, guttural moan came out.

' "Hail Mary, full of grace, the Lord is with you," ' I was praying aloud, very quickly . . .

When all at once the girl's head lolled over to the right, and that deep, smoky voice emerged again. 'I—am—I—am—!'

One of the folding chairs skidded across the floor, then crashed into the wall, nearly striking Burke. Suzanne shrieked. Another chair spontaneously toppled over, then violently started folding and unfolding, the sound of its rusty metal squeaking and straining under the pressure. As the chair fell still at last, our eyes quickly turned to the opposite wall, where rows and rows of conduits began creaking and straining under some rising external pressure, the pipes starting to buckle inward. It felt as though even the musty air was pressing in on us.

'Jesus Christ!' Dodd's voice rang out behind me.

I turned to the girl and said forcefully, 'Who *are* you?'

The girl's head fell backward. 'I am—NOT—!'

I waited for the voice to complete its sentence, but it had gotten clogged up somehow. 'Not what?' I hollered, addressing the entity as though it was some rabid dog.

'I am—NOT!'

Her face contorted into a look of utter agony, and somewhere to one side began a low, incessant vibration—like a gigantic motor-housing running on faulty bearings. It rose up from below, and sent violent tremors through the floor and walls till the desk and chairs started to vibrate wildly. Then the noise subsided.

And the girl spoke again in that guttural voice: 'I am . . . *forgotten.*'

Her head jerked back, and that terrible sound bellowed out again. It sounded so tormented, so full of rage and hatred, that I almost vomited. More than just a moaning sound, it was *alive*; it had a shape, it had a density to it. It was like an atonal symphony pouring out of her, and I had never before heard anything like it.

At that moment, I sensed it was working its effect on the others too.

'I'm here, Melissa!' Suzanne was trying to get near her child, but Dodd was restraining her.

Burke and Redding had meanwhile turned away, training their guns on the trembling walls.

'What do you mean "forgotten"?' I yelled at the girl.

But she didn't answer.

I genuflected again, the crucifix extended, and started to declaim, ' "In the Name of Jesus Christ Our Lord—" '

She suddenly snapped her attention back toward me, her eyes feverish and glassy, with a flood of words bursting out of her: '*Les hommes étranges et enterrés reviendront, en-fleurs-et-en-feuilles, les hommes étranges et enterrés—!*'

'I can't understand!' I yelled at her.

Her head drooped for a moment, obscuring her face. Then she started whispering hard and fast: '*Je suis vivante, à présent, et je vais vous faire payer!*'

'In English, please!' I commanded, following the protocol that had been drummed into me. According to the Jesuits, an invading spirit was like a spoiled child, and one should always address it as such.

Burke's startled voice behind me: 'What the hell language is that?'

The girl's face snapped upward suddenly, her baleful glare again fixing on me. The voice that boomed out of her was not even close to human. '. . . *VOUS FAIRE PAYER!*'

'Who are you?' I cried.

'. . . *VOUS FAIRE PAYER!*'

'Answer me in English!'

Then the current was cut again, and once more the girl's head lolled from side to side, her expression anguished. As her head became still, a low sound emerged. At first I thought she was merely moaning, the sound of it so soft and low. But soon I realized she was singing an off-key rendition of some familiar tune. What was it? By that point I could hear Suzanne Fallon crying faintly behind me. The woman was in agony, watching her daughter. But I couldn't place that familiar melody. What in God's name was it? It sounded obscene, flat and dissonant enough to hurt your ears—but so familiar.

It was the Ave Maria.

'—aaaaaaavveeehhhhhh—mmmmaaarrrrrrrreeeeeeeeah-hhhhh—'

I reached into my satchel and pulled out an ampulla of holy water. Anger was boiling inside me. I couldn't listen to any more of that hideous voice desecrating such a sacred hymn. I thumbed the container open and flicked a first droplet at the girl. ' "In the Name of Jesus Christ and the Almighty Father—" '

'—*VOUS FAIRRRRRE!*' The voice which exploded out of her sent her head sprawling backward, nearly snapping her neck, and the whole cellar seemed to react simultaneously, the plumbing overhead shivering, vibrations resonating through the concrete. I tried to continue with my litany, but by then I was transfixed and could only stare at that poor child, springing to her feet as though the floor were electrified.

She uttered an unearthly howl of pain, her mouth gaping wider and wider and wider and—

'MY GOD!' Suzanne began screaming.

The girl's jaw kept gaping wider and wider, as if it wouldn't stop . . . and we all thought it must stop, but still it didn't. It was though her entire skull was about to tear in two, and for another crazy, horrible moment I couldn't move. All I could do was stare at that grotesque sight . . .

As the girl's face began splitting open like a ripe melon.

It was at that point that I managed to drop my satchel and rush across the space between us. I grabbed her with one arm, hugging her head against my shoulder with the other. She felt like a wounded bird in its final death throes, but I wasn't going to let her be harmed. Her skinny body was trembling in my arms, but I wasn't going to lose her. Her jaw kept cracking ominously as I pressed her against me, anything to prevent her skull from splitting apart. And I continued to recite the holy litany as quickly and forcefully as my rusty old lungs would allow: ' "Lord-hear-my-prayer-so-that-this-innocent-servant-of-Yours-may-be-mercifully-freed—!" '

In that horrifying instant, the girl convulsing against me, I reached another level of clarity. I could hear all sorts of different sounds around me: The strangled mewling of her mother sobbing into her hands, the very walls vibrating dangerously, the gouts of stone dust raining down—but above all this I seemed to hear the girl's heartbeat fibrillating wildly.

I wasn't going to lose her.

So I shouted out my litany.

' "Dear-God-Creator-Defender-of-the-human-race, You-made-this-girl-in-Your-own-image: Look-on-this-girl-Your-servant-Melissa-who-is-assaulted-by-the-cunning-of-this-dark-spirit! The-primeval-adversary-the-ancient-enemy-of-earth-surrounds-her-with-the-horror-of-fear-and-paralyzes-her-mind-with-darkness-and-strikes-her-with-terror! Repel-O-Lord-the-power-of-Evil-and-dissolve-the-fallacies-of-its-plots-and-may-the-unholy-tempter-take-flight! May-Your-servant-be-protected-in-soul-and-body-by-the-sign-of-Your-Name!" '

Hoarse and breathless, I traced the sign of the cross on her damp forehead . . .

And I felt a spark, as though I had just touched a live socket. I jerked back my hand, a tingling sensation shooting along the tendons of my arm. And then I saw something extraordinary: A radiant blue spark flickered off the crown of the girl's head. It sputtered and flashed like a swirl of static electricity—and then it shot up into the rafters. I heard a collective gasp from the others.

For just a split second, I saw the luminous blue current—or whatever it was—slithering upward, penetrating the guts of the ceiling, then vanishing. Then the sound of something shifting upstairs.

The girl sagged suddenly in my arms like a rag doll.

Again, it was as though someone had flipped off a switch. The basement fell abruptly silent, and you could almost hear our collective breaths pause in our throats. Our bizarre tableau remained frozen like that for several moments, the only sound the ticking of some nearby furnace element.

Then I managed to say, 'Amen.'

They all came rushing toward us as I carried the girl back over to the chairs and gently laid her down. Suzanne knelt down by her daughter and tenderly dabbed her jaw with a handkerchief. There were spots of blood at the corners of the girl's mouth, where the skin of her face had begun to tear apart. The men hovered nearby, nervously watching.

I knelt down to examine her closely.

Whatever had been inside her had fled.

She was now coming awake, her brow creased with pain. She reached up a hand to touch her jaw, as sensitively as though she had just taken a punch from Evander Holyfield.

'Don't try to talk, sport,' I murmured, figuring she would be black and blue by morning.

Her eyes focused on me for a moment. They were back to normal. She spoke very softly, in a hoarse croak, 'The funky father,' and smiled a painful smile.

Then I knew she was back with us.

2. Into the Dark

'I'm a little rusty on my French,' Dodd murmured nervously, rubbing a hand through his sandy hair. Only a few minutes had transpired since the incident, and we were all still jumpy. 'Haven't studied it since I was at Cornell,' he went on. I was huddling next to him, trying to suppress my own anxiety. Across the room, Melissa was now sitting up, trying to recover. Her face was drawn, bruised, but otherwise she looked pretty normal. The others were hovering over her. Burke had found a first-aid kit in one of the desk drawers, and Suzanne dabbed an alcohol-drenched swab at the corners of her daughter's mouth.

Dodd gave me a questioning look. 'Okay, don't hold me to this, but I think *vous faire payer* means "make you pay."'

I nodded. 'Follow anything else?'

He looked over at the girl, then back at me. 'It was coming too fast and furious, but I did pick out one other thing.'

'Yeah?'

'*Reviendront.*'

I asked him what that meant.

' "Will come again" or "will live again," something like that.'

'Uh-huh,' I said noncommittally, but my stomach was reacting again. My stomach was flaring up, a hot poker turning inside me, deep down in my bowels. The basement ceiling seemed closer, the walls tighter. The light coming from the bare bulbs seemed dingier, gloomier.

By that point I was sure we were dealing with a lot more than merely a dislocated spirit. More than a mere haunting. My guess was that it was some higher form of demonic influence. Something the Old Church used to call an 'unclean spirit.' All the signs were there. The girl had never properly learned French—according to her mother—and yet French words had streamed out of her. That kind of evidence had always constituted a major criterion in the Church for the authentication of a demonic possession. Add to that all the other phenomena—including the way the house was reacting to me and to my holy equipment— and you had the recipe for one mother of an infestation. But how deep did it go? How bad was it? When I thought of the checkered history of that house, all the lives destroyed through decisions made there, all the wars planned there,

I got the feeling that there was something genuinely monstrous lurking within it.

I gave Dodd's arm a reassuring squeeze, then walked over to Melissa and her mother. 'How's it going, sport?'

She looked up at me. 'I've been better,' she croaked.

'You remember anything?'

She shook her head. 'It's all like a blur, like a bad acid trip.'

'It doesn't matter, honey,' Suzanne said, nervously stroking the girl's spiky hair, 'because we're getting you out of here right now.'

'That's correct,' Burke confirmed, standing over us. 'And the sooner, the better.'

I could hear the dry friction of Burke's palms rubbing against each other, and it occurred to me just how silent it was down here in the basement. I could no longer hear any moaning wind, rattling windows, or creaking sounds. It seemed as though it had turned silent since the girl had snapped out of her violent fit.

Like the stillness just before a twister hits?

'That's probably a good idea,' I said, giving the girl an enquiring glance.

They raised her to her feet, then helped her into the down-lined parka she had rejected earlier.

As they crossed to the tunnel entrance, they paused. Suzanne looked back around the cellar for a moment. She looked defeated, like a boxer who has been training for months, only to have his match canceled at the last minute. Next to her, Melissa stood shivering in her parka, her eyes glazed and distant.

Burke murmured something to Redding—I think it was something like this: 'Take them out through the Jackson Place tunnel, and when you reach Blair House, call me on the satellite line. And make sure you get Tactical over here on the double.'

Redding nodded.

I turned to Dodd. 'You know, Jimmy, you probably ought to go with them, while you've got the chance.'

Dodd gave me an odd look, part dread, part surrender. 'What are you talking about, Father?'

I assured him he didn't have to stay, he didn't have to be a hero.

He stared at me then, his eyes glistening with emotion, and I could tell that he would have preferred to go with the others. He would be very happy to leave that place. But there was something stronger inside him binding him to the task at hand, binding him to me, his old neighborhood padre.

Finally he looked into my eyes and said softly, 'I know I don't have to stay, Father.'

And that's all I needed. I didn't need to hear anything else.

I turned and watched Redding, Suzanne and Melissa entering the tunnel. They headed off into the shadows, passing through regular pools of illumination cast by the overhead fluorescent lights. Walking briskly, stiffly—till they got about fifty feet away. Then Melissa told them to wait for her a second. She turned round and padded back toward us, limping a little bit, but moving with a purpose.

At first I thought she might be relapsing into some kind of daze, but as she approached I could see her face was clear, her eyes lucid. She managed another weak smile.

'Kick this thing's ass, Father,' she said softly, then leaned forward on her tiptoes and gave me a peck on the cheek. Before I could even respond, she whirled back toward the tunnel and rejoined her mother.

I watched them vanish into its darker reaches.

And then there were three. Burke, Jimmy Dodd, and myself.

'Gentlemen,' Burke announced, 'the White House is all yours.'

Part III

THE RITUAL

It is important to remember that the Exorcism Ritual is not a Sacrament. Its integrity and efficacy do not depend, therefore, as in Sacraments, on the rigid use of an unchanging formula or on the ordered sequence of prescribed actions. Its efficacy depends on one element: The faith of the exorcist.

Introduction to the Roman Ritual

CHAPTER FOURTEEN

Fatal Mistakes and Mortal Sins

1. Bad Memories

I can hear them knocking on the door. They're out in the hallway. Angry, frantic voices calling for me, some of them in Spanish, some of them in thick street drawl. 'He sick! Yo-yo-yo—that boy sick as dog! He dying! He dying!'

But I can't go to them. I can't open the door.

The battle is still raging inside the room, and I'm alone with the boy, and the demon is still inside him, and we're both on the floor, and I cannot relax until I'm sure the unclean spirit is cast out. I cannot open the door until I'm sure. And I keep reciting the litany—' "Lord hear my prayer! The power of Christ commands you!" '—and I'm cradling the boy in my lap now, restraining him like an animal trainer restraining a wild dog, and the knocking rises up behind me, piercing the heat and the stench of the tawdry little bedroom—

'Open the door!'

And I feel my strength ebbing away. I feel like an old man, even though I'm only twenty-nine, and this is only the second exorcism ritual I've ever performed. The boy is now silent and still in my arms.

' "Through Christ our Lord, Amen," ' I say, and loosen my

*grip on him. He collapses to the floor, unconscious. His face
is bluish, ashen-colored.*

*I feel for a pulse, trying to ignore the pounding at the
door.*

There is nothing.

Nothing.

2. Battle Plans

Those memories never leave me, wherever I go. The smells,
the sounds, the texture of the light and the air in that little
boy's bedroom. But mostly what I remember are the words.

The words have always been straightforward, very
simple ones full of fire and brimstone—the sort of melo-
dramatic call-and-response that's been lampooned in
countless B-movies and pulp novels. But the premise cuts
to the heart of our existence in this world: The battle
between opposing moral forces, the big brawl between good
and evil. But beneath all the drama is a fairly ordinary set
of instructions, in many ways no different from any other
Christian rite such as a baptism, Holy Communion or
marriage.

The only thing that differentiates the Roman Ritual of
Exorcism is the fudge factor.

For some reason that I've never fully understood, the
original Catholic Church fathers—dating all the way back
to the year 200 AD—designed the original text with flexi-
bility in mind. I guess they figured the Devil was a dirty
fighter, and more often than not the priests would have to
improvise. If the possessed fled into the Syrian desert, the
clergy would have to be handy with a camel and abbreviate
the litanies. If the possessed dove into the Tigris, the priests
would need to learn to swim. Thus the rites were custom-
ized, and they evolved through the years. But the most

amazing part about the ritual is that it has pretty much survived intact for nineteen centuries. Even the reforms of Vatican II in the 1950s left the exorcism text pretty much unchanged. The Roman Ritual of Exorcism is a stubborn, iron-clad part of the Catholic religion, and no amount of modern psychology or humanism is going to mess with that particular tradition.

Lately, though, most mainstream Catholic priests are becoming more and more embarrassed by this antique Roman ritual. As though the mere existence of such a medieval text—with references to such sinister forces as demons and unclean spirits—weakens the credibility of the entire Church. It goes against today's kinder, gentler Church, and it flies in the face of the ecumenical, psycho-therapeutic approach to priesthood. In fact, a lot of my peers back in the seminary predicted that the exorcism rites would soon go the way of human sacrifices and public stonings. But guess what? It's now the twenty-first century, and this ancient ritual is still part of the secret liturgy of the Catholic Church, and that's good enough for me. As long as the Devil is still hanging around, dragging us all down into the shit, I'm glad we've still got a battle plan.

As a defrocked priest, though, I'm not exactly authorized to practice the ritual. When I was excommunicated, I lost all sanctions and privileges. But over the years, as my brain started to pickle and my drinking took charge of my better judgment, I started incorporating little bits and pieces of the same ritual into the occasional cleansing. I did the firehouse in Ravenswood, and I did a study hall at Loyola, and I did a few split-levels out in Barrington. I figured God wouldn't mind if I practiced a few kitchen-table blessings, just so long as my heart was in the right place. Even though I was probably committing about half a dozen venial sins— if not mortal ones.

But on this angry winter night, as I walked with Dodd

down that cold, empty corridor on the ground floor, the thing that was bothering me most had nothing to do with Church authority.

What concerned me then had nothing to do with the noises issuing from behind the walls as we strode toward the creaking shadows of the east end, or the incessant creaking, shifting sounds in the foundation. Or the room temperature plummeting with each passing minute, making me wonder when we would start to see our breath coming out in puffs of white vapor. Or my terrible feeling of isolation now that the White House had been completely deserted—except for us three fools. Or my senses that had been electrified by that deep-indigo burst of voltage that had shot out of the girl, and was now permeating everything in the mansion. No, none of these things was bothering me as much as the prospects of the summoning itself.

The summoning was the exorcist's starter pistol, his way of shaking the tree and getting the prey to take flight. And ordinarily it would be nerve-racking in the extreme, but that night . . . that night it seemed criminally irresponsible. It seemed as though I were about to open a doorway and let something hellish loose inside the most important residence in the country. But, in a way, the thing had been lurking there—behind the marble and the mortar—for over two hundred years.

All I was going to do was ferret it out and destroy it. At least, that was my plan.

We paused outside the library again. I had a weird gut feeling about that room, so I wanted to start the ritual there.

'I gotta tell ya something, Father.' Dodd kept his arms folded nervously, probably to hide his trembling. The back of his tailored shirt was sweat-soaked and clung to him despite the surrounding chill. His body odor smelled of fear.

Burke was away in the communication center, fiddling with dead circuits, no doubt trying to rationalize how the hell he had got himself in this mess.

'What is it, Jimmy?' I leaned against a decorative marble column near the stairs, my bowels in turmoil again. My satchel felt as though somebody had slipped a couple of hundred-pound barbells into it.

'You don't look so hot.' Dodd eyed me up and down.

'I'll be honest with you, Jimmy: I could use a drink something fierce right now.'

He wiped his mouth. 'Under the circumstances, I think I might join you.'

Somewhere upstairs there was a crash. It sounded like a giant church bell had fallen to the floor and shattered. The aftershock rang with discordant melodies fading into the awful silence. Dodd spun around, his gaze shifting everywhere. Even though there were plenty of sconce lights in the hallway—not to mention a couple of chandeliers glowing with dozens of forty-watt flame bulbs—the place seemed peculiarly gloomy.

'Try to stay calm, Jimmy,' I uttered, although I'm sure I looked as spooked as a sacrificial lamb myself.

He glanced at me and said, 'How does one do that?'

'Just . . . try to concentrate.' Right then I realized what that crash had been. I remembered the elegant grand piano in the ballroom above us—Truman's piano, shoved into the corner of the room. The lid had been propped open when I had last seen it. Now it must have come crashing down, and that's what had made the racket.

Dodd put his hand on my shoulder. 'The kitchen's just down the hall; you sure you don't want something to eat before we start?'

I shook my head and explained that I should be fasting.

He stared at me. 'Fasting?'

I explained: 'It's part of the first phase of performing an

159

exorcism. It's a tradition going back all the way to the seventeenth century, and it's pretty much still practiced today. The exorcist goes into seclusion before the ritual, where he prays, and he fasts, and he prepares.'

'I would think a priest would need all his strength,' Dodd said after a moment's thought.

'This is not about physical strength, Jimmy.'

'Whattya mean?'

'It's really all about faith,' I said.

He swallowed hard. 'Faith, huh?'

'Don't worry, Jimmy,' I said. 'You're doing fine.'

Something shifted above us. It sounded like a body being dragged along the floor—or at least that's how my hyperactive imagination interpreted it. I glanced over at Dodd and saw him lick his lips.

'Smoke and mirrors, Jimmy,' I told him. 'It just wants to spook you.'

'It's succeeding,' Dodd said.

'It cannot physically hurt you,' I said.

'How about mentally?' he asked.

'Like I said, this takes concentration. It ain't easy.'

'You said it cannot hurt me, and you've been talking earlier about this "unclean spirit." I've been working here for eleven months, Father, and I still don't have a handle on this thing. What do you think it is?'

I told him I had no idea, and that it was possible we might never find out.

There was a long pause before I finally said, 'I think we ought to begin, Jimmy.'

Dodd nodded.

I knelt down by my satchel, my knees stiff and sore. My chest felt tight again, as though there was a weight pressing down on my heart. 'Okay, there's a prescribed set of responses that the assistant needs to pay attention to,' I said, digging into the satchel.

'I understand,' Dodd said.

'We're both gonna need to wear the appropriate vestments.' I pulled out the purple stole, unfolding it carefully and draping it around my neck. I realized I was breaking at least half a dozen Church laws by wearing these vestments—not to mention sinning against the Lord Himself—but, again, I was rationalizing that it was all about faith. And I knew my faith was strong—maybe stronger than it had ever been.

I was reaching into the satchel for the yellow assistant's shawl when a new noise pierced the silence. It came from the corridor behind us: A horrible scratching noise like enormous claws scraping the underside of the floor. It seemed to go on for ever, as Dodd and I stood up, instinctively backing away. It came closer and, for one crazy instant, I remembered a huge old German Shepherd that one of the boys in the Catholic charities home used to keep locked up in a pen in the back alley, and every night that mutt would scratch incessantly at the aluminum door. But these clawing noises seemed a thousand times louder and more violent; a herky-jerky rhythm like a shark devouring the floorboards in a feeding frenzy.

The noise raced past us, then faded away down the opposite end of the corridor. Then something shifted behind the door of the library. Though muffled and indistinct, it sounded like fabric ripping.

I looked towards Dodd.

'I'm okay, Father,' he said quickly, trying to get a decent gulp of air into his lungs.

I unfolded the yellow shawl and gently hung it around Dodd's neck. He was shaking pretty badly, but at this point I figured that was probably a good sign. It meant he was focused, he was sharp. 'Okay,' I said, kneeling down by the satchel, 'the way we're gonna do this is, I'm going to explain the ground rules as we go along. Do you understand, Jimmy? Do you understand?'

He was listening intently to the muffled ripping noises behind the library door. 'Yeah—yeah, yeah, I understand. I'm ready. Let's do it.'

I reached into the satchel and found two small, dog-eared Roman Rituals in worn black-leather bindings, so old and musty that their smell was almost overwhelming. That smell reminded me of the cloakroom at St. Mikey's, and it was bracing, kind of comforting. An image came to mind of my Aunt Edith with her ivory-handled cane, taking me and my cousin Declan to Mass in Quincy, Illinois.

I had jury-rigged the books with nylon cords glued into their bindings, and I handed one of them to Dodd and said, 'This is the text, Jimmy. I'll shout out the pages as we go, and the rest is self-explanatory. Wrap the safety cord around your wrist. In case it gets rough-and-tumble, you won't lose the book.'

Outside the bay windows, the hungry wind was still going berserk, brutalizing the outer walls of the building. Floorboards shifted above us, window frames creaking, joists cracking, but I couldn't tell if the storm was responsible, or the presence inside the house.

It was almost as if the two forces had melded into one.

I dug into the satchel and found the cigar box full of brass cruets filled with holy water. I had already emptied one of them, which left five. I pulled them out, one at a time, and handed two of them to Dodd. I kept the other three, stuffing them inside my belt like so many bullet cartridges. I guess that's what they were: God's bullets.

Another noise from beneath us: A terrible racket, a metallic grinding like shrapnel being chewed up in a shredder. Then the sound deteriorated into convulsive vibrations rising up behind the walls.

I stood up. 'The Roman Ritual is in three parts, or chapters, Jimmy,' I said, trying to keep things focused. He was shaking like a palsied old man, but he was listening. 'Chapter Three is the text for exorcizing *places*,' I explained loudly.

Dodd began fumbling through his tattered little ritual book.

'We'll start here in the library,' I went on, 'and work our way up.'

Dodd nodded silently, then followed me over to the library door.

We paused for a second, gathering ourselves, not knowing what in hell's half-acre we would find on the other side of it. Muffled sounds were seeping under the bottom of the door, shuffling noises as though something large and soft was sliding across the floor. I positioned the ritual book in my left hand and the crucifix in my right, then took a deep breath. 'The rites are usually read in the original Latin,' I said. 'But we're going to be using the English translation you'll find at the end of the chapter. Do you understand, Jimmy?'

Dodd assured me that he did.

I prepared to turn the door handle.

'Another thing to remember, Jimmy, is that this house is under the influence of a force antithetical to Christ—antithetical to the truth. The house will make every attempt to throw us off and scare us and trick us. Do you understand?'

'I do, yeah.'

'It might even appear to have been cleansed in order to throw us off track. Don't trust it. Understand?'

'Yes,' he mumbled.

'A house under the influence of an unclean spirit can get into your head. It can tap into your fears, it can press your buttons. Do you understand what I'm saying?'

'I understand,' Dodd said.
'Good,' I said. 'Let's start this thing.'
I opened the door.
And the process started.

CHAPTER FIFTEEN

Voices Boiling in the Light

1. Talking to a Corpse

The library was empty, silent, still.

And so cold.

We stepped inside.

Its Victorian tables and chairs and tidy bookshelves sat undisturbed. And yet . . . I noticed a weird kind of hush in the frigid air, as though something big had happened there the split second before we opened the door, but we arrived just too late and all that was left were the echoes. Or maybe the echoes were in my brain. Or maybe they were merely traumatic memories from the first time I had set foot in that room.

'Go ahead, turn to the summoning, Jimmy,' I said. 'And get ready to repeat the assistant's litany, and do not say anything out of sequence, no matter what happens—you understand?'

'I'm ready, Father.'

'Here we go,' I said, and glanced around the wainscoted walls and book-lined shelves. Every single light in the room was blazing: Hundred-watt bulbs—at least—in every fixture; every Tiffany lamp on every end table; every jeweled chandelier; every sconce. Something about all that light was bothering me.

' "Do not remember, O Lord," ' I began reciting, ' "our sins or those of our forefathers." '

' "And do not punish us for our offenses," ' Dodd replied.

' "And lead us not into temptation," ' I said, my voice strained and hoarse.

' "But deliver us from evil," ' Dodd answered.

' "Save this house, the home of Your servants," ' I recited, gripping the Bible so tightly it was bending backward. I realized I was starting to perspire under my sweater.

But the room seemed dead all of a sudden, like we were talking to a corpse.

' "Because it exists in your name," ' Dodd answered, his voice sharp with tension.

' "Lord, hear my prayer," ' I said.

' "And let our cries reach You," ' Dodd replied.

' "Unclean spirit, whoever you are, and all your companions who possess this place," ' I said, ' "I command you, show yourself." '

I paused, and felt nothing.

' "In the Name of Jesus Christ, we summon you to show us a sign, your name, and the day and hour of your damnation." '

Another pause. Nothing.

' "In the Name of Jesus Christ, we summon you. Show us a sign. Make yourself known." '

Still nothing.

And it went on like that for nearly fifteen minutes.

2. Dead Flowers

At one point I thought Dodd was going to collapse, he was so wired; nervous tension was radiating off him like an odor. I felt sorry for him, but there was nothing I could do. In many ways, this was the hardest part: The smoking out of the spirit. I remember reading about one case in Naples in which the spirit lay dormant, like a fox in a hole, for a whole six days in order to throw the exorcist off the scent. I had heard of another situation—in the Deep South in the 1950s—where the entity slipped quietly into the assistant the moment the ritual had begun and then proceeded, in a hideous mocking voice, to exorcize itself.

I'm not claiming I was the world's wisest practitioner, or the world's bravest man—far from it—but I was experienced enough to know the Devil was a trickster, and that a fallen spirit tended to dance around the ring a little bit before engaging in the fight. But that didn't make it any easier that night. We were all juiced up with adrenaline, and scared to death, and full of righteous anger and the Holy Spirit, but we had to wait. We had to wait it out. And we had no idea how long that was going to take, or exactly how the thing was going to come at us. It was like entering the boxing ring and waiting for your opponent to make up the rules.

We kept repeating the litany for another fifteen minutes or so, and then decided to take a break.

We went back into the hall and found a small settee against the frosted bay windows of the south wall, and both sat down. I found the flask at the bottom of my satchel, and we passed it back and forth as we listened to the storm assaulting the house. There wasn't much whiskey left, but it was enough to wet our whistles. Apart from that, the cheap store-brand booze was doing very little to bolster my courage. Right then I really needed about half a dozen boilermakers to take the edge off. But that wasn't going to happen. Not in that house. Not on that night.

I glanced around the corridor and found myself marveling at where I was. I was in America's premier house:

The most famous residence in the western hemisphere. And it had turned out to be the most profoundly haunted place that I had ever visited. Who would have thought? But then again, maybe I shouldn't have been so surprised. After all, the White House was like America's attic: A place we store our collective memories. A repository of lost hopes and political disasters. Of course it was haunted. How could it not be haunted?

Directly across from where we were sitting was a portrait of Betty Ford in a flowing blue dress. Looking almost dreamy, with a Mona Lisa smile and piercing eyes, she held a kind of mythic quality. But I found myself wondering about the real woman who had wandered those halls. Had she been a heavy drinker before she moved in there? Or had her troubles started after this same house got its hooks into her? I wondered about FDR's illnesses, Bill Clinton's reckless affairs, Abe Lincoln's depression. I wondered about all those tragic misadventures that had occurred in that mansion. Were they because of the same dark spirit? Was there some centuries-old curse on the White House?

In the dim light of the Regency chandeliers, this ground-floor hallway had the feel of a marble catacomb. Its vaulted ceiling rose in great arches above each doorway and, upon closer scrutiny, all the bronze statuary and presidential antiques were covered with a film of age. The air smelled of dust and fatigue, and the entire place radiated a brooding kind of sadness. There was sadness in the fabric of the place, in the joins between the marble, in the seams of the floor. And I soon started noticing things that I hadn't noticed before. Like water-damage bumps along the edge of the carpet running the length of the hall. Maybe eight or ten of them. Had there been that many of them when I had made a tour earlier that day?

And what about all those antique vases? There were several of them distributed around that ground-floor corridor, on side tables and pedestals. But there was something odd about the flower arrangements that I hadn't noticed earlier.

'What's the deal with the vases?' I said, motioning at one nearby floral arrangement.

'What?' Dodd was taking a last sip of whiskey.

'The flower vases,' I said, pointing up and down the corridor. 'The bouquets—they're all clipped. You see what I'm saying? No blossoms.'

'Oh . . . yeah.' Dodd nodded, glancing at a vase set on a mahogany pedestal near the settee. It was a fire-glazed pot the color of a salmon's belly, with delicate hand-scrawled leaves, and from the top rose some spindly green stalks already starting to turn brown. 'The flower thing,' Dodd commented, 'it's been a problem for as long as anybody can remember.'

'What problem?'

He nodded. 'Flowers will never stay fresh in this place. You put them in the vase; five minutes later they're wilting.'

'Could've sworn I saw flowers here in press photographs, news broadcasts . . .'

'Plastic,' he said with a shrug.

I took my last pull of the flask, staring at those barren bouquets, and buttoned the top button of my flannel shirt. I was exhausted already, but I knew the worst was yet to come.

'Tell me something, Jimmy,' I said. 'And be honest.'

'About what?'

'About why you picked *me* for this job.'

He looked at me for a moment. 'In all honesty?'

I nodded.

'You have no current ties to the Church, so obviously you were less of a security risk . . .'

I looked at him. 'Is that all?'

'Yeah, I guess. That . . . and the fact that you're one of the few people I trust.'

We sat there in tense silence for a few moments. Dodd reached into his pocket, pulled out a cigarette and lit it with the last match in a soggy matchbook. Then he turned to me and said, 'What really happened that night, Father?'

'Pardon me?'

He looked at me. 'You know what I'm talking about: Your exorcism of that little boy.'

I glanced across the corridor and sighed. The last thing I wanted to do now was dredge up my past. But, then again, I had never stopped thinking about it. Never. Especially here in this mansion.

'It was almost exactly twenty years ago,' I said softly.

Then I told Dodd everything.

3. Blank Verse

It happened back when I was assigned to the Water Tower parish in Chicago. One day, this poor black woman named Letitia Rivers came to me and asked me if I would perform an exorcism on her son. Of course, the lady wasn't even a member of the Church, but, after investigating her claims, I became convinced that her boy was in the grip of real evil. The child was speaking in tongues and chewing his own fingers off. He didn't need drugs. He didn't need a psychiatrist. He needed God. But I just couldn't get it past the archdiocese committee. I don't know what the problem was—maybe it was because the boy was a non-Catholic—but I couldn't get the authorization to proceed.

So I just went ahead and did it on my own.

Looking back on it, there was one particular image from that night that stuck with me—always flickering, unbidden, across the back of my mind. An indelible memory: *The door*. It lurked at the end of that squalid tenement hallway, illuminated by a single bare light bulb buzzing with flies, almost as though it were waiting for me. The ugliest door in the world, made of cheap particle-board oak, probably purchased at some discount lumber yard decades earlier, but now ravaged by age, blackened with filth, scarred by generations of dogs clawing at it. It was symbolic in many ways of the sad, pathetic world inhabited by the Rivers family: Dirt-poor, disenfranchised, cut off from the rest of society, forgotten.

It was the same big, black, ugly door that materialized in a snowstorm twenty years later on the second floor of the White House. And maybe that was why I was feeling an overwhelming sensation washing over me that the mansion itself was listening. The White House was *listening* to me tell my tale. The house *knew* things about me.

Things that I didn't want it to know.

'Anyway, Jimmy, what happened was, that exorcism got away from me,' I said at last, gazing at the frosted-over windows. Dodd sat there, listening intently, smoking another cigarette down to the nub. 'The ritual went on for hours,' I said, 'but the boy's body just couldn't take it. He expired on his bed sometime after midnight. But I should have known that. I should have been aware.' I felt my eyes welling up, and I pressed my thumb against the bridge of my nose to quell the tears.

Dodd was watching me. 'How could you have known? The boy was weak already, right?'

I said very softly, 'Minutes before I locked myself into the boy's bedroom with him, the neighbors had called an ambulance. The paramedics were already outside the door, but I wouldn't let them in. I didn't want to lose my battle with the monster inside that child. Was that the sin of pride? Was it ego?' I paused. 'Whatever the reason, it was a fatal mistake,' I said.

It was because the boy had been an epileptic. His uncle had been trying to tell me that in his own simple language, but I just didn't get it. 'The boy died swallowing his own tongue,' I added, staring down at my empty flask.

Dodd just smoked his cigarette and thought about it. After a while, he put his hand comfortingly on my shoulder, and we sat like that for another eternity.

'Anyway, that's all ancient history,' I said finally, and longed for another swig of hooch, wanting to drown in it. 'What I really want to know is, why are you still single?'

He wiped his mouth and shrugged. 'Guess it's the job, the hours. How about you? Why didn't you ever get married?'

I managed a sad smile. 'Once upon a time, Jimmy, I was a priest. It's like you said the other day. Old habits die hard.'

He nodded, then took another drag of his cigarette.

I asked him if he had a current girlfriend.

He gave me another one of those odd looks, a mixture of awkwardness and pride. 'Are you interviewing me for a new altar-boy job?'

I could tell I was delving into something he didn't want to discuss. 'I'm sorry, Jimmy,' I said. 'Just making chit-chat.'

'It's okay, Father.' He looked at me openly. 'The reason I don't have a girlfriend is because I'm gay.'

There was a pause, and I was a little taken aback for a moment. I'm sure Dodd construed my silence as some kind of disapproval. He turned away, looking a little embarrassed, and I wanted so badly to say something to him, but I just couldn't figure out what in God's name my response should be. My mind had just gone blank.

Finally I managed to say, 'Jimmy, there's no—'

'I probably should have told you the minute I saw you,' he interrupted.

'Jimmy—'

'I won't blame you if you want me to leave now,' he said, staring at the floor.

As he looked at me, I saw all sorts of contrary emotions on his face. I saw pride and I saw shame, and I saw defiance, and I saw sadness. And I just couldn't imagine all the hard roads he had been down, coming from that blue-blood conservative Catholic family. And even though it was hard for me to reconcile the gay world with my own ingrained beliefs, I felt no malice toward homosexuals. After all, who was I to judge? Who was I to say it was right or wrong? And I certainly felt nothing but fondness for this bright, good-hearted man sitting next to me. He would always be little Jimmy Dodd to me. The kid that wore high-tops to High Mass. But what was I supposed to say to him? How was I going to ameliorate two thousand years of Catholic dogma? Whatever I said was going to sound phony. But I had to say something, and I had to say it sincerely. So I thought, and I thought, and it must have seemed like an eternity to Dodd, sitting there, smoking his next cigarette.

At last I turned to him and said, 'From 1956 to 1964, Bobby "The Hook" Carmichael was one of the greatest welterweight boxers ever to enter a ring, and he was gay, and nobody gave a shit about it.'

Dodd looked at me and smiled.

I smiled back at him and said, 'Who am I to argue with the World Boxing Association?'

I offered my hand, and he grasped it, and we shook—

—and that's when I heard music coming from some-where off in the darkness.

After a moment, I said, 'Is it me, or can you hear music?'

'What?'

'Music—like muffled, tinny music.'

Dodd listened hard, then shrugged. 'I don't hear anything.'

I cocked my head toward the sound. It was very faint,

and it seemed to be coming from the closet room next door to the library, that room with all the surveillance gear in it. 'I don't know,' I said. 'It's like a radio playing somewhere, or a record player or something.'

Dodd was nodding all of a sudden. 'Yeah—I hear it now—definitely.'

'Come on, Jimmy,' I said, and led him into the little room itself.

4. Funeral Dirge

The first thing I noticed was that in an entire wall of security monitors not one of them was operating properly. Each of the thirty-something screens was roiling with white noise. 'What's wrong with them?' I said, pointing at the screens.

Dodd shrugged, biting his fingernail. The little worn ritual book was still strapped to his wrist, dangling. 'Same thing that's happening with the phones?'

'Where the hell is that music coming from?' I looked down at the paint-spattered plastic radio on the work bench—the one on which I had heard the weather forecast earlier. It was turned off, but the muffled music kept droning faintly from somewhere nearby. I listened closely, trying to locate it. Was it Burke? Was somebody else still in the house? Somehow it sounded strangely organic, like a live orchestra seeping through the floor. It was the oddest tune I've ever heard: Slow and dirgelike, and completely out of tune, with a syrupy violin weeping some old fashioned melody over the top—almost like one of those annoying musical saws—and the more I listened to it, the more familiar it sounded.

'Sounds like it's coming from the basement,' I said.

'There's nobody down there,' Dodd argued.

For some strange reason I felt compelled to shove the desk out of the way and gaze down through the grating of the furnace vent behind it, as though I expected to see a little elfin orchestra down there jamming away in the dark. But all I could see was a couple of feet of spiderwebs, and then darkness.

But I could still hear that muffled music coming up from the darkness and, boy, did it sound familiar. The weird high notes, warbling painfully out of tune—what was it?

'Is it the house?' Dodd was saying. 'I mean, are we really hearing this?'

I confessed that I didn't know.

'It sounds familiar.'

'Yes, I know,' I said.

I looked back up at the assembled monitors and stared at the screens flickering with snow. When I was a kid I used to stay up late and wait for the national anthem to come on, and after that, when the station closed down for the night, I would scare myself half to death by staring at the snow-filled screen. The longer I looked at it, the more I would see things in that boiling light, and hear voices in the rushing white noise.

And right at that moment—as I flashed back to my misspent youth—I recognized the music coming from below. It was 'The Star-Spangled Banner.'

'I know what—' I started to say, but was interrupted by the phone as it began ringing.

We both froze.

It was one of those amazing moments when the entire universe seems to come to a halt, and the room around you seems to freeze in suspended animation, and you can't move or talk or do anything but just stare at your pal across the room like an idiot. The telephone rang a second time, miraculously, as I stared over at Dodd, and he stared back at me, and we stood there like statues as the phone shrilled a third time.

It was an old, black, ceramic Maryland Bell table model sitting on the corner of the cluttered desk. I told myself that Burke must have finally got the phones working again. Or maybe it was Redding calling from Blair House already. But something deep down inside me told me that it was something else altogether.

I managed to answer it on the fourth ring.

'The Star-Spangled Banner' was coming out of the receiver.

I felt a strange, feathery weight pressing down on my shoulders, like invisible mosquito netting. And I felt a wave of sheer dread come over me. Not fear, or panic, or terror . . . but dread. Like a surge of clinical depression settling suddenly in my bones.

I slammed the phone down.

Dodd was staring at me, eyes wide. 'Who was it? What's the matter?'

'Get your crucifix back out, Jimmy,' I said.

'Who was it?'

'It was the house calling,' I said.

'The what?'

It was time to go back into the library and finish what we had started.

CHAPTER SIXTEEN

The Summoning

1. Black Tar

' "By the mysteries of the incarnation, the sufferings and death," ' I recited softly. ' "By the resurrection, and the ascension of Our Lord Jesus Christ, and the coming of the Holy Spirit, we summon you." '

The library lay still and silent before us, almost as if it were taunting us, and the temperature seemed to drop as soon as we entered. I could feel the unclean spirit weighing down on me. I felt heavy and weak and useless and ugly and sick. I felt diseased. I felt repulsive. I felt like a slug. And it took a major amount of effort just to gather my thoughts.

Dodd was standing behind me. ' "In the Name of the Lord Almighty," ' he answered.

I repeated the summoning, and Dodd answered again, and we went on like that for several minutes before I noticed the odor.

In the frigid, dank air, the odor rolled in like an invisible fog.

I had smelled awful odors before—some in that very house, in that very room—but I had never encountered anything like the stench that was wafting through that room right then. It was the smell of rotten matter, decayed by time and sickness. It was a black, rancid odor teeming with disease. It was something cooked up in hell, and it attacked us like a living thing, penetrating our very lungs and choking us. My stomach heaved, and if it weren't for the Holy Litany I would have vomited my guts out.

But something kept me going at it.

' "Show yourself," ' I demanded as forcefully as I could manage, and as if in answer I caught my first sight of a black oily liquid dripping from a bookshelf.

' "In the Name of Jesus Christ," ' Dodd replied, and then he too noticed the black fluid. His eyes got big, but he didn't say anything, not wanting to interrupt the rite, but neither being able to tear his gaze from the shelf.

I watched the oily substance seeping out between the books that lined the east wall. Viscous, shiny and as black as pitch, it was dribbling lazily down from the spines of the antique books. I had read about that kind of stuff before, but I had never actually seen it. The Italian Franciscans called it *nettare del diavolo*—the nectar of the Devil—and, if I understood things correctly, it appeared only during particularly nasty exorcisms. Like this one.

' "The power of Christ summons you," ' I continued, staring at the wall of books.

The odor was intensifying, making the air almost too noxious to breathe. It was as though we were trapped in a slaughterhouse all of a sudden. Hell, it was like we were right inside a slaughtered animal that had been decaying in the sun for several days. But I couldn't stop staring at that black fluid. It had an obscene quality, as though it was the bile from some desecrated body. I was having trouble breathing, and so was Dodd, but we didn't stop our recitation. We just tried to ignore the black tar and kept on chanting.

' "The power of Christ summons you," ' we said in

unison, following ancient words written nearly two thousand years ago. The temperature was still plummeting. It was cold enough for me to see Dodd's breath erupting in white puffs with each word he uttered.

' "The power of Christ summons you." '

I felt tremors in the floor, and I heard otherworldly music rising up from beneath us—like a gigantic antique Victrola playing some dusty 78 rpm recording, warbling sickly—and just above the noise I heard a bizarre crackling sound all around me, like an electrical circuit overloading.

' "The power of Christ summons you." '

I looked around and blinked at the awful glare coming off stained-glass lampshades and crystal chandeliers and light fixtures. The light bulbs seemed to be glaring brighter and brighter, the sound of circuits frying and of static electricity melding now with the vibrations underneath us, and that infernal music rising from the darkness. I'll be damned if it wasn't a mish-mash of patriotic songs—'God Bless America,' even 'Hail to the Chief'—but all warped and hollow-sounding, rattling through the guts of the house as I squinted at the nimbus of dazzling light all around us.

'Father, what—?'

' "The power of Christ summons you!" ' I yelled at the room, still calling the spirit out.

One light bulb exploded behind me.

I spun around after a flash of silver light, like a photographer's strobe popping, and I saw that a Tiffany lamp on the side table by the door had overloaded, a thin tendril of blue smoke now rising off the top of the dark bulb inside it. I turned back toward Dodd and started to recite something else, when several more light bulbs erupted around us.

It was like the Chinese New Year for a few seconds, with light bulb after light bulb exploding violently in concussion blasts of glass-dust, driving us both to the floor, our hands clamped over our heads for protection. The air flickered brilliantly for several more minutes. But with each bulb that burst, it got darker and darker.

I heard others bursting out in the corridor, in rooms nearby, and panic started strangling me. You could hear the whole place dying, with fuses popping, the furnace blowing, the entire electrical system convulsing. It was like the house itself was having a stroke.

Then there came a deep, subsonic WHOOOMP!

And the thing that I had been dreading the most since the storm had started now finally happened. In that one deep paroxysm of sound, the entity knocked out the mansion's power.

And we were plunged into absolute darkness.

2. Death on My Fingertips

It's hard to explain, but there was a moment of sheer panic when I literally forgot where I was. It was a primal sort of terror, I guess. I was a baby again, alone in the middle of the night, and I was clawing, flailing, at the empty air, trying to grasp something, trying to find purchase, but then I heard Dodd's horrified whisper next to me, and everything came rushing back into my brain as I crouched down on the floor in the White House library.

'Father!'

'The satchel, Jimmy,' I hissed at him, clawing at the Persian rug, trying to locate my equipment.

'What—?'

'The little black satchel! There's a flashlight in it.'

'There's supposed to be an emergency generator—' Dodd was saying.

'Just help me find the satchel, Jimmy!'

I was still in a shocked state of blindness, my eyes trying

to adapt to the darkness. I couldn't see a thing, but I could hear something behind us, out in the corridor. It was such a horrible sound that I blocked it out of my mind—while I focused on locating that satchel, groping around on the floor. I felt something wet, brought my hand up to my face and sniffed at my fingers.

I almost gagged. It smelled like death on my fingertips, like a deadly, rotting super-bacteria from deep in the earth—the smell of blackness—and I realized at once that the black tar was probably seeping across the floor. It was the same nasty phenomenon that Father Lankester Merrin had discoursed on extensively: A sort of biological by-product of demonic infestation. Like pus from a wound. And it reminded me that we were still in the middle of our ritual.

'I can't find it, Father,' Jimmy whispered hoarsely across the darkness.

'Most important thing, Jimmy, is to keep the ritual going.'

'I understand,' he said.

Finally my hand brushed against something hard and cold: The handle of my satchel. I grabbed it and pulled it toward me and felt my way into it. I could feel all the odds and ends in the bottom of the bag—the rosary beads, the caffeine pills, the incense and my Bible.

And the small metal cylinder filled with two c-cell batteries.

I dug the flashlight out and flicked it on.

The room was an obscenity.

It was everywhere, gluey and thick and glistening like a cancerous infection, oozing down the bookcases and the gray-paneled walls, dripping off the edges of historic portraits, soaking the rug and even clinging to the ceiling. I had never seen anything like it. I shone the flashlight over toward Dodd. Crouching under a painting of a Pawnee

Indian chief, he seemed frozen with terror, gawking up at the black slime. I could tell by the way his head was cocked that he was hearing the same sounds coming from the corridor as I did.

'The ritual, Jimmy,' I urged, turning back to the little worn-out book strapped to my wrist.

'Yeah, right—' He tried to find the correct page, but it seemed pretty tough going.

'Page 496!' I prompted.

'Yeah.'

' "Most glorious prince of the heavenly army," ' I recited as I rose to my feet, shining the flashlight down on my book. My knees were rubbery and I felt dizzy, and I was having some trouble following the minuscule text on those delicate, yellowed pages. And the sound out in the corridor was intensifying. We had let an otherworldly animal out of its cage.

' "Holy Michael the Archangel," ' I murmured quickly. ' "Defend us in battle against the princes and powers and rulers of darkness—" '

All I could focus on was the sound out in the corridor, and the pinpoint of yellow light on my Bible.

' "Defend us against the spiritual inequities of this former angel," ' I recited, my breath visible to me in the slender beam of light. ' "Come to the help of men whom God made in His own image, and whom He bought from the tyranny of Satan at a great price." '

'Amen,' Dodd said softly, standing next to me, straining to see in the dim peripheral glow from my flashlight.

' "Pray to the God of peace that He crush this unclean spirit under our feet—" '

'Amen,' Dodd said.

' "Pray to the God of goodness that He give us strength to drive out this unclean spirit—" '

'Amen.'

The noise now filled the corridor, and we instinctively turned toward the open doorway. Had there been light and power, that same noise would not have rattled us quite as badly. But, plunged in darkness, it was the kind of noise that might haunt my sleep for the rest of my days. It seemed to emanate from everywhere and nowhere simultaneously, pouring out in great rhythmic waves—like noxious air pumped through gigantic bellows.

Something breathing?

Something *enormous* breathing?

' "Help us make captive that ancient spirit," ' I recited, my voice sounding tinny and weak in my own ears. ' "And reduce it to everlasting nothingness so that it no longer grips this place in evil." '

'Amen,' Dodd muttered through clenched teeth.

I took a step toward the corridor. ' "In the Name of Jesus Christ, God and Lord," ' I recited.

' "And through the intercession of the Immaculate Virgin, Mother of God, Mary," ' Dodd answered shakily, hovering right behind me.

' "And through Holy Michael the Archangel, the blessed apostles," ' I continued, stepping into the doorway, feeling the chill on my face.

' "And all the saints," ' Dodd answered.

' "We are about to undertake the expulsion of the diabolic," ' I said, clenching the book of rituals in bloodless fingers, my heart hammering in my chest.

In the darkness came creaking noises.

The breathing stopped.

I pointed the flashlight beam out into the corridor, sweeping it along toward the west end.

My breath caught in my throat.

'You gotta be kidding me,' Dodd uttered behind me, and I knew he had just seen the same thing as me.

3. Wax Before Fire

In the darkness it was quite hard to tell for sure, but of the six bumps along the floor of the corridor, where the water damage seemed to have buckled up through the parquet tiles, the one closest to my flashlight beam—among the largest of them, about the size of half a melon—had just moved position. It was so fast it made me jump, almost insectile in its jerking.

One second it was visible in the pool of light, the next second it was gone.

'This is not happening,' Dodd was mumbling. I shone the light in his face.

'Gotta stay on track, Jimmy.'

'I know, I know, I'm just saying—'

'Don't look at it, Jimmy. Just don't look at it,' I said, gripping the book tighter. The renewed silence was horrible. We couldn't even hear the storm anymore. The only sound was that violent creaking noise echoing intermittently down the dark corridor.

I shone the light back along the hallway.

They were slithering toward us from the west end of the corridor, just barely visible in the skinny little light-beam. Dozens of them, some also as huge as watermelon halves, others as tiny as walnut shells. It was almost too surreal to register: Lumps in the floor moving directly toward us. Coming at us like little animals burrowing under the tiles, and making the most hideous noises. Something like old arthritic bones creaking.

For a moment I went a little crazy, spinning around desperately on the spot, shining my flashlight this way and that, focusing on one slithering lump after another—each of them seeming to deliberately seek us out.

Yet I stood my ground in that doorway. 'The opening

prayer now, Jimmy. The fourth part of the ritual, the fourth part—do you see it?' I noticed Dodd seemed short of breath. 'Breathe in, Jimmy, deep breaths. Come on, concentrate on the text, I need you.'

In the darkness, the bumps converged from all angles. You could hear them shift like cartilage tearing. I gripped my book and started reciting the call-and-response: ' "May God rise up, and may His enemies be dissipated." '

' "And let those who hate Him—" ' Dodd replied in a halting, quivering voice. ' "Let those who hate Him flee— let them flee before Him." '

' "Let them be dissipated like smoke," ' I recited. I could feel the floor vibrating faintly as those things burrowed toward us.

' "As wax flows before fire, so let—" ' um, "so let sinners perish before God," ' Dodd uttered frantically in response. The creaking sounds were all around us now. The wooden floor tiles groaned.

' "Look upon the Cross of the Lord," ' I said, ' "and be defeated, all enemies." '

' "The ancient strength will conquer," ' Dodd replied, ' "through the . . . through the King of Kings." '

The flooring was bubbling with movement as the lumps approached my feet, insectlike under the parquet. The stench of that black infection was overwhelming.

' "Let Your mercy be with us, O Lord," ' I called out above the din, reaching down to my belt to locate one of the cruets of holy water.

' "According to our hopes in You, O Lord!" ' Dodd rejoined frantically.

' "We exorcize you!" ' I said, trying to hold both the cruet and the flashlight with the same hand, while struggling to get the top of the cruet open with my thumb. I eventually flung a dollop of holy water at the floor—first to the left, then to the right. I could barely see the scattered liquid shimmering.

The instant the sacred water touched it, the floor reacted violently.

4. Nerve Endings

In retrospect, I think it was all mostly taking place in our minds—although that didn't make things any easier to accept. It happened so quickly, with so much coming at us all at once, that our brains probably shut down a little bit through some kind of innate defense mechanism. I think it was at that precise moment that the thing that had been lurking in that place truly came out of hiding.

The best way to describe it is that the floor erupted with arms.

I know how crazy that sounds, but it seemed true. Dozens of black, spindly arms erupted out of those blisters in the parquet, shooting straight up at us like cobras striking. It was a little bit like one of those high-tech virtual-reality games—except that it wasn't like that either. It was something more tangible, decidedly more real. In that brief instant of utter horror, those arms *existed* in space and time—I noticed scars on them, and networks of delicate veins, and their shriveled, callused skin—and I got the sense that they *belonged* to somebody. In fact, in that single insane moment that seemed to stretch on for ever, it occurred to me that those arms all belonged to a single entity.

The flashlight slipped out of my hand and clattered to the floor. Its yellow beam rolled about, and wobbled, casting oblong shadows across the walls, and we reacted instinctively, shielding our faces from those terrible outstretched hands. And simultaneously our senses were attacked by a kind of weird, rushing chorus of screams—accompanied by that rotten, black, earthy odor. And it all happened so quickly that I never even noticed when precisely the grasping arms ceased to exist.

I stumbled backward and fell hard on my ass, the wind knocked out of my lungs.

In panic, Dodd tripped over his feet and also went down hard.

For several frenzied moments I clawed around in the dark for that flashlight. Luminous dots flashed across my field of vision, and I thought for a moment my heart might explode. Then I finally located the flashlight.

I trained it on the floor, searching for those ragged holes through which the arms had exploded. But there was nothing there: The floor was now one smooth, unblemished plane.

Even the bumps were gone.

'Father?' Dodd's voice rang out next to me, close to hysterical.

'I'm okay, Jimmy. You all right?' I turned the flashlight towards his face. He looked like a ghost, his eyes moist with terror.

'Yeah . . . I guess,' he said.

A moment passed, then we both struggled to our feet, and stood there in the darkness. I could hear my own heart beating in my ears, and I was developing a splitting headache. My knees were complaining, and my stomach felt as though it had been scoured internally with a wire whisk. But I couldn't think more about my discomforts because the house was now awake.

The spirit had been summoned.

I flashed the light down the length of the corridor and saw its reflection glittering up by the ceiling, sparkling amid the dead chandeliers, gleaming off marble on the walls. It was like looking down the length of a sunken ship—a ghost ship. I could feel the spirit's presence as thick and dark as ink clouding in water. Outside, the storm continued to rage, the winds moaning, rattling the windows. But somehow the house had taken on a new complexion. The darkness had deepened further, and the air felt prickly as though charged with negative ions.

'What's next?' Dodd said suddenly.

'Wait here, Jimmy,' I said, and went back into the library to recover my satchel. I tried not to look up at the walls or the ceiling, or at the glistening tarlike patches staining the floor. And I simultaneously tried not to inhale that foul odor of death. I grabbed up my satchel and rejoined Dodd.

'What now?' he asked, nervously fingering the edge of his ritual book.

'We continue the rite of exorcism, Jimmy, harder than ever—while we've still got the presence on the run. It's a good sign.' I inserted my right wrist through the satchel's handle, so I could keep holding the flashlight with that hand.

'Let's do it,' Dodd said with forced enthusiasm. He was jittery, terrified. The dark energy in that place was really getting to him.

'Stay close,' I said.

'You don't have to worry about that, Father.' There was no humor in his voice.

I played the flashlight back along the dark corridor, its beam piercing through a haze of dust motes. I then froze for a brief instant, as I thought I heard some new sound beneath the falsetto whining of the blizzard. Was it floor-boards creaking rhythmically somewhere in the distance?

'What is it, Father?'

I assured him it was nothing.

I inhaled a deep breath, stretching my neck from side to side—an old boxing technique to calm me down, to get me centered and ready to fight. The trouble was, I was already exhausted, and I had barely set foot in the ring yet. Hallucinations will do that: They'll sap your energy. But that was how it worked with exorcisms. They were like marathons, and you had to pace yourself.

The section of text I was reading—'The Expulsion of Apostate Spirits from a Place or Domicile'—fell into six parts: The Invocation, the Summoning, the Exorcism Address, the Closing Prayer, and the Blessing. We had now completed the Invocation and the Summoning, but the most grueling part was still ahead of us, as I knew only too well.

I started heading toward the west end of the hall.

Dodd followed.

'Wait a minute!' he uttered in the dark beside me.

'What's up, Jimmy?'

'Just listen.' In the flashlight beam, his eyes looked shiny and huge. He spun around and glanced back toward the east end. 'Sounds like—'

He didn't have to finish, because I now heard it too, louder and more distinct than before. There were footsteps echoing up from the basement, moving up the stairs. Chills brushed up the backs of my legs. The footsteps were slow and clumsy, dragging heavily up the worn iron steps, taking their sweet time. And for an instant my rattled brain cast back to images from those old Universal horror movies that had scared the piss out of me when I was a kid. I thought of a wrinkled, stiff-armed Boris Karloff in *The Mummy*, shuffling through the shadows, and I thought of how stupid those archeologists had been for reading aloud the ancient scroll of Thoth and bringing the monster to life. I wondered if that's what we had done here too—awakened a monster.

I flashed the light across the top of the staircase as the footsteps were coming ever closer, echoing up from the dark—*thud, drrrraaaag, thud, drrrraaaaag*. They ascended the steps so slowly that I became sure the spirit must be deliberately taunting me, trying to destroy my nerve.

'Turn to section three now, Jimmy,' I said, digging another cruet of holy water out of my belt. 'It's on page 498, "the Address to Satan and the Apostate Spirits." ' I then took a few steps toward the top of the staircase.

'What if it's only Burke?' Dodd said, fumbling in the dark with his ritual book.

'It isn't Burke,' I said firmly, though not sure how I could know that.

Dodd grabbed me, pulling me back. 'How do you know it's not him?'

'The Address, Jimmy—the Exorcism Address.'

Dodd yelled toward the stairs: 'Who's there? Who is it? Please identify yourself.'

But there was no answer.

'Burke?' he cried out.

Still no answer.

'Burke!'

My light was now focused on the top of the stairs, forming a luminous ring about three feet in diameter, but we still couldn't see anything. The footsteps were reaching the ground-floor level, and now we could hear a thick breathing noise. Whoever or whatever it was would be stepping into the pool of light any moment now.

I approached the stairs, my ritual book already open.

' "Each unclean spirit, each power of Satan," ' I recited loudly.

' "Each infestation of the Enemy," ' Dodd responded from the darkness behind me. ' "Each legion, each Satanic sect . . ." '

Something was finally coming into view. In my peripheral vision I could sense a deeper shadow emerging from the dark.

' "In the Name and by the power of our Lord Jesus

Christ," ' I said, genuflecting with the flashlight, so that the items in my satchel rattled, ' "we exorcize you." '

But Dodd was staring transfixed at the deep shadow emerging against the wall.

'Jimmy, the answer! Read the answer!' I waved my flashlight at his book.

'Yeah . . . I'm sorry, um . . . "Be uprooted and put to flight from this place of God," ' he added finally.

' "From the souls that were made in the image of God," ' I continued, holding the cruet up and thumbing it open. 'And from the innocents redeemed with the blood of the divine Lamb, we exorcize you." '

The apparition was coming into view.

' "Leave this place!" ' I shouted as I flung a drop of holy water at it.

My light-beam landed for just an instant on a pale, drawn face.

'Oh my God!' Dodd gasped next to me.

I raised the trembling beam of the flashlight up into the creature's face, and finally I saw who it was. For one terrible moment I couldn't move, nor could I even compute what I was seeing. I just stood there staring as the light reflected off the figure's vacant gaze.

'Suzanne!' Dodd blurted from the darkness.

But the First Lady just stood there with a dazed, faraway stare. There were tears glistening on her cheeks, and her face was as white as porcelain. Her eyes were like marbles, and clearly something had frightened her stupid.

We both went over to her, and I put a supporting arm around her. She felt as cold as if she had just emerged from a walk-in freezer. In the light shining onto her face she now resembled a very old woman.

'It got my daughter,' she finally said, in an utterly toneless, bloodless voice.

I gaped at her. 'What's got your daughter?'

But she didn't answer—just kept staring with those glassy, marble eyes.

'Suzanne,' Dodd said softly. 'We're here now, and we'll help you.'

I asked again, 'What got your daughter, Mrs. Fallon?'

Fresh tears welled in her eyes, and tracked down those alabaster cheeks. Then her voice came out in a strangled whisper. 'Redding's dead.'

Dodd flinched. 'What?'

'Mrs. Fallon,' I persisted. 'Try to concentrate. You just said *it* got your daughter,' I said. 'What is it that's got your daughter?'

She took a long time to answer, her traumatized gaze never wavering from the darkness straight ahead of her.

Finally she replied in a choking voice: 'The black man.'

CHAPTER SEVENTEEN

Into the Dark

1. Dead End

Arm in arm with her daughter, she had been following the secret-service agent through the damp, gloomy world of the emergency tunnels. Built to withstand everything from stubborn rodents to nuclear attack, the passageway was lined with grime-covered lead and other metal alloys that had aged over the years to a dull, slimy gray, like the skin of an earthworm. Legend had it that LBJ used these tunnels to avoid the press, and rumors were plentiful about Nixon's disappearing acts underground. But Suzanne was not aware of any of that—she just wanted to get her daughter out of harm's way as quickly as possible. And at first it had seemed that was not going to be a problem.

As they had made their way north toward Pennsylvania Avenue, their footsteps echoing dully in the confined space, the storm was barely audible above them, merely a faint humming noise coming in waves, and the sound of dripping could be heard somewhere nearby. Every few yards, a light hanging down from the ceiling would illuminate the tunnel in a pool of harsh, dirty light.

At one point, she asked Redding how much further they needed to go. When he failed to answer, Suzanne asked *him again, but he requested her to be quiet. She realized immediately that something was very wrong.*

They paused in mid-tunnel as Redding studied a rusty electrical box fixed on the wall. Melissa kept glancing nervously around, as though something might jump out at her at any moment. After a minute, Suzanne again asked Redding what the hell was the problem, and why had they stopped here, and shouldn't they be out of there by now? Redding turned to her then and confessed the truth.

As far as he could determine, they had got lost somehow.

Suzanne couldn't believe her ears, but Redding went on to explain that something very weird was going on. Something was not right about the tunnel. What the hell was he talking about, she demanded, and Redding explained further. They had been proceeding under the north lawn for altogether too long now, with no sign of reaching their destination.

The tunnel was supposed to be laid out in regular sections, with junctions occurring about every five hundred feet. The first of these sections should lead them all the way under the north lawn, and the next below Lafayette Park, then another would take a ninety-degree turn to the east, toward Jackson Place, and after that a series of steps would lead up to a garage adjacent to Blair House. Each junction was marked by a visible seam in the lead wall, as well as a metal call-box and a distinctive sign stenciled in military-style block letters on the floor—announcing exactly where they were. Judging from the amount of time elapsed, and the distance they had already covered, they should have been right under Pennsylvania Avenue by now. But they had not come upon the first seam yet, so had been walking for a good fifteen minutes without reaching a single junction.

It was as though the first section of tunnel was going on for ever.

Suzanne felt dizzy herself, but begged her daughter to

stay calm. Melissa was mumbling to herself, and Suzanne feared the girl was starting to zone out again.

Redding held his gun arm out, and began turning around in circles, scanning every wall surface. 'Wait a minute. Stand by.' He pointed out a shadowy patch in the wall some fifty feet ahead of them, and told Suzanne to stay put with her daughter while he investigated it. Reluctantly she agreed.

Redding approached the spot he'd indicated, and then called back to them to explain. The shadow was actually an opening in the tunnel wall which wasn't marked on the map. He had decided he was going to climb through and check it out. Suzanne yelled back, 'You're not leaving us here,' but he was already gone.

Redding had vanished inside the hole.

For a few moments she just stood there, clutching her daughter and agonizing over what to do. Melissa was mumbling something about the house not letting them leave, but Suzanne was not paying her much attention as she was too busy figuring out what to do next.

And that's when she heard a scream ring out.

It came from inside the hole in the wall, and if Suzanne had not known Redding was somewhere inside there, she never would have guessed it was his voice: High-pitched and blood-curdling, it sounded like the cry of an animal being skinned alive.

Grabbing her daughter by the arm, she started backing away from that awful keening scream. Suddenly the two women turned round, and tried to flee back along the way they had come.

But they didn't get far, for the tunnel simply ended. A dead-end wall that hadn't been there before now loomed up in front of their faces. The two of them gasped, nearly colliding with it. Suzanne reached out and touched this obstruction, finding that it was rough cinderblock and cold to the touch. And it was real—as real as anything. Suzanne's heart started racing.

Melissa had fallen completely silent, as if drifting into some kind of trauma. The shrieking sounds from the hole behind were dwindling now, and Suzanne had no choice but to take her daughter's hand and start heading back towards it.

As they got nearer to the hole, she told Melissa to wait under one of the lights for a second while Suzanne herself investigated.

Creeping toward the hole with her heart pumping furiously, she had no idea at all what she would find there. But she was certain about one thing: She didn't want Melissa to witness it. Slowly approaching the cavity, she leaned forward and peered inside; the opening was about four feet in diameter. At first she saw nothing because it was so dark. But then came some faint, watery gasping sounds, and she detected something moving, about ten feet further in.

As her eyes adjusted to the darkness, Suzanne was finally able to make out Redding's face.

The house was eating him alive!

That's the only way she could describe it: The house was swallowing him whole. Flailing wildly, his mouth gaping open in terror, Redding looked as if he was being strangled by countless shriveled black arms protruding from the tunnel wall itself. For a brief, terrible instant, his eyes met Suzanne's. He tried to call to her, but the arms kept slithering all around him. One black hand was clasped around his throat, while several zombie arms were entwined around his solar plexus. Ultimately the pressure of them became too much, and Redding was slowly crushed alive, his eyes bulging, blood oozing from his nostrils, his purple tongue protruding . . .

And that's when Suzanne heard Melissa call out behind her.

She snapped her shocked attention back toward her daughter.

At first glance it seemed as though Melissa was engulfed in a cloud of black smoke. But then Suzanne realized something grotesque was hovering over her daughter. It was something huge and black . . . and it happened so fast that Suzanne could hardly manage to scream. Her daughter was being engulfed by a shadow of pure evil.

Suzanne howled, 'No!' and started running back along the main tunnel—

But she just couldn't get her legs to work. Like in a dream, her body was seizing up, as if her joints were clogged with molasses. She tried to cry out, the words catching in her terror-constricted throat, and struggled to reach her daughter. But all her efforts were futile. Melissa seemed to have fainted away, and the great dark figure had seized her in its arms. Suzanne caught a glimpse of the figure's face: It was straight out of a nightmare—like black, chiseled onyx, with a flash of ivory teeth.

Either grimacing or smiling at her.

And then Suzanne finally found the breath to scream.

2. The Black Man

'It took her right into the wall,' Suzanne choked in a whisper. She was nearly at the point of total exhaustion, and I wasn't sure how much longer she could go on talking.

'Into the wall?' Dodd's gaze flitted from her to me and back to her.

We were huddled in the rear of the service kitchen, in the pool of dim yellow light from a Coleman gas lantern. We had locked the door—as if that was going to provide us with any comfort—and we had laid Suzanne down on the cot we had found in Henry's office. The kitchen was full of hulking stainless-steel shadows and ticking noises, and the muffled whining of the storm outside. The temperature had already dropped ten degrees or more, and it wouldn't be long before we needed our coats. But, right then, our attention was focused intensely on the thin, patrician-looking woman on the cot.

'I watched it lift her off the ground,' she whispered hoarsely, holding in a lot of agonizing pain and fear. She was one tough nut, this woman. 'It seemed like she was floating,' she repeated, as though trying to convince herself. 'Then it carried her across the tunnel to another hole into the wall. And there was nothing I could do, I couldn't move. Oh Jesus, I was completely frozen to the spot.'

'We'll find her for you, Suzanne,' Dodd said firmly.

'I was frozen,' she said again.

I asked what happened next.

She swallowed and said, 'I don't really know. I stumbled around down in the tunnel for a while, trying to find her, but I got lost, and then the lights went out, and I kind of lost my mind a little bit, I don't know, but then somehow I found the stairs . . .'

'Mrs. Fallon, try to describe this figure,' I said. 'It may be important.'

She closed her eyes and put her face in her hands. 'I . . . I don't . . . I don't know what else to say,' she stammered.

Dodd looked at me for a moment, then back at her. 'You said it was a black man? You mean like African-American?'

She looked up. 'No, not African-American,' she said. '*Black*. What I mean is, this thing was black. The color *black*.'

I broke in, 'Was it similar to a hole in the air?'

She stared at me. 'A what?'

I explained about how I had heard of several witness sightings that had reported a sort of absence, as if cut out of the air. She shivered at the mention of it, reacting involuntarily to the remembered image.

Then she nodded. 'I suppose that's what it was.'

I then asked if she had ever seen an apparition like this one before.

She shook her head slowly. 'Nothing even remotely like it.'

There was a tense pause before I started to ask, 'Can you describe the feeling you—'

'This is something you guys did, isn't it?' Suzanne blurted, suddenly sitting up on the edge of the cot.

I asked what she meant.

'With your rituals and your—your goddamn ceremonies.'

Dodd started to say, 'Suzanne—'

'Let her speak, Jimmy.'

Her gaze, now suddenly intense, scorched me. 'Maybe we should have gotten a real priest,' she said. 'How do we know you're not just making it worse? With *your* background.'

I shrugged. 'You might be right, Mrs. Fallon, but the wheels are in motion—'

'*Something's* in motion,' she snapped at me. 'Something terrible's in motion, and a man is dead, and my daughter is missing—and whatever's been tormenting this house, it's worse than ever. Who's to say we're not playing right into its hands?'

I tried to control my anger. 'I promise you, Mrs. Fallon, I'm going to cast this thing out, and I'm gonna get your daughter back.'

'The father's right, Suzanne,' Dodd interceded.

'The father? The *father*?' she said, her frantic eyes shimmering in the flickering light. 'This was all your big idea, James—bringing in some alcoholic ex-priest.'

'Suzanne, come on!' Dodd knelt down beside her, his face ashen.

'Who the hell do you people think you are?' she snarled, nearly breaking down again.

'Mrs. Fallon, I'm gonna get your daughter back,' I repeated, my stomach churning. I was trying to keep my emotions in check and it wasn't easy.

She looked at me with liquid rage. 'Well, you don't have a very good track record, do you?'

'I told you, I'm going to get your daughter back!' I shouted back at her.

'Stop it, both of you!' Dodd yelled at us.

Suzanne then put her face in her hands again and started weeping. I turned away, my heart thumping like a ball-peen hammer in my chest. I was breathing quickly, so much energy and pressure building up inside me. I could feel the house around us like a living thing, and we were stewing in its acids. The house wanted to digest us, as it had already digested Redding. I had been through this before—with the Rivers family, and the haunted wing at Loyola. The dark energy gets into your soul and it stirs up rage.

A long, excruciating moment passed. Then something across the kitchen caught my eye: A huge butcher's block hunched in the shadows, stained with decades of sacrificial blood—roasts for Eisenhower receptions, ducks for Carter Christmases—and flanked by the tarnished silver doors of walk-in freezers and refrigerators. Beneath the butcher's block, the floor was a tacky, linoleum-style surface that had seen better days. There was a drain embedded in the floor, a huge, dented workman's toolbox sitting next to it.

Even in the darkness, I could discern the black substance oozing out of the drain.

'Stay here,' I said under my breath to Dodd, and dug in my satchel for the flashlight.

I went over to the butcher's block, sweeping the beam of light across the greasy floor. The bottoms of my shoes were sticking slightly with each step. I knelt down by the drain to take a closer look. It was the same black fluid that had been oozing out of the bookshelves of the library. I heard something gurgling up from below.

A whisper?

Somebody laughing?

I ignored the gooseflesh surging over me and touched the black liquid with my fingertips. Again I smelled that deathly rotten, earthy smell, and something inside me clicked. Of course. *Of course.* I sniffed at my fingers again as I listened to that soft, distant sound of whispered laughter echoing up from deep inside the drain. It was the secret laughter of a predator, cruel and mocking and uncontrollable.

A tide of black despair rose up in me.

I stared at the toolbox.

Of course.

' "Let no one fear death," ' I murmured, reaching deep inside my own heart, asking for the goodness of Christ to give me courage and strength.

'Father, what is it?' came Dodd's voice from the other side of the kitchen.

' "For the Savior's death has set us free," ' I went on with the prayer, ' "and Christ, having risen from the dead, has become the first fruits for those who have fallen asleep." '

I sprang to my feet, then hurried back over to where Suzanne sat huddled on the cot, shivering with her arms wrapped tightly around herself. Dodd stood beside her in the flickering gaslight.

'What is it?' he asked again. 'Talk to me, Father.'

I pulled him away from the First Lady, so she wouldn't be able to hear us, and then spoke in a low voice: 'I think I figured it out, Jimmy.'

'Figured what out?'

'I don't know why I didn't see it earlier.'

'What are you talking about?'

'The haunting, Jimmy.' I glanced over my shoulder at the drain in the floor . . . at the black sticky tar oozing out of it . . . the weird feelings of dread emanating from it.

I turned back to him. 'I think I know the source.'

CHAPTER EIGHTEEN

Last Rites

1. Swallowed Up in Darkness

'Tooms told us there is a sub-sub-basement here, right?'

'What?'

'A basement beneath the sub-basement,' I said, my chest tight, buzzing with adrenaline. The kitchen was teeming with flickering shadows. 'Something about Harry Truman's CIA building being a classified space, a bomb shelter, something like that, right? Right?'

Dodd nodded.

'It all comes from below us, Jimmy. From *below*. I don't know why I didn't realize it before.'

'How do you—?'

'The black tar that stinks like rotten earth.'

'Yes—'

'It's evident in all the different phenomena, Jimmy. Just think about it. The plumbing going haywire, the heating vents, the water damage—everything connects, everything.'

I could tell Jimmy was thinking about it, and during that awkward pause I could feel Suzanne's hot gaze on me.

'Okay, fine, whatever,' he finally said, ' but I still don't see how this knowledge helps us.'

I took him by the shoulders. 'Because it means that's where *I'm* gonna find the girl, Jimmy.'

Dodd cocked his head. 'What do you mean, *you're* gonna do it?'

'Because you're gonna stay here with Mrs. Fallon, Jimmy.'

'No, Father, uh-uh, no way,' Jimmy said.

'Jimmy, listen to me.' I squeezed his shoulder for emphasis. 'The next phase of the exorcism, the Address—it's not a call-and-response type of ritual.'

'Meaning?'

I explained I didn't therefore need an assistant for that part.

'No, Father, we stick together.'

'Jimmy, it's something I should have noticed right off the bat, but the underground is where the trouble lies.'

'All the more reason for us to stick together.'

'I'm trying to tell you, it's probably safer up here.'

'What? What's safer? That we stay here while you go off alone on some suicide mission from God? No way, we stick together.'

I glanced over at the First Lady, whose face was unreadable in the dull light. I turned back to Dodd. 'Jimmy, I'm just saying I don't want to go through another episode with Mrs. Fallon like we went through with the girl. God only knows what I'll find down there.'

Dodd rubbed his eyes. I could tell he was now exasperated on top of being terrified. 'It doesn't matter anymore that—'

'Yes, Jimmy, it matters more than ever.'

'No! Damnit! I don't want—'

'We are not splitting up!' the woman's voice suddenly cut us short.

We both whirled round. Suzanne had risen to her feet, her jaw set, and her cold hard gaze told me everything. She was a strong lady, who had never suffered fools gladly and wasn't about to start now. She had three academic degrees, and was a licensed attorney, and had been through four senatorial and two presidential campaigns. She was a tough character who usually got what she wanted, and right now she wanted her daughter back.

'Mrs. Fallon, this is for the best—' I started in an attempt to reason with her.

'We're *not* splitting up,' she said again, sounding more adamant than before.

I glanced around the dark kitchen, my heart thumping painfully. Why was I so anxious to go at the beast *alone*? What was I trying to prove to myself? For a moment, I saw the gaslight shimmering off a row of butcher's knives, and I felt that horrible black dread settling over me. I had to do something quickly. I felt as though I had finally made a breakthrough in my little war with the house and now I had to act. I had to go on the offensive. Just like those grizzled old Jesuits had taught me a million years earlier— *never let up, and never give the Devil any quarter.*

I turned to Dodd. 'I got an idea,' I said. 'We'll go find Burke.'

Both of them looked at me, but said nothing.

'We'll find Burke,' I went on, 'then we'll have the *three* of you stay together until the power comes back on, and meanwhile I'll go finish the ritual.'

Dodd and Suzanne exchanged a brief look, and finally Suzanne said, 'I just want my daughter back.'

'That's the idea,' I said, scooping up my satchel and turning my flashlight at the exit. 'Come on, then.'

I led them out of the kitchen.

Until we were swallowed up in darkness.

2. Alive with Ghosts

Halfway up the staircase of the north hall, the batteries in my flashlight started to go. The beam was changing colors as it swept across the red carpet runner, turning from a silvery yellow to a dull urine color. That was bad, really bad, because the mansion was turning into a haunted castle straight out of some brooding fairy tale. The air was bone-chillingly cold, the temperature dropping thirty degrees or so in the last half hour. We were each wearing a winter parka, since Suzanne had insisted we stop at the coat closet on the first floor where she kept some spare jackets, and our breath was increasingly visible. Above us, the vaulted ceiling gave the impression of some subterranean cave, and the noises coming from behind the walls were indescribable—like rats having an orgy. God only knew how much longer the flashlight would last me.

Dodd and Suzanne had noticed it too.

'Mrs. Whittaker left us one of her care packages in the communication office,' Suzanne spoke up in a drained, whispery monotone that made both of us jump. She sounded like a victim recovering from some terrible trauma. I later realized that she had swallowed a couple of Valium from her purse. 'I think there were some batteries in it,' she muttered.

I nodded, and continued on, focusing the dying beam on the top of the stairs.

We had already searched the first floor pretty thoroughly. Each room seemed alive with hallucinations, the air crackling with fragments of sounds and ghostly vestiges of past residents. In the Green Room, Suzanne thought she saw the clawfoot legs of a Duncan Phyfe table coming to life, clawing at the Persian rug, its caryatid heads becoming animated, shrieking in terror. In the Blue Room,

Dodd thought he saw the portrait-eyes of President James Monroe blink and turn luminous yellow when the flashlight hit it. The East-Room floor was also boiling with lumps. I kept admonishing my companions to ignore it all, to block it out, and just stay focused on finding Burke. But that was easier said than done. Every time we called out his name, the answering silence only made things worse. The house was subtly tapping into our fears. Every sound, every groaning floorboard, every surge of winter winds outside was magnified in the darkness.

At last we reached the top of the stairs.

I pointed the dying beam along the shadowy corridor. 'Burke!' I hollered again.

Only the dark silence replied.

The second-floor corridor seemed narrower than I remembered from my first view of it earlier, and also the feel of the place was completely different. No longer did the floor have the look of some quaint, run-down Victorian hotel. In the power blackout it had taken on a sinister quality, like an enormous broken dollhouse filled with corpses.

Or a forgotten waiting room.

I suppose it was the spirit working on me, but I stood there for a second, unable to make my old legs work. I just couldn't move. And all I could think of was a weird little memory: When I was thirteen, and in the eighth grade at Pope John School, Father Karras had caught me smoking on the playground and had made me write the Jesus prayer a thousand times on the blackboard: *Lord Jesus Christ, have mercy on me, a sinner*. That line would not stop running through my head now and, before I knew it, Dodd and Suzanne were eyeing me with alarm. So I took a deep breath and willed myself to start moving along that narrow-seeming corridor.

The communication room was the last door on the left,

in the corner office across from the President's dining room. You had to go through the west sitting hall to get there, and in the darkness it felt as though we were burglars creeping across someone's living room. I supposed the west sitting hall was the closest thing to a living room the White House had, and right then, in the pitch dark, it was alive with ghosts. I kept expecting to shine my pitiful light over at one of the velvet armchairs and see the ghost of Eleanor Roosevelt sitting there in her burial dress.

Dodd was betting the farm that Agent Burke would be found here in the communication room. Before we had split up in the basement, the older secret-service man had said that he was going to try to locate the source of the telephone problem, so the communication room was obviously the most likely place to start. Transformed in 1982 by Ronald Reagan into a quick-response media center, the room was designed for easy after-hours access to the President. It was equipped with a whole array of state-of-the-art communication gear and, according to Dodd, it was a combination Oval Office and Cabinet room squeezed into two hundred square feet of Victorian boudoir. Supposedly there were things in there that could alter global affairs with a flip of a switch.

We paused outside its closed door.

'Burke?' I called out, trying the doorknob. The door was locked. I then tried knocking. 'Burke? It's Delaney. I'm with Dodd and Mrs. Fallon. You in there?'

No answer.

'For God's sake, where the hell is he?' said Suzanne in a strained whisper.

'Maybe he's up on the third floor,' Dodd suggested in a puff of white vapor.

'Wait a minute, wait a minute,' I said, pressing my ear against the door. All I could hear on the other side was the wind whistling through the keyhole, yet I sensed there was something else inside that room.

I jiggled the knob, trying to force the door open.

'Father, what are you doing?' Dodd demanded.

'There *is* something in there,' I said, still fiddling with the knob. It was an old door, so I thought I might be able to worry it open with a little wrist action. But the lock held firm, and eventually I told the others to stand back.

'What the hell are you doing now?' Dodd demanded.

'There's something in there,' I insisted, and I slammed my shoulder into the door.

It hurt like a son of a bitch. I grabbed my shoulder and let out a sigh of pain. I'd been wrong about this door being so old; it was probably in fact a steel-reinforced repro-duction designed to withstand some terrorist strike force. Dodd and Suzanne began backing away, as if aghast at what I was doing. But by that point I was all juiced up with adrenaline, so I tried it again, banging my aching shoulder into the damned door. This time I heard it shifting slightly, so I put all my weight behind my third attempt.

Wham!

—and the door gave way.

I crashed into the room, stumbling to the floor, my flashlight careening across the carpet. Its shaft of dim light danced off the wall, and at first I couldn't see anything but the dark bulky shapes of computer gear. I swallowed back my pain and crawled across the room after the flash-light. Then I heard something odd behind me, and I heard Suzanne's strangled whisper saying something like, 'OhmyGod-ohmyGod-ohmyGod,' and I finally got my hand around the flashlight.

I managed to sit up on my heels and aim the flash-light around the room.

The man in the swivel chair had been dead for at least an hour.

But the worst part was the face—and the terror etched upon it.

3. Book of the Dead

'OhmyGod-myGod-myGod-myGod-myGod . . .' Suzanne stood pinned to the doorway, her hands pressed to her face. Her gaze was locked onto the body across the room.

Dodd put an arm around her. 'Okay, okay, okay, Suzanne, calm down, calm down,' he was saying, trying to persuade her to tear her gaze away from the corpse.

I couldn't stop staring at it either. With the fading yellow light trembling in my hand, I rose to my feet and looked closer at Burke's remains.

He was sprawled at a forty-five-degree angle, the swivel chair canted backward against a rack of charred computer drives. He seemed as stiff as a block of ice, his arms and legs splayed outward. His flesh was the color of boiled egg-white, and his eyes had erupted, leaving sockets full of gray mulch. But it was the frozen expression on his dead face that really got to me, his lips curled back into the horrible rictus of a scream, his ruined eyes wide open in terror.

'He must have been—what?—electrocuted?' Dodd gibbered.

I stared at the scorched computer drives. 'There must have been a power spike.'

'Yeah, but how? I mean how did all that voltage get into him?'

'Are you sure he's dead?' Suzanne asked nervously.

I eyed the corpse. 'Yeah, unfortunately, that's a pretty safe bet.'

Suzanne was now looking away, and murmured, 'But you said the spirit couldn't harm anybody.'

'I don't know what's happened here,' I said dumbly,

playing the light up and down over the stack of burned-out equipment. There was a blossom of soot behind Burke's skull, and I noticed that some hair had been singed off the top of his head. His left arm rested stiffly against the edge of the desk, near a row of twelve-inch computer screens, most of them cracked and blackened. The power surge must have been tremendous. I wondered if that was also why his face had frozen in that expression of terror. I had heard that involuntary facial tics at the point of death could sometimes resemble extreme fear, but I had never seen anything like the fright I saw on Burke's face.

'You said it couldn't hurt us,' she repeated hoarsely.

'Come on, Suzanne,' Dodd said, putting an arm around her. 'The spirit didn't do this.'

'The house did it!' she snapped.

'Okay, easy, easy, everybody.' I reached down and pressed my fingertips against the cold flesh of Burke's neck, feeling for the pulse I knew would not be there. Sure enough, it was like touching a slab of cold meat. 'He's definitely dead,' I muttered, kneeling down beside him.

Behind me, Suzanne began to weep softly.

I set my satchel down, unbuckled it and dug into it for my tattered copy of *The Catholic Book of the Dead*. I wanted to give Burke the Last Rites at least.

'What are you doing now, Father?'

I turned to Dodd. 'Was Burke a Catholic?'

'No—I mean, I don't know.'

Suzanne glanced at the corpse and said, 'He was baptized as a baby, I know that much. His wife once told me, for some reason.' Suzanne's tears were returning. 'He had two kids, both in high school.' She sobbed again.

I nodded. 'Okay, thank you. I'm going to administer the baptism for a tranquil death. It'll just take a second, Jimmy.'

'No, no, no, wait a minute, wait a minute—oh my God.'

Dodd sounded panicky. He was pointing at the corpse, his eyes widening. 'Oh my God, he's got the football.'

'The what?'

'The football, the football . . .'

'What are you talking about?'

He pointed to Burke's right hand, which was sort of pinned behind his body. I hadn't noticed before, but his fingers clutched a small, black metal box about the size of a Walkman. Dodd was pointing at that black box and saying, 'That thing in his hand—it's an electronic coding device, and it's—it's—it's—it's always supposed to be with the President.'

I urged him to calm down, since Burke was not going anywhere with it.

'No, no, no, you don't understand,' Dodd continued frantically. 'The football's always supposed to be with the President and no one else. It's a signaling device—a hold-over from Reagan and the Cold War. But for some reason Mr. Fallon decided to keep it operative.'

'Oh, Jesus,' Suzanne muttered, realizing what Dodd was talking about.

'It's linked through microwave technology to an uplink from NORAD headquarters,' Dodd went on. 'And nobody—I mean *nobody*—is supposed to have it outside of the President's immediate presence.'

'Jimmy, you lost me.'

'The football signals ICBMs—'

'Wait, wait.' I looked at him hard. 'You're talking about missiles? Nuclear missiles?'

'They're still out there, Father, though people don't realize it. With all the troubles in Europe lately, and China—you know—the silos are ready, locked and loaded.'

I looked at Burke's bloodless hand gripped around that black box, and I thought: *The football?* Good Lord in heaven, another obscene euphemism from the shadow government. But it didn't seem possible in this cozy post-Cold War era. And yet . . . and yet there it was, like a black tumor nestling on a dead man's hand. How the hell did Burke get a hold of it? Had he stumbled upon it by chance in the White House? Was he trying to get it back to where it belonged?

But I had a feeling the house was responsible somehow.

'What in God's name is happening, James?' Suzanne was raving again.

'Get away from it, Father,' Dodd said, and went over to Burke's body.

I stepped away to let Dodd remove the black box, carefully making sure that the dead thumb—the stiffness of rigor mortis already setting in—was not pressed against any vital part of the keypad. It was like extracting a molar, the lifeless hand was frozen so tightly around the little box, and Dodd had to literally root it out. Finally the device came free.

Dodd set it down to one side and emitted a pained sigh.

'Let me finish this one thing, Jimmy,' I said, wanting to provide some kind of closure for Burke's death. I really wanted to do the same for Redding. They were both innocent men just trying to do their jobs, and they deserved at least a final blessing.

I turned back to the corpse and genuflected, then looked down at my book and recited the Last Rites aloud. ' "Jesus, Mary and Joseph, assist this man in his last agony; Jesus, Mary and Joseph, may he breathe forth his soul in peace with you." '

I reached down to my belt. There was a droplet or so of holy water left in the last cruet I had used. I dabbed a little on my finger.

' "From this sudden and unprepared death, deliver him, O Lord, Amen." '

I reached out to the cold skin of his forehead to gently make the sign of the cross.

And something sparked at the point of contact.

And Burke's ruined eyes flashed to life.

And Suzanne screamed.

CHAPTER NINETEEN

The Black Box

1. The Puppeteer

It happened all at once—the sudden movement, the reawakened eyes, the sound coming out of his mouth—and it was nothing like any explanations provided in pathology texts about how gases get trapped in a dead body, and how sometimes they can cause the corpse to move slightly, so most coroners can tell you macabre anecdotes about cadavers suddenly sitting up on the mortuary slab. It was nothing like that. What happened with Burke was more like a puppeteer thrusting a hand inside his spine, making his eyes flare brightly and his body sit forward with a sudden jerk.

We all instinctively jumped back with a start, and every fiber of my being was warning me to get the hell out of there, get out of that dark room, to run for my life, but the sheer grotesque fascination of it all kept me motionless, crouching just a few feet away, clutching the flashlight, my Roman Ritual dangling from my wrist, as I gaped at the reanimated corpse. Something between a sigh and a moan came out of Burke as he jerked upright in the swivel chair. I could hear Suzanne's gasp behind me, as she huddled in the doorway, Dodd beside her.

'Burke? Can you hear me?' I called out naively, not expecting him to answer.

His head snapped backward almost to the point of wrenching his neck off. '*Aaaaaaiiidezzzzz—mmmmmmoi—je vooooouus ennnn prieeee!*' An unnatural shriek poured out of him in a piercing howl. Then something drove him, and his chair, backward against the computers, and he slammed right into the electronic gear, his skull shivering as though a million volts were coursing through it. His body nearly slipped off the chair.

'Stop it, stop it, stop it, someone!' Suzanne sobbed.

The thing that was once Burke stiffened again like a lightning rod, the chair groaning beneath him. An invisible current was running through his body, his scorched face lit up with madness. '*Crrrrèeeeve—crève-crève-crève-CRÈVE!*' he bellowed, cocking his face toward the ceiling as though summoning some pagan god. '*Ffff—ffffaaaites—lllles—paaaayerrrrr—Faites—les—PAYYYYEERRR!*'

In the doorway Dodd was shielding Suzanne's face from these horrors. Staring at Burke completely transfixed, he cried out: '*Crève* means "break"! *Crève* means "break" in French!'

I managed to rise to my feet, on wobbly knees, training that feeble beam of dim light on this monster that was once a man. I fumbled for a cruet of holy water with my other hand. I was shaking wildly, repulsed and entranced at the same time. I couldn't tear my gaze from the spectacle, but I knew I must do something.

'*Non!—non!—non!—NON!!—NON!—NON!*' the same voice yammered out of Burke. His chest was heaving like a tortured animal. His blackened eyes were widening.

I flung a drop of the holy water at him. ' "God the Father commands you!" ' I cried. ' "God the Son commands you!" '

The body started shivering convulsively, then quaking wildly as though about to explode. He seemed to be rising up. Examining the base of the swivel chair, I saw that it was already several inches off the ground.

' "The sacrament of the Cross commands you!" ' I yelled at him and threw another splash of holy water.

Burke whiplashed back again, smashing hard into the computer gear, shattering components, his dead face twitching seizurelike. His head lolled for a moment, and I heard something deep and gravelly emerging from the base of his throat. It was like an animal growling, some warning call, a rabid dog about to strike.

' "The most exalted mother of God, Mary the Virgin, commands you," ' I said and started to hurl another drop when I heard Dodd cry out.

'No! No! Look out!'

I turned away from the beast for a moment.

'The football! THE FOOTBALL!'

I turned back to Burke, and saw he had grabbed the black box and was gripping it in his left hand. There was a tiny red light blinking on it.

Suzanne's voice sounded behind me: 'Oh, Jesus, Jesus, Jesus . . .'

My flashlight flickered and dimmed further.

'Watch out!' Dodd screamed.

I continued to recite, ' "In the name of the blessed apostles—" '

Then I froze stiff. Burke was pressed hard against the bank of computers, his burnt-out eyes blinking, a defiant look coming over him. His chin jutted, his neck bulged, and I swear to God Almighty he almost looked familiar as a new voice came bellowing out: 'I'm going to splinter this world into a thousand pieces and scatter it to the wind!' But that voice was the rich New England tenor of John F. Kennedy. 'The Bay of Pigs is nothing! Cuba is nothing!' it shrieked on.

I was paralyzed, my mind seizing up. I couldn't think of

what to do next. I couldn't remember any prayers, I couldn't move. Burke was like an enormous moth pinned to a board, trembling with dark electricity running through him. He was gripping the little black box like a totem.

'Father!' Dodd yelled from the doorway. 'The football! Get the football!'

'Watch this goddamn trail they're coming down!' Burke barked in a new voice, raising his face again to the ceiling. It was a thick Texas drawl, full of spite and rage. I recognized it from my early adulthood: LBJ discussing the Ho Chi Minh trail, the bombing of North Vietnam. 'Bomb them out of there! Bomb them until the whole country bleeds!'

I took a step closer, then made the sign of the cross with a trembling hand. ' "In the Name of Jesus Christ—" '

'Shoot the little faggots and whores!' Burke cried suddenly, raised his arms to the heavens, his face sloughing into a completely new shape. Those jowls, that humorless, paranoid scowl, it had to be Nixon. I swear it was Nixon's expression—and Nixon's voice ordering the National Guard to move in on Kent State University. 'We'll show them what it means to be an American,' it growled, 'to be shot at from the trees.'

I tried to compete by shouting out the litany, but it was futile. A wave of poisonous black doom had rolled over me, making me practically double over in pain and grief. I struggled to breathe as the revelation struck me in the gut. It was all that bad karma over the years, which had been festering in this place, influencing our leaders, tainting our country—and it was all now pouring out of a dead man. It was almost too surreal and horrible to take in. Like stumbling upon a catastrophic traffic accident to find the wreckage of the last two hundred years piled up along the side of the road. All the lost innocence, all the death and destruction . . .

All at once, there was sudden movement behind me. Before I could turn round, Dodd was diving toward Burke.

'The pilot light—it's on!' he cried out in a strangled voice as he lunged.

My flashlight flickered again. I could barely take in the blur of movement, Burke's unnatural howl like a chorus of wolves, and Dodd grasping desperately for the metal box. Burke's arm shot out like a huge piston—I had seen nothing like it since George Foreman knocked out Joe Frazier in the second round in Kingston, Jamaica—backhanding Dodd with a mean blow. Dodd's head snapped to one side, and then he stumbled backward, tripping over his own legs. Suzanne shrieked as Dodd went down hard, landing against the door-jamb next to her, all the breath knocked out of him.

I went over to help, but Dodd pushed me away.

'The football! The black box! Gotta get it before . . . before . . .'

I heard something new across the room.

Burke had now slumped back in his chair, still clutching the metal device in his lap in dead white hands. His head lolled just like Melissa's had done, that deep growling in the base of his throat like an engine idling. But his hands were moving over the black box, like a blind man reading Braille. And before I could motivate my legs again, a new voice bubbled out of him.

'They have evil in their past, evil in their present, evil in their future.'

I recognized the modulated baritone of Ronald Reagan.

I took a step toward him.

'They are the evil empire,' Reagan's voice went on, 'and I for one believe it is God's plan for us to wipe them off the face of the earth.'

Burke's face snapped up to stare at me with those black eye-sockets, and I was frozen with dread. I could feel all the hate that had been seeping out of the walls of that place now radiating from those empty, ruined eyes. He raised the metal box over his head in both hands, as though celebrating some repulsive victory.

I took another step. ' "Christ orders you!" ' I shouted, now reciting the exorcism address from memory, and made the sign of the cross, sweeping the almost defunct beam of light across that abomination. ' "He who is the eternal Word of God become man!" '

Burke howled again.

' "Christ orders you!" ' I thumbed open another cruet and struck him with another splash of holy water.

Dodd's voice behind me: 'Stop him, Father. Stop him!'

Burke held the box in front of his dead face, and another voice was heard. 'In this day and age, in this environment, the key is peace through strength . . .'

It was the voice of President Daniel Fallon, causing Suzanne to moan in the darkness: 'Oh, Jesus, no, no . . .'

'The box, Father!' Dodd screamed at me.

I went straight for it, lunging at the corpse. Its right arm leapt up and tagged me in the jaw, ringing my skull like a bell. I staggered backward and saw stars in the darkness, with the coppery tang of blood on my tongue. I felt the emotions roiling up inside me. 'The power of Christ compels you, you son of a bitch!'

I lurched at him again. This time he backhanded me.

It was like being struck by a freight train. The impact lifted me off my feet and sent me sprawling. I collapsed to the floor, punch-drunk and gasping, my flashlight rolling under a file cabinet. After a minute, I scrambled across the floor on my hands and knees, trying to locate the damn flashlight. It had gotten wedged under a credenza, so I clawed at it desperately, trying to free it as the darkness behind me filled up with movement and sound. I could hear Dodd's frenzied pleas, and Suzanne's shrill cries . . . and a shuffling movement.

And also I could hear that strange ventriloquist's voice coming out of Burke, sounding just like our current President droning robotically: '. . . alpha, sierra, tango, Charley, x-ray, Lima, November, kilo, foxtrot . . .'

Dodd's frantic voice: 'Good God—'

'. . . Oscar, Romeo, whiskey . . .'

'—those are launch codes!'

I finally got a hold of the flashlight and turned it on Burke.

He was speaking into the metal device, his dead thumbs tapping its keypad: '. . . uniform, Zulu, bravo . . .'

'No!'

Dodd made one last lurch across to tear the black box away from the dead man.

And something invisible popped in the air like a crackle of static electricity. The box slipped out of Burke's grasp and went flying end-over-end across the room, bouncing off the window blinds and clattering to the floor.

Burke seemed to collapse suddenly like a balloon bursting, all the air puffing out of him, his body turned limp as a rag doll. He collapsed forward into Dodd's arms like a drunken sailor, and as cold and dead as if nothing had happened.

Dodd let the corpse slide to the floor, and just stood there panting.

The room was plunged into a horrible silence.

It took me some time to rise to my feet.

I could hear the howling of the winds again, and my own heart beating in my ears.

Burke's body lay in a crumpled heap at the foot of the computer rack, its face now slack and expressionless and the eyes finally closed in death. The dark spirit had relinquished its grip on him. Then I tracked the dim light across the floor in search of the black box.

'Oh, no, no, no, no,' Dodd was muttering as he approached it. He knelt down and picked it up with trembling hands. After examining it for a moment, he looked up at me, his eyes shimmering like diamonds.

'We are in very deep trouble,' he said softly.

CHAPTER TWENTY

Tick-Tock

1. Down into Hell

The tortured moaning of the wind.

The constant thump of my pulse.

My footsteps echoing down a dark corridor, my flashlight scanning painted panels.

. . . tick-tock . . .

'We should all go together,' Dodd had urged me only minutes earlier, trying to get the last cigarette out of his crumpled pack. His hands were trembling too violently to get a proper hold of it. 'All three of us together.'

We had been huddling in the west reception hall, the only light coming from my flashlight. We had finally found fresh batteries in one of Mrs. Whittaker's care packages, and I had then set the flashlight down on a coffee table where its beam sliced through the musty-seeming air, throwing a pool of pale yellow onto the iced-over Palladian window. There was a cold, wet draft streaming through the room from an open transom above the window. Dodd had managed to pry open this small vent with a screwdriver. He had then tried calling out through it, and tried blinking SOS with the flashlight, and had even lit a nineteenth-century kerosene *lantern and hurled the flaming object out onto the lawn, but all had proved futile. The storm was altogether too loud and opaque, and the surrounding area seemed deserted.*

Dodd had even suggested—with deadly seriousness—that we set one of the big house's wings on fire to draw attention. But Suzanne was too afraid that Melissa might get caught in the blaze. Not that we didn't each relish the thought of seeing that cursed old building go up in flames.

That's when we decided that the only way out of the place must still be through the underground tunnel. So that's why I had taken a seat on an old velvet armchair, and started sorting through the contents of my satchel, to prepare myself for what lay ahead of me. Suzanne was pacing back and forth in front of a massive Hepplewhite bookcase, wringing her cold slender hands.

'I don't care who goes down there,' she muttered. 'I just want my daughter.'

'It's not that simple anymore, Suzanne. The code has been uplinked—'

'I don't care. I don't care about any fucking code,' she said. 'I just want my daughter back.'

'Then you'd better care,' Dodd snapped. 'Because, as we now speak, that fucking code is on its way—'

Floorboards groaning beneath me. The light trained on an old carpet runner. The sound of my heavy breathing swallowed by the darkness ahead of me.

I'm hurrying toward the private staircase.

. . . tick-tock, tick-tock . . .

'My baby is down there in the dark—alone!' Her voice sounded stretched to the limit.

Dodd was still trying to root that one, lone cigarette out of the crumpled pack. 'I understand, Suzanne, but it won't matter anymore if that code gets to the silos. Nothing will

*matter. You understand what I'm saying? The Chinese are on
high alert.'*

'I don't care—'

*'You're not listening to me!' Dodd yelled suddenly. 'I said
the Chinese are on high alert. They have been for five years
now. So is Iraq.'*

'James—'

*'These defense systems are all automated. The general
public has no idea. They're automated, Suzanne. Senator
Leahy tried to overhaul the whole system last year, but he
couldn't get it out of the armed services committee. When
that code is downlinked, a hundred other codes are automatically launched in response. We have no idea how many, but
we know for sure that China and Iraq are on the system. We
know this for a fact.'*

There was a tense pause.

*'So what are you saying, James?' Suzanne said finally. 'We
just started World War III?'*

Through a private door and down some marble steps.

My flashlight glimmering off the walls.

My heart pumping.

. . . tick-tock . . .

*'If that code gets downlinked, hundreds—maybe thousands—
of other missiles will fire automatically at targets all across
North America,' Dodd had explained, finally rooting the cigarette out of its container. He stuck the bent butt in his mouth
and searched for his lighter. 'The only way to cancel it is a
voice command from your husband the President, but we
have no way of contacting him. I'd say we're pretty much
fucked.'*

Suzanne chewed her fingernail for a moment.

I'm not really sure if she—or any of us, for that matter—
truly realized what was happening right then. There seemed

to be only that dark sitting room, and that single beam of light, and that corner door, locked from the outside, with Burke's body now safely sealed in the room beyond. And that black box sitting on the coffee table next to the flashlight, its tiny green LED light blinking. And of course, the house itself. The haunted mansion. Sitting there in the darkness, trying to ratchet up my courage, I could sense the spirit everywhere like an airborne virus, infecting us, metastasizing inside us. We were responsible. We had unleashed it from the bowels of that house. And all of a sudden it had a name. Maybe the worst boogyman of them all: Thermonuclear war. Just thinking about it made my skin go cold. But maybe that was all part of the dark power that had been growing there since the place was constructed over two centuries ago. Maybe this was the logical conclusion.

But why? I wanted to know. I wanted to know how it all began. I was convinced the answer lay somewhere beneath us. In the soil. In the ground itself. I was convinced it all started there, but I had a feeling it wasn't because of any of the routine: The house being built on an Indian burial ground, or the foundations dug in desecrated soil, or whatever. I had a gut feeling it was specific and unique to the White House— the Executive Mansion. That weird language which had sputtered out of both Melissa and Burke—sounding maybe like French, maybe even Portuguese, but altered slightly—was the key. But I couldn't figure it out. And I realized the only way to figure it out—the only way to prevent it—was to go to the heart of it.

Downstairs.

Nothing had ever been more clear to me. I was going to have to now go down into the sub-sub-basement, and I was going to go there alone. It was a hunch that had been building in me ever since I had first heard those whispered words in the back of my brain: Tonight . . . Damn right, tonight. It was now just me versus that house, however egocentric that sounds. I was brought to that place for a reason. I knew that, and the house knew it, and I wasn't going to back down. But, after all was said and done, I was not trying to be a hero, and I was sure as hell not trying to win a place in heaven. Hell, I wasn't even a priest anymore.

What I was was a washed-up old club boxer who never turned down a fight.

Descending the marble steps, my entire body racked with chills.

Approaching the first floor.

Sensing the passing of valuable time like a ghost on my heels, dogging me, breathing down my neck.

. . . tick-tock, tick-tock, tick-tock . . .

'Jimmy, listen to me. Please, both of you listen to me. The only way we're going to get out of this mess is by going back down into the tunnels. Back into the sub-sub-basement. That is how we will find your daughter, Mrs. Fallon, and that is how we will get word to the President. By getting out through the underground route.'

'Father—'

'Most importantly, Jimmy, only one of us is trained to deal with what's down there. Only one of us.'

There was a long pause.

Then Suzanne looked at me and said in a thin voice, 'What do you think is down there?'

I told her I thought it was the source of everything bad in that huge place.

Dodd finally let out a pained sigh. 'What do you want us to do, Father?'

I told them I wanted both of them to stay there in the sitting room and keep signaling for help, and somebody should be along pretty quickly. After all, this was the White House.

Dodd took a quick drag, then stared at me questioningly. 'You don't have to do this, Father.'

I managed a thin smile. 'I know I don't have to, Jimmy, I know.'

Dodd shrugged. 'Okay, okay. Fine.' He went over to the coffee table and picked up the black box. 'You should probably take this with you,' he said, 'and keep track of the elapsed time.'

He handed it to me.

It was heavier than I expected, cold and heavy, and it felt like a malignant growth. I looked down at it and studied its little digital display. The tiny red diodes were clicking off the time that elapsed until the uplink would be completed.

Behind me, the wind whistled like a railway engine bearing down on us.

'You know how to get down there?' Dodd asked.

I assured him I remembered the way from Tooms' guided tour.

Dodd nodded, glancing nervously at his watch. 'Remember, when you get to the end of the sub-sub-tunnel, there's only one way on, and that's to the right.'

I told him I remembered.

I unbuckled my satchel and dropped the device into it. Then I buckled it back up. I looked at Suzanne, then back at Dodd. 'If you guys are looking for something to do while I'm gone,' I said, 'you might say a few prayers for me.'

Dodd managed a smile.

Suzanne came over and hugged me. I could feel her shaking in my arms. She looked at me through her tears. 'I'm sorry I got a little crazy back there,' she said.

I told her to forget it.

'Will you do something for me?' she said then. 'Will you find my daughter?'

I told her that's exactly what I was going to do, then kissed her on the cheek.

Then I turned and started down the dark corridor. I looked back only once and saw them both watching me with similar expressions: Mortified parents watching their child go off to war. I will admit it didn't do much to bolster my courage. I gave a final wave, and they waved back. Then I turned down the stairwell and descended the steps as quickly as possible in the pitch dark.

Approaching the bottom of the stairs, I glanced inside my satchel.

The little black box, its indicator glowing.

As it rolled backwards, it read one hour, forty-one minutes and twenty-three seconds to go.

Part IV

THE LAST HUNDRED MINUTES

Then I saw an angel coming down from heaven, holding in his hand the key of the bottomless pit.

Revelation 20:1

CHAPTER TWENTY-ONE

Archangel Descending

1. The Fabric of Smoke

At the foot of the marble staircase, I began hearing a low humming noise—almost like one of those old console radios warming up. It came from somewhere in the deep darkness of the first-floor corridor, and I realized what was happening immediately.

I couldn't discern if it was coming from the east ballroom to my left or the central hall to my right, but it was clearly there, just beneath the tortured winds; a droning, buzzing hum as real as the heartbeat in my ears. It meant the house was still tapping into me, working on my psyche. I was already expecting this. Hell, it had happened to forty-three presidents, countless members of their families and staff, and God knows how many others, so why should I be any different?

The beam of my resuscitated flashlight glimmered off the edges of great marble columns, throwing a pool of light onto the gilded wall of the state dining room seventy feet away, the same dining room where Ulysses S. Grant had wined and dined Mark Twain, where Franklin D. Roosevelt served cold dill pickles to Winston Churchill. The dining room was as dark and still as a morgue, and as cold as a freezer. I couldn't see anything moving, but the humming sound was coming from somewhere nearby. It had a hollow sound, like bumblebees in a drum. I told myself to ignore it. I asked God to give me the strength to ignore it. I needed to keep moving and to get down to the sub-level as soon as possible.

I glanced inside my satchel and saw the indicator glowing in the dark.

Ninety-nine minutes and thirty-one seconds left.

Okay, no problem. With the power off, there was only one way into the sub-levels from the first floor, and that was down the private staircase on the other side of the north entrance hall, and then across the ground floor, and then down another staircase. *No big deal, right?* I told myself to get moving, but there was still that horrible humming. I realized it came from just across the entrance foyer.

In fact, it seemed to be coming from inside the grounded elevator.

I directed the light at the elevator doors, thirty feet away, but I couldn't figure out what it was about that humming that was spooking me so much.

I walked cautiously over towards it.

The hum was so loud now, it sounded like an enormous electrical terminal overloading. I couldn't identify it yet, but I knew with every cell of my being that it was a *bad* noise. It meant danger and pain and awful things happening in the shadows. The sound resonated down through my bones, touching some deep-rooted fear inside me that I wasn't even aware of. I forced myself to turn away from it.

The private stairs lay only a few feet beyond the elevator shaft, roped off by a velvet cordon. I carefully stepped over the rope, and I was just entering the stairwell when I heard something click behind me, then the whirr of a motor, which was impossible since the power was still out, and yet I heard it as plainly as the roaring winds outside.

The elevator doors were opening.

I wish I could say I bravely turned around to confront whatever was in the elevator, but I just stood there frozen with terror as the humming noise rose in pitch behind me, and that same black, rancid odor engulfed me, and dread coursed through my veins. And in that instant I flashed back to my childhood: A single white-hot moment of panic, when I was ten years old and climbing a tree in my grandparents' backyard in Quincy, and I stumbled against a wasp nest and kicked it apart, instantly to be surrounded by a cloud of buzzing menace. That *same* sound was coming from inside the elevator.

I turned to focus my light on the figure standing in the shadows of the elevator.

Through the gap between the doors I saw a man made entirely of flies.

I staggered back horrified, away from that thing shaped like a man.

It was huge and glistening, and seethed with flies of all shapes and sizes—greenbacks and bluebottles, horseflies and gnats—which seemed to hover and orbit around it like a magnetic field as it came toward me, buzzing and sizzling with each lumbering stride. Then it was reaching out for me, like some long-lost lover, and in that brief instant of feverish panic I finally looked into its face. Its features boiled with hectic movement, its eyes luminous green. But underneath all the seething flies was leathery flesh of purest, blackest onyx.

The black man from the tunnel!

Before I had a chance to shout out a litany or make any move, or even to scream, I tripped over my own feet and got tangled in the cordon rope. I careened backward to the floor, my satchel and flashlight sliding across the top of the stairwell. I turned and started frantically crawling toward my equipment before it tumbled all the way down the stairs. I grabbed the satchel just in time, then scooped up the flashlight and turned it back on the elevator.

The fly-man had completely vanished.

The whole incident was so jarring, so abrupt, that it took my breath away, and I flinched with shock in the stone-silent darkness. I paused to sit for a moment, trying to slow my thudding heart.

The house was obviously drawing on my personal fears, my phobias, my childhood terrors. How was I going to shut it down? How was I going to keep it out of my head? I sat there breathing hard, praying to God: *Please, Blessed Father, let me get past this thing. Give me an extra measure of courage so that I can finish Your work.*

Flies were a symbol of the Devil. They always had been and always would be. Legend dictated that Satan adopted the form of flies when pressured by a holy person. But I was starting to wonder if there was more going on here than simply infestation of evil.

I rose to my feet.

I could still hear the buzzing rising up from the darkness below. I felt dizzy, and the cold was getting into my joints. I had to squint to see clearly through the breath clouding in front of my face. I aimed the light down the staircase, toward the bottom steps. Surely there was something moving down there? I couldn't get a good look at it in the thin beam, but I could tell it was something huge and dark. And it was waiting for me; waiting to block my path. I opened my satchel and glanced again at the black box.

Ninety-five minutes and eleven seconds left.

I wasn't going to let that bastard beat me. I wasn't ready to quit. I closed the satchel and started down the stairs.

The buzzing increased in the darkness below, and the light beam fell suddenly on a ghostly leg pulsating with insects. I grabbed a container of holy water from my belt, and kept descending.

'You're not stopping me, because Christ orders you.' I found as firm a voice as I could muster; I might be on the ropes now but I still had some juice left in me. 'He is the eternal Word of God become man—and you're not stopping me!'

I flung a drop of the water at the apparition, the passage of the liquid glimmering briefly.

It struck its target and sizzled as though coming into contact with a hot griddle. All at once an enormous surge of sound and motion erupted from the darkness and, before I knew what was happening, a dark shape leapt up at me. I had no time even to duck, and I screamed as the solid swarm of flies slammed into me.

It was like being struck by black napalm, the sheer energy radiating through me in veins of poisonous black emotion and pure unadulterated hate.

It knocked me on my ass.

I slid down the remaining ten steps on my tailbone, and landed on the marble floor. If it weren't for the extra padding in my parka, I might even have broken my back, but fortunately there was plenty of my ass to absorb the fall too. I blinked away stars and gasped for breath. I still had the satchel clutched in one hand but the cruet of holy water was gone.

'Come on!' I shouted into the darkness of the corridor. 'Is that the best you can do?'

As I tried to stand up, my tailbone screaming in pain, I noticed countless more of those lumps in the flooring, like cancerous tumors, bubbling languidly, menacingly. They were getting bigger with each passing moment, so the internal clock in my brain was shrieking at me to get up and get moving.

I closed my eyes and asked the Good Lord and Saint Christopher to protect me.

2. Strange Fruit

When I opened my eyes again, the floor surface was still, the corridor silent and empty. My breath still came out as rapid puffs of vapor, and I sat back up against the wall for a moment, gathering myself. I had sustained some major bruises from my tumble down the stairs, but I still felt in fairly good working order.

Finally I rose up on my sore knees, and looked around. The ground-floor corridor had gone through a subtle trans-formation since I had first arrived at the White House. Initially, it had resembled a tasteful Italian mortuary, with all its marble and vaulted ceilings, and its soft lighting and museum-quality decor. But then, after the power had futzed out, the same corridor had taken on a darker, more sinister quality—like being in an ancient catacomb. Now, as I stood there in that cold, silent darkness, the place had become a haunted cave.

Or a predator's lair.

I started moving toward the western end of the corridor, toward the private staircase leading down to the lower levels. Tooms had indicated these stairs to us briefly, explaining how they were used mostly by workmen and maintenance staff, but I realized it was the only way down without using power. Smelling something musky and rotten, like rancid blood, as I moved stiffly along, I passed an elegant oval reception room on the left, and then the kitchen on the right, and then the map room on the left, where President Clinton had delivered his infamous 'inap-propriate sex' testimonial to the independent counsel. For some reason, all the doors were now ajar, and it almost felt as though the house was making some kind of obscene gesture at me—daring me to look into those various rooms. Daring me to confront whatever was inhabiting them.

I made it to a door marked 'ACCESS RESTRICTED,' right beside the freight elevator.

Thank God the power outage had disabled all the electronic deadbolts—otherwise, I wasn't sure how I was ever going to get downstairs. In fact, since the days of the Truman renovations, access to the lower levels had been severely restricted—probably due to Cold War paranoia. But on this fateful night I fortunately found the maintenance door unlocked, so I nudged it open and stepped inside.

The stairwell itself was narrow, with white-painted walls and iron steps, and I started carefully descending. It's hard to explain, but the renewed silence seemed even worse inside that stairwell. There was now no sound of humming, no buzzing, no distant, muffled winds, no creaking floorboards. *Nothing*. Just the dead thudding sound of my footsteps against the stone-cold silence, and a terrible certainty that the man made of flies would be waiting for me at the bottom. The air smelled of mold and old cigarette butts, and before long I could almost hear my own heartbeat. I realized I had to calm down if I was going to break through that wall of evil—and find the girl, and get to the outside world in time to shut down the weapons launch. I was going to have to find some deep, hidden reserve inside me.

And that's when an idea occurred to me.

The music.

If the house could play games, then so could I. Music was part of the fabric of my spiritual life, and that's why I had brought along my battered little tape recorder. It was the same one I used to always take along with me on blessings and cleansings, with the same old worn-out cassette inside it. One side contained hymns from St.

Michael's Church itself, along with various other bits and pieces that might help me through a long, hard ritual. The other side had more personal stuff: Some favorite tunes that comforted me. Mostly old blues and torch songs.

Mostly Billie Holiday.

I reached the bottom of the stairs and pointed the light straight ahead of me. There was an unmarked door flanked by metal shelves crammed with old paint cans and cleaning products. My heart was now racing. I just stared at the door. I needed to calm down. I need an extra jolt of courage. *I needed a drink.* But the only thing I could think of was to fish around inside my satchel for my old tape recorder.

Once I found it, I checked the cassette, then turned it over and rewound it. The batteries were pretty old, but they still had some life in them. I put the recorder back in my satchel, then pressed the play button.

The melancholy moaning of Billie Holiday suddenly warbled out of the bag.

I can't find the right words to express how her voice affected me at that moment. It was a somber, bluesy ballad called 'Strange Fruit,' a mournful lament about lynchings in the Deep South, about bodies swinging in the breeze, and strange fruit suspended from poplar trees, and it bathed me in goosepimples. I felt stronger all of a sudden, and I was filled with a new burst of anger—and anger can be your friend when you're fighting the Devil.

I went over to the door.

My pulse was ragged in my ears again, and my throat felt raw and dry, but I was ready. I was ready. The tinny music sizzling out of my satchel was fueling me, driving me on. I thumbed through the tiny ritual book still attached to my left wrist, till I found the place where I had left off in the Exorcism Address. I gripped the flashlight a little tighter, took a deep breath, and glanced at my watch. It was 12:29 a.m.

Eighty-nine minutes left.

I pushed the door open and stepped into the basement.

Chapter Twenty-Two

The Worst Place on Earth

1. Blood on the Leaves

The basement was empty, silent and still—just as we had left it. But it was colder down there, as cold as an ice cave, and my breath fairly fogged in front of my face. But there seemed nothing out of the ordinary: No apparition waiting for me. No man made of flies. No undulating floor. No black tide of dread.

Just a basement.

Billie Holiday echoed through the gloom.

I shivered in my parka and tried to get my bearings. Turning my light to the left, it fell on a plaster wall where an outdated calendar hung next to a portrait of Daniel Fallon. Then I shone it to the right, moving past a service window and a metal door that was hanging open. I could see the passageway beyond, a narrow tunnel full of exposed plumbing and furnace ducts. It was the same passage down which we had gone rushing to Melissa's side earlier that night. The same passage along which we had heard those hysterical cries. The same one that had pulsed and quaked with such hellish energy.

But now that same passageway was completely silent, almost as though the house was playing possum.

I crossed the threshold and entered the tunnel.

Tooms had said there was a staircase at the end of it, used mostly by workmen and maintenance crew. I panned my flashlight across the darkness ahead of me, searching for a door or stairwell, but all I could see was yet more pipes and conduits snaking the length of the tunnel, so old and filthy they were jacketed with a gray fur of mold. I passed a doorway which led into the furnace room, and trained the light on an overturned desk and chairs. The pipes along the ceiling were still warped and dented from the explosive energy that had erupted off of Melissa Fallon.

The Billie Holiday music continued to crackle out of my satchel, her smoky voice crooning about blood on the leaves of poplar trees.

I did then notice a door up ahead of me, over to the right, and marked 'SUB-A/RESTRICTED.'

I approached it cautiously, half expecting the black fly-man to lurch out at me. The door was slightly ajar, and when I pushed it open it squeaked stubbornly. There was a narrow landing of stained concrete, about five feet wide. The stairs beyond were of grimy iron, and they led down into even deeper darkness. Someone had left a push-broom leaning against the wall nearby.

For a moment I felt compelled to call out for Melissa. It was an absurd urge, more wishful thinking than anything else. As though a simple summons toward those shadows— *Melissa, it's time for supper!*—could solve all my problems. But the compulsion passed quickly when I glanced down at my watch, and realized how quickly time was passing. I didn't realize it then, but somewhere in Maryland, at that very moment, a couple of Air Force specialists, along with a commander and a CIA operative, were assembled in a sealed room at Fort Meade, staring at the sequence of log codes flickering on their computer screens. Designated as one of the failsafe points in the outmoded E-STRAD program (Emergency Strategic Defense System), these gentlemen were confirming the same launch orders that had earlier emanated from the black box sitting in my satchel.

I wasted no more time, and started down the stairs. My boots made a dull clanking noise on the iron treads as I descended, and soon I felt dizzy with fear. I needed to concentrate furiously just to keep my slender light fixed and steady on the steps, as my hand was shaking so badly. Instead I tried to focus my thoughts on the girl herself, and the dwindling time, and the escape route out from under that mansion. Tooms had explained earlier how the sub-sub-level—the crawlspace underneath the sub-level—featured a 300-foot-long tunnel terminating at Pennsylvania Avenue, where there was an iron ladder that led back up to street level. At that point, it seemed I needed to achieve just three simple things, then—if I succeeded I would finally be able to cleanse this house, and rescue the missing girl . . . and maybe even save myself into the bargain. Just three things: One, to complete my ritual of exorcism here in the sub-sub-level; two, to rescue Melissa; and three, to make it out of that house in time for someone in appropriate authority to override the launch codes. They seemed so straightforward . . . three simple things.

I finally reached the bottom level.

There was another door in front of me, which I noticed was also ajar by several inches. Enough for me to peer through, as the beam of my flashlight fell on a shape.

As I stared at it, a sudden bolt of revulsion and panic shot through me.

I was looking at a headless woman.

2. Brutalized Possessions

I flinched away from the open door, barely registering in my mind the figure standing in the pitch blackness beyond, waiting for me there like some kind of exotic fluorescent denizen of the deep—in that faded royal-blue gown and bodice, the puff sleeves and rosy pink chemisette, slightly plump, her posture erect. I braced myself for the assault.

Except nothing happened, the headless woman didn't move or make a sound. She just stood there beyond the door like a sad sentry in the darkness. And my body relaxed in stages, my breath returning to me, my heart dropping back into its normal position. I moved back toward the half-open door, peering through it with my flashlight sweeping again across the immobile figure.

It was merely a mannequin in period costume.

I stepped through into the sub-level and found myself in the middle of a cavernous, cluttered storage room. And the mannequin that had given me such a start was just a dusty relic, garbed in its nineteenth-century finery, probably belonging to a First Lady of the early 1800s, and no doubt bound for some folk museum. And as I stood there in the cold, with Billie Holiday crackling out of my satchel, playing my flashlight across the remnants of forty-two presidential administrations, I could see the discards from the house above like sediment in an archeological dig. I was staring at Hannah Van Buren's cracked punchbowls, and Abigail Fillmore's busted upright piano, and Mary Todd Lincoln's torn umbrella, and Ida McKinley's broken rollerskates, and Helen Taft's discarded wigs, and Eleanor Roosevelt's warped ukelele, and Mamie Eisenhower's water-damaged rugs. And all at once it hit me: The house itself had wreaked this damage. The house had ruined those things. I was looking at a graveyard of forgotten possessions, each one of them brutalized by the house.

And that's when the dread returned, like a toxic tide rolling over me.

So I stood there in that musty, cold, sewer-like stench—the smell of old things decaying in damp darkness—and tried to swallow back my fear. I fought it with everything I had. I stood and I prayed to Jesus Christ and the Lord Almighty and Michael the Archangel, and I asked for strength, and I asked for wisdom and vision and stamina.

For the house was swallowing me.

It wasn't anything tangible that I could see or hear. It was purely in my brain, but it was no less palpable for that. I felt myself shrinking into the sub-level's darkness, my body shriveling, the sound of Billie Holiday fading as though draining down a hole. It was a feverish feeling, making me think back to the sixth grade, when I would lie in my sickbed at night and feel as though my arms were as thin as threads, my head as big as a watermelon. I had made a big mistake coming down here to the sub-basement, and I felt myself drowning in the fear. I'm convinced that if I had stayed there in that storage room I would have literally melted into the floor.

Instead I managed to make my way through all the clutter toward the far corner.

Tooms had mentioned a hatch embedded in the concrete floor, near the north-east corner, so I swam through ancient boxes and wardrobes toward it. I ignored strange objects brushing against me as I scrambled through the dark—the wire claws of coat hangers, the feathery tendrils of ladies' hats, and the bony carapaces of lampshades. I scanned the blackened, leprous cement floor with my light, searching for that hatch, but couldn't find it. Only when I reached the wall, and traced its base along the floor did I finally discover it.

It was concealed behind a huge steamer trunk that looked as though it dated back to the First World War. I had to shove this heavy object aside with my hip, and it made a horrible rasping noise on the cement. Something dark glistened beneath it. I shone the light down onto a colony of grub worms oozing and pulsating slowly from their uncovered hiding place. My stomach flopped, and my mouth filled with saliva. I told myself to stay focused on the game, to stay focused on the ultimate goal, the President's 'football.' Just get that football over the goal line.

I went over to the hatch.

It was an old corrugated flap of iron covered in rust and filth. The words 'MARYLAND IRONWORKS' were stamped into it, and it had a round metal ring tucked into one corner for a handle. It resembled the door of a furnace or oven: *Out of the frying pan and into the fire!*

I crouched down by the hatch and grasped its handle. It was like taking hold of an icicle. A jolt of energy shot up my arm like electric current, and I flinched, my eyes slamming shut. I saw a flicker of something indistinct in my mind, and I heard that terrible ghost-voice again in my head. It was beyond words, beyond human language—like an echo of a scream in reverse. I was going down into the worst place on earth. I was going exactly where the house wanted me to go, and I felt so terrified I could hardly move. But I was also seething with righteous anger, and somehow God filled me with strength, and I thought of the litany, the sacred litany of exorcism. I said the prayer silently under my breath.

So I opened the hatch.

A sigh of cool air engulfed me momentarily, smelling like once-living things that had long ago died and decomposed, and I swallowed my revulsion, willing my stomach to hold down its contents. My mind was sparking and sputtering with impressions of things so horrible I can't even describe them, so I reached for my prayerbook, still attached by its cord to my left wrist, and I focused the flashlight on the page: *From the ambushes of evil spirits, free us, O Lord.*

The Billie Holiday tape shifted between songs, and the crackle of the tone arm on the old record was chillingly clear in the silence. I clenched the flashlight in my teeth, put the satchel under my arm, and started down the iron steps.

Halfway down, Billie started her next song, about her body and soul, and being so lonely. It seemed as though the house's spirit was reacting to Billie's words, reaching into my gut and twisting my innards, as I could feel it waiting for me down below. But I knew the girl must be down there somewhere, too. All the evil energy in that house was coming from there—and I knew it had the girl in its possession. The foul odor was getting stronger as I approached the bottom step. It was a peppery, metallic, rotting ammonia smell, like the smell of a morgue's refrigerator.

My foot hit something solid.

I grabbed the flashlight out of my mouth and trained it on the floor. The concrete, caked with dried filth, was all cracked and moldering, looking like the floor of an archeological dig. The air itself was rancid, and seemed even colder and meaner down there, if that could be possible. I shone the light up at the walls, and saw gray, petrified earth broken only by huge iron beams—load-bearing I-beams sunken into the walls themselves—and the narrow tunnel stretching off to my right.

But my mind was still sharp with anger as I stood softly murmuring the litany. ' "Humiliate the enemies of the Lord," ' I whispered, barely loud enough to hear above the music. ' "We pray you hear us." '

I then started moving along the tunnel.

If there were any lights down there, I don't know where they were mounted. It felt like a catacomb or an old abandoned salt mine, and I'm sure nobody ever ventured down there normally. But I knew the girl was there somewhere, because I could feel the presence, radiating out from the darkness beyond the reach of my flashlight, pungent like the spoor of a wild animal. I now drew on my own anger, and most of all I drew on my affection for the girl named Melissa, and I drew on the thought of that ticking indicator in my satchel. I forced myself to walk on down that tunnel, reciting the lines of the exorcism Address from memory.

' "Accursed spirit," ' I recited as I moved along, the blues music echoing off the walls. ' "We enjoin you under penalty, cease to deceive human beings and to offer them the poison of eternal perdition!" '

From the beam of my flashlight I could see that I was approaching a bend in the tunnel, and registered that there was a ninety-degree turn to the right. I reached into my coat with my free hand, dug behind my belt and pulled out another cruet of holy water. I thumbed it open and raised it, ready.

Then I addressed the darkness ahead of me: ' "Cease to injure the innocent, and to set traps for the Church's liberty! Go, spirit! Give way to Christ!" '

I flung a sprinkle of holy water at the darkness.

As it landed on the floor about ten feet away, I braced myself for that pop in my head, that sudden eruption of energy . . . but nothing happened. The water just landed on the filthy cement with no effect. No reaction. No apparition. No man made of flies. No stomach cramps or vomitous waves of dread.

Nothing.

My nerve endings tingled with righteous anger. On top of everything else, this bastard spirit was a coward. I could feel the same rage cooking inside me. My watch now said

12:38. There were eighty minutes left (and at Fort Meade the specialists would no doubt still be collating the data on their screens, frantically trying to verify the launch order).

I navigated the bend in the tunnel, aiming the flashlight ahead of me, and the light fell on the thing at the end of the tunnel. And I nearly jumped out of my boots.

I dropped the satchel, the contents spilling across the tunnel floor.

CHAPTER TWENTY-THREE

The Seraphim

1. An Old Enemy

As I dropped my satchel again, I was hardly aware that the tape recorder shattered on impact, sending shards and pieces of plastic across the filthy cement, cutting off the music for ever, cutting off my connection to Billie Holiday and my better angels.

I was oblivious to anything but the door at the end of the tunnel.

I stood there in terrible silence, staring at that door, which seemed to stare back at me in the dusky beam of my flashlight and, for a brief instant, time seemed to stand still as my traumatized brain spun its wheels, trying to understand, trying to process everything, trying to make sense of how the same door from little Eric Rivers' tenement bedroom had gotten down there in the sub-sub-level of the White House.

It was like seeing an old enemy looming. Rising up to the ceiling, about fifteen feet away, the door was framed by the antiquated timbers of the cellar. It was a muscular door, hewn from cheap oak, its black lacquer finish cracked and peeling, its stained porcelain knob looking like exposed bone. It was the ugliest door in the world, and it radiated a kind of unmitigated evil. And it hated me as much as I hated it. But the worst part was that this was a real door, not some recurring nightmare, or even some druggy hallucination. I was standing before a real door. The claw marks from the dogs looked exactly the same as they had done twenty years earlier. The scarred wooden panels were precisely the same. The dull gleam of the doorknob was the same.

I willed myself to take a step forward, though my legs were shaky and weak, and my balance was uncertain. I felt so dizzy, it was a major effort just to stay standing. The light seemed to dwindle—or maybe it was my vision—and the door seemed impossibly horrible and threatening to me. How could one single door be so repellent, considering everything I had already encountered in that mansion? I tried another step—

That's when I heard a new sound.

It was only a muffled rustling from behind the battered door, but it touched some elemental chord in my nervous system. My flashlight began trembling convulsively.

' "Behold the Word of the Lord," ' I muttered breathlessly. ' "Depart, enemy of the innocent—" '

The rustling behind the door increased as I approached, much clearer now. It was delicate, dry and husky, like someone giggling. Someone very small, giggling behind that door.

'You can't get rid of me!' I shrieked suddenly, my voice exploding like a depth-charge in the passage.

The giggling stopped suddenly.

Then came a voice from behind the door—scratchy and faint, yet very familiar.

'Come in.'

I was paralyzed. That was the voice of little Eric Rivers. Back from the dead. The same voice I had been hearing in my nightmares for over twenty years.

'*We been waiting for you,*' it whispered, as though imparting some deep childhood secret.

'Who—who are you?' I addressed the door.

The voice: '*You know.*'

'No, I don't, I don't know, I don't know who you are! Identify yourself now!'

'*We been waiting for you, Father,*' it whispered in the sing-song tones of a demented child.

'Who are you?' I cried, now close enough to reach out and touch the bone-white doorknob.

There was no answer.

I could feel the time dwindling away, but I knew Melissa was somewhere behind the same door, so I was going to have to go through it, but I hadn't bargained on hearing that particular voice. There was something really terrible there, and I did not want to encounter whatever it was.

'WHO ARE YOU?' I bellowed at the top of my lungs.

The giggling rose up again, then the husky child's voice. '*Guess who.*'

I reached for the doorknob.

A lightning bolt shot up my arm.

I staggered backward, my brain filled with a paroxysm of ghastly images, surging so quickly and fiercely they stole my breath away. I saw a hideous black face contorted into the most malevolent expression I had ever witnessed . . . I saw blood burst out of the ground like an oil geyser . . . I saw a flash of huge white incisor teeth lunging toward me . . . But mostly I felt my soul being sodomized by a torrent of hate pouring into and through me, metastasizing like the fastest-growing cancer possible.

I landed on my ass ten feet away.

Gasping for breath, flailing at the darkness, I became conscious of the fact that I could easily die there. I could asphyxiate, or pass out from hypothermia, or maybe even suffer a heart attack from the shock alone. I was immersed in two kinds of darkness suddenly—one from outside, and one from the inside. I felt a black, hopeless wave of self-loathing; I felt useless and diseased and ugly and weak— that same horrible wave that had crashed over me earlier. But, worst of all, I could feel the fight drain out of me.

Tears streaming down my face, I then turned and stumbled back along the tunnel the same way I had come. I was reacting to some kind of primal, lizard-brain flight-instinct. I just had to get out of there, or I was going to die.

I made it to the ladder and scurried up it like a frightened child.

I didn't look back.

2. The Valley of the Shadow

I don't remember how I found my way back up to ground level. I remember stumbling back across that cluttered storage room, ramming into Victorian wardrobes and nearly toppling over a rusty old shelving unit filled with broken dolls. I remember stumbling up the iron steps, banging my shins, starbursts of pain popping behind my eyes. I remember careening through the basement corridor, hyperventilating in my panic, my mind swimming with unwelcome dark thoughts and images.

There was an engine inside my head, revving out of control. Pain and self-doubt bombarded me in equal measure, half-formed memories flickering across my brain. I saw myself filling those empty years after my excommunication: Driving cabs, working the loading dock down at Navy Pier, spending more and more time in taverns, alone, bellied up to the bar. I saw myself searching for redemption, volunteering my time at the Catholic charities, working with the kids down at Gold's gym, doing blessings for poor families. But mostly I saw myself *alone*, shoulders slumped, dressed in an old pea-coat, wandering home under the 'El' tracks to spend another night alone in my little fleabag apartment, wondering what might have been. I was a loser. I was a failure. And now I had no idea how I was going to cleanse the Executive Mansion of the United States.

Somehow I made it back up to the ground-floor corridor. I lumbered across the marble hallway, scanning the walls with my flashlight, searching for the door to the kitchen. The hall was silent and dark, and its stillness seemed to mock me. I finally reached the last door on the right and stumbled into the dark kitchen itself.

There was a large pantry area to one side, and I hurried into it. My brain was on fire. I shone the flashlight up at the white enamel cabinets.

' "The Lord is my shepherd, I shall not want," ' I muttered.

I threw open the door of one cabinet. Inside it were hundreds of crystal goblets, water glasses and juice glasses, glimmering in the beam of the flashlight. I slammed the door shut.

' "He maketh me to lie down in green pastures," ' I continued in a sort of half-grunt, half-sob.

I threw open the next cabinet, full of bulk foods and bottles, kitchen staples such as molasses, olive oil, vinegar, and ketchup. I angrily clawed at these items, knocking them off their shelves, sending them toppling to the floor. Some of the bottles shattered, spilling liquids across the parquet tiles.

' "Even though I walk through the valley—!" ' I cried, turning away.

I turned my light down on a bottle of cooking sherry with a metal cap.

' "Even though I walk through the valley of the shadow of death," ' I sobbed.

Twisting the cap, I put the mouth of the bottle to my lips and chugged the over-sweet liquid.

I drank half the bottle before coming up for air.

' "I shall fear no evil," ' I murmured.

I felt myself shrinking, shriveling up. The building had won, and I was going to die in that dark place, and I didn't care anymore. My cover had been blown, my façade broken through. I was a worthless coward. I was worse than that. I was a liar, and I was about to allow the house to destroy the people close around me. Perhaps the rest of the world, too?

I looked at my watch: It said five minutes to one. Sixty-five minutes left.

At that moment, the black box was still down there in the sub-sub-level, where it had fallen out of my satchel. Those indicator lights would be glowing unheeded in the darkness. And I just didn't care anymore.

I downed the rest of the sherry.

' "I shall fear no evil!" ' I screamed, and hurled the now-empty bottle against the row of cabinets. As the glass shattered, it resounded like a cymbal clash, almost musical in the stillness. And I sensed the entire house laughing at me, the floorboards guffawing, the ceilings giggling uncontrollably, the foundations chortling.

I clumsily climbed to my feet, my head spinning, the rage now seething in me again. ' "I SHALL FEAR NO EVIL!" ' I shrieked.

The house roared with laughter in response.

'GO BACK WHERE YOU CAME FROM!' I wailed, starting toward the exit. But my feet became foolishly tangled, and I sprawled headlong.

I think I hit my head on the corner of a sink. Pain exploded in my left temple as I tumbled to the floor. I lay there gasping.

It never occurred to me that I was passing out, it happened so fast. It just seemed as though my head were sinking into the floor.

Into the dark nothing.

The lights fading, fading . . . gone.

3. From Hell

Best I could figure, it came from the ground, and it rose up through the crawlspace, three levels below my inert body, moving like a cloud of pollen on the wind, or a storm front, floating with that kind of ephemeral certainty. Up through the fossilized joists of the lowermost foundation, penetrating the concrete of the sub-level floor, then up through the darkness and penetrating the parquet floor of the ground level.

As it moved, it picked up speed, soaring up staircases, swirling around corners and winging along the corridors, faster and faster, homing toward its ultimate destination.

Me.

It was coming for *me*.

It approached the kitchen, narrowing into a bolt of black lightning, then coursed through the kitchen door, passing through stainless-steel barriers, through shadows, and finally diving toward the pantry.

And it struck me, a direct hit, dead center in the brain, exploding inside me.

Taking me to a horrible place.

CHAPTER TWENTY-FOUR

Faustian Aaman

1. The Curse

The sound is excruciating at first—squeeeeek!-squeeeek!-squeeek!—and I look down and I realize the source of it is a potter's wheel. And then I realize it's my own potter's wheel—it's mine—and I'm working a wet slab of clay with my long brown fingers, creating another masterpiece: A vase to display my sweet Jocelyn's beloved orchids. I'm covered with sweat, dressed only in my linen pants, and my eyes burn from the intense concentration. I can hear a commotion outside my work hut, and I get up to peer through the bamboo slats.

I see French sailors heading down our path, coming with weapons, long knives and broadswords. I can't believe they would really intrude on my property, my sanctuary, but then again I have been hearing of recent raids on Port de Paix and Pointe Jean Rabel, nasty attacks on fisherman and their families, kidnappings—slavers taking people across the Windward Passage to other islands.

I hurry to my cache and find my machete. I can hear them yelling now, and I can hear Jocelyn's voice keening frantically. My heart starts racing. I hurry to the door, and slam myself against the frame, peering out the slats, with sweat streaming down my back.

They're now coming toward my work hut. The two younger men are in ordinary sailors' garb, but the older one wears a tattered frockcoat, boots and a scabbard, like an officer. Their faces are weatherbeaten sea faces, grim and twisted with a cruel purpose. My heart thumps. My grip is moist on the machete's pigskin handle. I am not a warrior, but I will not let them take me away from my family. I will not.

I kick open the door of my hut, as Jocelyn screams again. I run out at them with my machete raised, and the two younger sailors engage me. Their swords flash in the hot Haitian sun, and one of the blades strikes my machete and the sparks fly. I fight back as hard as I can, but they are strong and experienced. Then I hear my little bébé, Stenio, coming down the path behind me, shouting for his father. I see Jocelyn grab him and hold him away.

While I'm distracted, the net comes out of nowhere.

In the blink of an eye I am covered with a trawling net, and I get tangled up and fall into the dust. Jocelyn shrieks as I try to tear free, but the more I struggle, the tighter the net draws around me. I'm only twenty-six, a respected craftsman in my village, with a new family—and they're taking me. The damned slavers are taking me.

'Faustian! Faustian!' Jocelyn screams, Stenio crying in her arms. 'Retounin! Pa Ale'! S'il vous plaît—s'il vous plaît—RETOUNINNNN!'

I'm now being dragged down the seaward trail like a bundle of booty, through the plantain fields toward Port Margot. Behind me, Stenio has torn free from his mother and is clamoring after me. I can see him through the mesh of the trawling net, and my heart is rent, burning tears fill my eyes, tears of rage, tears of sudden horror.

'Pitit moin!' I howl in our native creole, the Frenchman laughing at me, laughing at my ignorance. 'Pitit moin!' I scream, calling out for my baby.

Then a club comes down on my head and everything goes dark.

I wake up later, maybe hours later, maybe days later—I'm not certain—but now I'm in the hold of a ship, obviously a slaver, and there are many others like me crowded in rows of bunks, chained to the floor. The floor is slick with vomit and blood. It's dark, except for a single porthole, through which a shaft of daylight bleeds into the hold. I can just barely see the ocean through it, and it's the color of olives, roiling with whitecaps, and I recognize the Sargasso Sea.

We are obviously heading for the new American colonies.

My heart sinks, and my soul feels as though it's melting away. I'm being sold into slavery. Me, Faustian Aaman, the pride of Saint-Raphael! Sculptor, artisan, educated man, apprentice to the great mystic Dartiguenior! Me, father of sweet little Stenio Palo! I feel madness swirling through my brain, the heavens cracking apart, the world sliding out of balance. A furious rage erupts in me. All the spiritual knowledge and power inside me is poisoned and curdled and focused into hate.

A guard is sitting in the shadows across the hold, a big hairy Frenchman in stained britches and leathers. He has a broken nose, his eyes glimmer with cruelty. I can barely speak, but I manage to whisper something to him: 'Min tone' ou pran' de pitit moin!'

It is a curse, and I growl it low like a wolf, cursing him for taking me from my baby. He comes over and strikes me with the hilt of his sword, which sends me reeling into unconsciousness again.

Sometime later we arrive at the Virginia Colony.

The next few days pass in a blur. The weather is hard. The early spring rains have turned the land into a hellish place of mudslides and floods.

They take us in huge carts to a new city on a river, where buildings are being erected. I am sold to a construction concern, and my new owners find out I have skills, and they put me on a work crew. They feed us worm-infested grain and tainted water, and they whip us if we go too slow.

We are digging the foundation of a giant palace now, the largest building I have ever seen. But the going is tough. The ground is soft and swampy, and it takes for ever to dig a hole. The foreman is a cruel Englishman called Hacknell, and he lashes us regularly. We work through the night, through the rain, through the floods. This is hell on earth. I vow to escape. I vow to see vengeance visited on these white devils.

On the third day, the underworld finally opens its mouth and swallows me.

It happens in torrential rain, as I am standing a hundred hands below ground level, pounding a post into the soupy earth. The hole in the ground is nearing completion, but the foundation is flawed. It has been too hurried, it is compromised. The framing beams are uncertain and dangerously sodden from the rains. And, as I pause to take a breath, I hear the telltale sound of earth shifting—like a vast wave washing toward me—and I barely have enough time to cry out.

It's a cave-in.

It's like being eaten by the walls, a tidal wave of wet earth devouring me, swallowing me, sucking me down into its depths. I instinctively reach up toward the sky, but there's nothing anybody can do. The cave-in is too furious, too swift. In no time at all, I'm completely buried up to my neck, then am quickly being sucked under. The pressure is tremendous. It's squeezing the life out of me.

I cannot breathe, cannot cry, cannot move; I can only feel the hate.

The next-to-last thing I see in a veil of gray mist is Hacknell the foreman, staring down at me, and doing nothing. The plans for the great palace—which were once under his arm—have blown away on a gust of wind and rain, and I *see Hacknell staring at me, and I stare back at him. And with my last breath, I utter, in a strangled voice, 'Tone' leu caye ca'!'*

A curse on this house.

Then the earth is rolling over me, I can't breathe and I'm dying. The last thing I see is the builder's plans, the soaked parchment pages on which the blueprints of the palace are marked. They tumble across my dwindling line of vision on a gust of wind, and I glimpse them briefly before sinking under.

I glimpse the title heading one of the pages, and I read it, unable to understand the language, but memorizing it nonetheless for eternity—

'The President's House.'

That's the last thing I see before gray light fades to complete and utter blackness.

2. Maelstrom

Something was moving in the darkness . . . a couple of tiny pin-pricks of light.

I came awake with a gasp.

For a moment I was in a state of complete disorientation. It felt as though something or somebody was standing on my chest, but I couldn't see a thing. I couldn't even see my own hand in front of my face. I had a feeling there was a dark presence looming over me, but I had no sense of direction—or anything else, for that matter. Thank God, though, for those two tiny scintillae of white light off to my left coming toward me.

That gave me something to lock onto.

I tried to sit up, but my back was wrenched pretty good. My brain was buzzing with a horrible kind of exhilaration— the sights and sounds of Haiti and slave ships and cave-ins echoing in my head. I couldn't remember exactly what had happened, but I could still taste that awful nutty-sour tang of sherry in my mouth, and I realized I was still in the White House kitchen. I could smell the yeasty after-odors of bread, and something else, like a trace of hickory smoke or an old fireplace flue. The last thing I could recall was bursting into the pantry but, after that, everything got pretty bleary.

The specks of white light had now grown into slender beams threading the shadows, till I realized a couple of flashlights were approaching through the darkness.

All at once the memory hit me. *The door. That damned door.* And the sound of Eric Rivers' voice coming from behind it. And the tidal wave of terror crashing down, when I had chickened out like a scared little schoolboy. And I had turned tail.

Then another memory: The potter. The young man from that dream, or vision, or whatever it was. *He* had to be the primary spirit inhabiting this mansion. And he had revealed himself to me for a reason. He had even shown me the manner of his death. He had shown me that he was no demon, no fallen angel, no emissary from hell.

He was a just an ordinary man whose spirit had become twisted into evil shapes.

'Faustian Aaman,' I managed in a strangled whisper.

The shadows crackled suddenly around me like a cat's fur standing up with static, as though the very words touched off some sort of electrical charge in the air. I felt that wave of dread crash over me again, and my body ached from the immense weight pressing down on it. Somewhere in the back of my mind, I had the feeling that I had forgotten something very important.

In the darkness ahead of me, those twin beams had grown into beacons slicing through the open doorway of the kitchen. I could hear two sets of footsteps coming toward me—and something else. I could hear a strange noise off in the dark recesses of the house, one that I hadn't heard before. Almost like a whip cracking. And that smell—that charcoal-smoke smell permeating the air.

'Father?' Dodd's voice pierced the stillness, just as one of the lightbeams exploded like a silver sunburst in my eyes.

I managed to sit up against the steel cabinet, my back shrieking in agony, the ritual book still dangling from my wrist. I called Jimmy's name, but my voice came out sounding shredded and weak. I couldn't see a thing other than the harsh glare of his flashlight.

'Jimmy? Is that really you?'

Dodd loomed over me in a nimbus of light. Suzanne Fallon was with him, holding the other flashlight. 'Father, what happened? Jesus, we're in deep trouble here! What happened?'

I started to answer, when all of a sudden Suzanne burst out of the shadows.

'Where is she? Where's my daughter?' She lurched toward me, clutching at the collar of my parka, and shaking me. My head was pounding, and I had trouble seeing clearly.

'Haven't found her yet . . .'

'Don't tell me that!' she wailed, aiming her flashlight straight into my face.

'Suzanne, stay back!' Dodd yelled, pulling her off me.

I noticed something flicker in the hallway behind them. It was something bright yellow. But I couldn't be sure if it was real or some flashing artifact of my imagination. My head was spinning. Things were happening too fast.

Dodd grabbed me. 'Father, come on, where's the black box? Where is it?'

I swallowed hard as I realized what I had forgotten. The black box . . . the indicator light . . . 'Jimmy, it's still down below.'

'What?'

'Wait, wait! Listen to me!' I tried to stand up, but felt too sore and disoriented. I glanced at my watch and saw that it was 12:56, and I silently thanked God that only eighteen minutes had elapsed since I had stumbled upon the ghost-door . . . and chickened out . . . and come back upstairs . . . and passed out here in the pantry. The spirit's assault on my mind must have happened in the space of an instant, and that meant that there was still enough time—not a lot, but enough to try one last campaign against the underground.

'Father, you don't understand!' Dodd said, with a strange urgency glittering in his eyes. 'The White House is burning!'

'What do you mean?'

'The lantern, damnit! The lantern!' Suzanne cried out from the shadows behind him. 'The one James threw out the window . . . the kerosene . . .'

Dodd nodded frantically. 'It led the flames right back to the first floor.'

I finally managed to rise to my feet. 'Isn't there some way to—?'

'No, no, there's no way out!' Dodd said. 'The bulletproof windows will not break! We tried! We wrapped ourselves in blankets, and we tried to bust through.'

'But what about the emergency—?'

'Father, listen to me! There's no way the E-units will make it in time. The north entrance is blazing already. The doors and windows are impenetrable. There's no safe way out of here!'

I stared at him, then asked, 'Who is Aaman, Jimmy?'

He glanced at Suzanne in surprise. 'What? Who?'

'Faustian Aaman,' I said.

The odor of woodsmoke was becoming so thick in there, it was getting hard to breathe.

'What the hell are you talking about, Father? Look, we have to find a way out of here.'

Suzanne pushed toward me again, her eyes flashing hysterically. 'My daughter is going to die in this place if we don't find her soon!'

I grabbed Suzanne and held her still. 'Listen to me. I'm going to find her. I'm going to find your daughter. I just need you to tell me, have you ever heard of Faustian Aaman?'

'LET GO OF ME!' she screamed. 'You've been drinking! I can smell it on your breath, for God's sake!'

Dodd was trying to extricate her from my grasp. 'Father, what the hell's the matter with you?'

Right then there was the sound of timber cracking outside in the corridor, like a pistol shot. There followed a huge thud, and we all jumped. The crackling sound of the blaze grew louder, and I realized the fire was completely out of control. I also felt sure that fire engines and E-units were already circling the perimeter of the north lawn, or careening down East Executive Avenue, coming across Pennsylvania, fishtailing in the blizzard. And I'm sure the auxiliary secret-service agents stationed at Blair House were already snapping into action. In fact, I'm pretty certain the whole country was about to learn about this whole drama, as it unfolded on CNN. But none of that mattered. None of that mattered because the ground-floor corridor immediately outside the kitchen was alight, blocking any hope of escape that way, and we all knew the only way out of there was back downstairs.

And time was still ticking away.

'Faustian Aaman!' I yelled, almost shaking her. 'Does it mean anything to you?'

'No—Jesus! No! What are you talking about?'

I finally let her go. 'I'm talking about the spirit.'

Dodd was looking horrorstruck. 'Faustian what?'

'Aaman. Faustian Aaman. I think he's the source.'

There was another crash from the corridor, louder and closer, and it sounded like glass exploding. The fire must have been just gobbling the carved and gilded wood in the ceiling out there, chewing through those antique mahogany furnishings. The White House was a tinderbox.

Suzanne's voice pierced through the din. 'Well, whoever it is, whatever it is, my daughter is *not* going to die in this house!'

'Come on, both of you!' I grabbed her flashlight, then guided her by the elbow out of the pantry and across the kitchen toward the door. Dodd was following close on our heels.

'Father, we can't make it out that—'

'Come on, before it's too late!' I was moving on pure, righteous adrenaline. I was not going to quit. I was not going to let that place beat me. I yanked them through the doorway.

'What are you doing, Delaney?' Suzanne demanded, her voice cracking up with terror.

'This way!' I yelled, leading them toward the west hall.

The corridor flickered with firelight from a collapsed ceiling joist that had fallen behind us, and the air temperature was rising, and the sound was like firecrackers snapping and popping. But I set my sights on a door marked 'ACCESS RESTRICTED' beside the freight elevator. I certainly didn't want to waste any more time here at ground level. There was no telling when the ceiling might collapse on top of us, and I didn't want to lose the battle that way.

I wanted my one last chance.

We hurried through the service door, then clambered down the narrow stairs, stumbling in the darkness, my flashlight slashing this way and that.

'We'll never make it out through the tunnel!' Suzanne cried out.

I didn't even reply. Something was boiling in me now,

more than mere rage, more than any pure emotion. Maybe it was some kind of holy spirit filling me. Maybe it was Michael the Archangel himself.

Or maybe it was just foolish pride.

We reached the bottom of the stairs where the rusty shelves rose all the way up to the low ceiling. The sounds of the fire above us had dwindled to a muffled hiss, and I wondered for one crazy instant whether the others could hear my heart thumping in my ribcage.

We pushed the door open and entered a dusty maintenance office, the silence in the empty room screaming back at us. It was almost excruciating.

'MELISSA!' Suzanne wailed, as though the sheer force of her will could roust the girl. But only that horrible indifferent silence answered.

'I want you two to follow the Truman tunnel,' I instructed them, quickly assessing my watch. It was now 1:02 a.m.: Just fifty-six minutes to go.

Suzanne started to protest.

'Don't argue with me!' I yelled at her. 'I want you two to head straight for Blair House! That's the only way. No arguments! You will be able to get out.'

'How do you know?'

'Because I'm going to be keeping the spirit busy, Jimmy. And that's why you two have to get word to the outside world as soon as possible. You've got only fifty-five minutes. Now go! GO!'

Suzanne was in such a daze that Dodd had to drag her over there and kick open the door leading to the passage.

I watched as they vanished into the grimy shadows.

I looked at my watch.

Fifty-four minutes left.

CHAPTER TWENTY-FIVE

River of No Return

1. The Rabbit Hole

It took me less than three minutes to make it back down the rabbit hole.

But it wasn't easy, as the house was fighting me all the way.

As I crossed the cracked cement floor of the basement, the old concrete rippled and crawled with tiny goosebumps, like the dry gray flesh of some giant. I tried to ignore it by repeating those lines Father Karras had made me write across the blackboard back in grade school—*Lord Jesus Christ, have mercy on me, a sinner*—and it worked fairly well. But when I descended the iron steps leading down into sub-level A, I heard the strangled breathing of a child, a small child in the throes of a seizure, and when I shifted my light from side to side, I saw the faded plasterboard walls breathing in and out very quickly, like the lungs of a child. Dizziness rocked me and threatened to send me tumbling, but I held firmly onto the handrail and made it to the bottom of the steps.

Finally, as I tried to cross the cavernous storage room of the sub-level, the house came at me with everything it had got. The dank air was filled with the most horrible moaning I had ever heard, a tortured human agony, and in my peripheral vision I saw the faces in old, torn paintings and busted mannequins and cracked bronze statuary— actually I *sensed* them more than saw them—contorting into expressions of utter horror. And blood oozed up from the cracks in the floor, and blackened fingers reached up for me, and diseased, shriveled arms flailed at me, and amorphous tangles of naked corpses fornicated in slime pits of burning oil. There were even fragments of very personal demons out of the corners of my eyes, fears from my childhood, secret phobias—festering knots of wasps, coffins filled with dead children, amputated sex organs on broken dinner plates.

I was in hell.

But I continued reciting the litany as I moved along, mouthing the sacred words from the eleventh century, my hot breath pluming as white vapor in the frigid temperature. And as I crossed the sub-level, a realization dawned on me: All these horrors were happening at the edges of my vision, and in the back of my mid-brain, and just out of sight, and that's exactly how the house had been working on me since I had first arrived, and that was the key to my survival. The sounds were mere echoes of sounds, the ghosts mere photo-strobe flashes of objects burned onto the backs of my retinas. Even the physical manifestations were fleeting and external: The door, the windows, the claw marks, the flowers dying. They were all virtual events—things merely going *bump*.

And that realization filled me with enough strength to make it across the sub-level room to the corner hatch.

Still gaping wide from my hasty retreat a half-hour earlier, the hatch looked like an open mouth. I wasted no time in climbing through, and then descended the steps beyond, the flashlight gripped in my teeth. I moved quicker than before, my mind completely focused, the most Zen-like state I had ever been in. Sixteen steps: I counted them as I descended. I ignored the odors of death around me.

I landed eventually on the petrified mortar floor. The ground seemed to vibrate beneath me, sending tremors through the foundations and up into the house above.

I aimed the light down the tunnel. My satchel was lying on the floor fifteen feet away, at the point where the tunnel turned ninety degrees to one side. I could see the broken shards of my tape recorder strewn across the cold cement. My rosary beads lay nearby, as well as a couple of brass cruets, my silver medallions, and my caffeine pills. The black box itself was lying against the base of one wall. I walked over to the fallen satchel.

Gathering up my things, I felt the tunnel contracting around me like some giant, obscene intestine. My flashlight flickered, which was impossible since I had just inserted some of Mrs. Whittaker's fresh batteries. I shook the light, and it flared brightly again. I quickly got everything back into the satchel—pausing only to look at the black box, now indicating fifty-two minutes and thirty-one seconds left—and I rose to my feet.

A sort of terrible hush had fallen over the tunnel. The sounds of the fire burning above, and the storm raging outside, and everything else for that matter, were all distant memories. It sort of felt like the house was coiled, silent and ready to strike. I stood for a moment, taking deep breaths, the satchel handle fastened around my right wrist, the ritual book in my left hand.

I recited the final lines of the Address aloud to the dark tunnel, my voice echoing.

' "Accursed spirit named Aaman! We enjoin you under penalty of the living God, fear and take flight when the Holy Name of Jesus is invoked by us!" '

I directed the light at the tunnel bend.

' "Be driven out by the powerful hand of God!" '

I took a few steps forward, then turned the corner and froze, my heart nearly skipping a beat.

2. Last Hope

I wasn't standing in the tunnel anymore. I wasn't in the White House. I wasn't even in Washington, D.C. anymore. I was somewhere else—another time, another place—the revelation nearly toppling me to the floor.

'Straight on down the hall, sir,' a gravelly voice burbled behind me.

I spun around and saw an old black man perched on a bar stool near the fire-escape door. A yellow bug light burned over his bald head, giving him a deathly pallor. Dressed in tattered denim overalls and a sweaty sleeveless T-shirt, the old man was little Eric Rivers' great-uncle, and he was keeping watch for me. It was exactly as it had been twenty years earlier, and the sight of it sent gooseflesh rippling over me.

'You must be Uncle William,' I said, and the sound of my own voice startled me.

I was young again. Dressed in a crisp black coat and clerical collar, I was fresh out of the seminary, wet behind the ears, and ready to change the world. I had a head full of unruly auburn hair and was clean shaven, and I walked with a spring in my step. I hadn't started drinking yet, and I was very fit. I felt I could do anything, and I guess that's why I was in the Robert Taylor projects that night with my Roman Ritual book—still brand spanking new—tucked under my arm.

'You the exorcist man, ain't ya?' the old man enquired, peering up at me through milky, hound-dog eyes. There was a weariness in his voice.

'Yessir, I guess I am. Name's Father Delaney. I'm from Saint Michael's.'

He nodded slowly. 'That boy is sick,' he said.

I told him I understood, and hoped I could do something about that.

He shook his ancient head. 'No, no sir, y'all don't get it,' he said. 'That boy got a sickness. He could die.'

I assured him I would do everything in my power to help.

He pointed a crooked brown finger at the hallway straight ahead. 'You want to help? Fetch a doctor.'

I looked at him for another moment, then turned and made my way down the hall.

It was so strange, walking down that airless little hallway, my footsteps creaking on the chipped and peeling linoleum. I was reliving the worst night of my life—completely conscious of the fact that it was a dream, or a vision, or some kind of horrible hallucination—and yet I was powerless to stop it. I was trapped, strapped on board a terrible rollercoaster, a passenger inside my younger body, and all I could do was watch myself go through the motions. And the worst part now was that I knew what was coming next.

I reached the Rivers' door—a heavy steel job with gang graffiti all over it—and knocked on it. The door clicked and swung open. A naked little black girl, who couldn't have been more than six years old, was standing there with tracks of mucus under her nose and her eyes shimmering with terror.

'Hello, sweetheart, I'm Father Delaney,' I said, and gently patted her head. She flinched at my touch, and I pushed past her to enter the apartment. 'I'm here to see your older brother—'

She was already pointing toward a narrow hallway leading from the living room.

I glanced around me. It was a typical two-bedroom apartment in the world's largest public-housing unit: A space designed with good intentions, then devoured, digested and shat out by poverty. The meager furnishings were all covered with tattered bedspreads. Windowpanes were missing, boarded over or covered with plastic. The air smelled of cheap canned food and bodily functions. Yet there was a tidiness to the place—the kitchenette was spotless and the floor was scrubbed—which suggested this family had not yet given up hope.

A strangled moan came fluttering out of the shadows of the hallway.

I made my way across the living room.

The boy's room lay at the end of the passage, behind the largest, ugliest black door I had ever seen. His mother was sitting with her head down in front of the door on a metal folding chair like a brooding sentry and flinching at every tortured sound from inside the room. She wore a cheap cotton shift over her portly body, her long frizzy hair pulled back inside a scarf, her caramel-colored face wet from tears. I felt so sorry for that woman.

She looked up at me as I approached; her eyes looked poached from endless crying. 'My baby boy is dying, Father,' she uttered in a dry whisper.

'I'm with you now, sister,' I said, touching her hand, which was ice-cold.

'They already called some kinda ambulance,' she said. Then she looked at me. 'You is our last hope.'

'The good Lord will help us,' I said, reaching into my jacket pocket. There was an ampulla of holy water there, and I gripped it tightly. I wanted to get this over with quickly. I was operating without a safety net, going against the express orders of the Church. I wanted to get in and get out. I was such a fool, so young and stupid and arrogant.

Right then a piercing cry came from inside the boy's room, a falsetto howl that rose up and then deteriorated in mad laughter. And I thought I heard my own name—Delaney. I *thought I heard that insane voice say my name. I looked back at Letitia Rivers questioningly.*

'Please save my baby,' she pleaded through choking sobs.

'Pray for me, sister,' I said, and saw her close her eyes and start to pray.

I opened the bedroom door and walked inside, locking it behind me.

The room was tiny—barely a hundred square feet—and the air was ripe. The odors of urine and sweat hung like a shroud. I could hear a panting sound, like a dog, and I glanced across the room and saw the cause: An eight-year-old black boy bound with stained sheets to a moldering lounge chair, and hyperventilating. Skinny as a rag doll, with close-cropped corn rows, Eric Rivers was dressed in a torn Star Wars T-shirt sodden with blood. His face was a road map of pure hate. His flesh was the color of ashes, his eyes were milky-gray, his teeth black. There was blood on his chin.

The moment he saw me, he let out a caterwauling like a lion being skinned alive.

I wore a gold crucifix around my neck, and now I took it off and raised it up in front of me. ' "Behold the cross of the Lord," ' I said firmly. ' "Depart, enemies! Be uprooted and expelled from this creature of God!" '

The boy stared at me, those milky-gray eyes burning into me. 'Fake!'

I flinched at the sound of his voice. It was a whiskey-cured voice full of adult wisdom, which took me by surprise. I knew immediately this was the real thing, and I felt as though it knew me. It knew my secrets. My heart started pumping as I made the sign of the cross. ' "I exorcize you, invading enemy!" ' I yelled. ' "In the name of our Lord, Jesus Christ!" '

I took a step closer to the chair, flinging a sprinkle of holy water.

The boy stiffened, gasping at the moment of contact, as

though the water were acid. Then he snapped his head back and laughter poured out of him: The most sinister, mocking laughter I had ever heard. The chair started vibrating, then shaking convulsively as though it too was laughing.

The boy looked at me. 'I know you, Father Hypocrite! Father Greenhorn!'

' "Enemy of the Faith, leave this child of God!" ' I said, trying to ignore the taunts, trying to stay on track. I hadn't expected such a direct assault. The truth was, I had expected a lot of screaming and writhing and foaming at the mouth, but I hadn't expected it to get so personal so quickly. But I was familiar enough with the procedure to remember the rules laid down in the original text: The exorcist must give no credence to the evil spirit, or engage in conversation, or give credence to any other vanities, mockeries or foolishness of the evil spirit. *The only problem was, I was young and scared all of a sudden. And I was way out of my element.*

'Look at yourself!' the boy yelled at me. 'The world's biggest hypocrite!'

I told the thing to be quiet.

'The great exorcist!' the boy jeered. 'With no church! No authority!'

I made the sign of the cross, and screamed at it to shut up.

'You're a phony!' the boy laughed. 'A phony and a liar!'

' "Jesus of Nazareth commands you!" ' I bellowed, genuflecting, before sprinkling more holy water.

He howled and laughed. 'Liar! Liar! Liar! Liar! Liar! Liar! Liar!'

I started the ritual.

'Liar! Liar! Liar! Liar—! it kept shrieking, answering every sacred word with that taunting cry.

And it went on like that for some time.

I went through an entire ampulla of holy water, and the thing inside the boy just kept growing more and more powerful. It started spitting at me, and making the chair levitate several inches off the ground, then slamming it back down with a crack. And the more I worked on it, the more active it became. The average exorcism usually lasts around forty-five minutes, but that night, in that tawdry little bedroom, I was losing all track of time. I had no idea how long I had been in there. Through sheer force of will, I managed to get through the first half of the ritual, shouting out the litany above the demon's voice until I was hoarse. But something was happening to me, something terrible. Something that I—in my naive arrogance—would never have expected in a million years.

Finally I heard the crackle of a paramedic's radio outside the door.

Inside the room there was pause for a tableau: A horrible frozen moment as the boy's body deflated for an instant, his chest cavity convulsing, his bloodless tongue protruding. The child's head lolled for a moment. The sound of the door handle jiggling, voices calling out to me. But I was so immersed in my ritual by then, I barely heard them.

' "Lord, hear my prayer!" ' I screamed. I was filmed in a cold sweat, trembling and nauseous. I raised the crucifix, made the sign of the cross. ' "Let my cry reach You!" '

I flung another drop of holy water.

His face snapped toward me suddenly, his lips curling away from his teeth. His facial features started spasming wildly. It was the most horrible thing I'd ever seen. His face was changing so rapidly, almost cartoonishly, from one expression to another—rage, amusement, hate, lust, terror— that I just stood there, paralyzed. It looked as though someone had photographed his face in different expressions and then sped up the film, these facial tics the work of a psychotic puppeteer, his mouth opening, closing, convulsing, smiling, or cringing in a death rictus. His eyes narrowing, or popping wide, then slamming shut. He looked like a subject in some terrible experiment, a million volts of electricity coursing through him.

I hollered: ' "Diabolical spirit! Invading enemy! The power of Christ compels you from this innocent child!" '

All at once, the boy's head stopped moving. His eyes narrowed and fixed me with a horrible steely gaze. His cracked lips peeled back into an obscene grin. 'I know your secret,' it whispered.

By that point I had forgotten my training, forgotten that I was dealing with a child, forgotten that I was supposed to be a man of the Lord. I was a cornered animal, and it was either fight or flight, and that's why I committed that one fatal mistake—going against thousands of years of training for both Catholic priests and smart lawyers—letting it see my one weakness.

Asking a question that I didn't know the answer to.

'What secret?' I said.

The thing that was once a boy sneered at me. 'Your secret bigotry,' it hissed.

I told it to shut up, my voice losing power. I realized I had made a critical blunder the moment that question had come out of my mouth. It was like I had punctured a hole in my side, and now all the strength of my conviction was leaking out.

'Your dirty little secret,' the demon said through the boy's bloody mouth, making little Eric's face contort into the hideous mockery of a lustful sexual predator.

'Shut up!'

'You know it's true,' it insisted.

'I said shut up!'

The demon's yellow gaze burned into me. 'You hate this little nigger as much as I do!'

'In the name of our Lord Jesus Chri—!'

'You're just like me!' the demon cut in, flicking the words at me like poison darts. 'You hate these little pickaninnies, *don't you? Don't you? You see them everywhere, on the street, in the subway. You can smell them. Jigaboos! Mud people!'*

'Shut up! Shut up! Shut up!'

'Your pity is another form of hate,' the demon barked at me. *'In your heart, you hate this little coon more than you hate me. In your heart, you hate him.'*

'SHUT UP!'

'You hate all the spooks because of what they're doing to your neighborhood: The drugs, the crime, the welfare mothers shitting out more little darkies every day. They're infecting the world, all those spades!'

I hurled the now empty cruet at him, but it banged against the wall behind his chair. My brain was on fire with rage. 'I TOLD YOU TO SHUT UP!'

The demon began laughing, making the child's body shiver and quake. *'My finest creation!'* the voice howled. *'A holy man full of hate and bigotry!'*

'THAT'S IT!'

I lurched at the boy.

The impact of my landing on the lounger propelled the chair slamming against the wall, but the restraints still held the boy's body in place. I slid across the floor. The boy kept laughing. I managed to climb on top of him, panting hard, my fists clenched white-knuckle tight, and seeing nothing but phosphorescent pink sunbursts obscuring my vision. And then I could see the boy beneath me, still emitting that hideous screechy laughter. Laughing at me. Laughing . . .

And that's when I started hitting him.

I lashed out at him insanely. I kept hitting—wham!—and crying out—'Shut up!'—wham!—'Shut up!'—wham!—'Shut up!' and he kept laughing, and I kept whaling blows to his temple, and that little head kept snapping backward like a toy, but still laughing and chortling, and I kept pummeling him, but with less effect each time. And then the boy swallowed his tongue.

Finally I paused in horror, gasping. The kid's head drooped, his face looked a disaster area, his mouth was bloody. I wiped my mouth clean of the sweat and drool mingling on my chin.

I slid off the chair.

My heart stopped as I gaped down at the child's body. The demon was gone, and the boy was now totally still. His eyes were closed, his skin had returned to its original gray pallor. Astonishingly, after my onslaught, he looked much the same. I leaned down and listened for a breath. My scalp crawled. He didn't seem to be breathing. I felt for a pulse, but detected none. My heart started hammering in panic.

I tried CPR—remembering bits of it from a church class I had attended—pressing down on the boy's skinny chest, then blowing my breath into his mouth. His lips tasted coppery from the seeping blood. I stared at him with utter horror and revulsion.

He was dead.

I had killed him.

I didn't know what to do. I grabbed handfuls of my own hair and gazed up at the filthy ceiling as though I might find an angry God up there looking down at me, but of course there were only the stained tiles. And a long, hoarse moan came out of me then, my eyes filling with tears of despair. It felt as though a gigantic knife sliced through my midsection, letting all that pain and horror and grief spill out.

I had killed the little boy.

I started sobbing.

The pounding on the door grew louder in my consciousness as I sat and sobbed uncontrollably for several minutes more. I had never wept so hard in my life. I collapsed on the floor next to the boy's body. I covered my face in my hands and I wailed for an eternity. Then I began to wipe the blood from the child's mouth.

When the paramedics finally burst in, they detected the

feeblest of heartbeats still, and they began to work on Eric Rivers in a frenzy . . . until Eric Rivers finally expired. Never suspecting what had really occurred, they peremptorily declared it death from heart failure—and I never argued with them.

I never found the courage to tell them what I had done.

3. Dark Threshold

When I opened my eyes, I was no longer in Eric Rivers' bedroom.

And I was no longer young.

I was on the floor of the narrow sub-sub-level tunnel, in pitch dark and thirty-five feet beneath the White House itself. The flashlight was lying on the petrified cement next to me, its beam flickering yellow, threatening to extinguish, but my satchel was still tied to my right wrist, and my book of rituals still attached to my left.

Wiping my eyes, I grabbed the flashlight to look at my watch. It was now 1:31 a.m. My mind was swimming, my body drained, my emotions wrung out, my soul cauterized by all the tortured memories, but I had still remembered the crucial countdown. I reckoned that my recent hallucination had only chewed up about twenty minutes or so of precious time. I wondered for one moment whether Dodd and Suzanne had made it out yet, and what the current status of the devastating launch sequence was.

I sucked in another breath and turned the dim yellow light on the darkness ahead of me, till I saw a new door.

The only way out.

CHAPTER TWENTY-SIX

Inhuman Remains

1. Flesh

I managed to stand, my flashlight pooled on the filthy surface of an iron door.

This was not the same door from the tenement building, but it was just as foreboding, battered and dented, filmed by cobwebs, stamped out of cheap post-war steel—and it had faded words stenciled across the top: 'CRAWL-SPACE—RESTRICTED ENTRY.' I played the trembling beam up and down it, and I saw the metal shift in the light as though refracting my fear: Veins slithering across its dusty surface; cracks snaking up and down, forming delicate tributaries; lumps boiling across the edges. This door was alive. This door was flesh and blood. I had to marshal every last ounce of spirit in order to move toward it—

(*Of course, I was completely oblivious to the fact that Dodd and Suzanne, at that same moment, were lost in the labyrinth of tunnels above me, madly calling out for help, their voices echoing down the dark passageways that seemed to stretch without end, as time ticked away: Twenty-seven minutes and sixteen seconds . . . fifteen seconds . . . fourteen seconds . . . thirteen seconds . . .*)

—and I lumbered up to the door, while hearing a choir

of agonized moaning in my brain. A mixture of ghostly cries from Aaman's native Haiti, and the wailing of little Eric Rivers, and something even more primal, something from my own soul. My soul was weeping.

I doubled over for a moment, only inches away from the door, as an orgasm of fear washed through me, the odors of death and decay and the deepest parts of the earth engulfing me. But I fought this terror with every last shred of strength—because I was a priest. I was a professional. Contrary to official Church bookkeeping, I was still a priest. And I was not going to let Melissa Fallon down. I was going to find her and get her out of there before the clock ran out on the weapons-launch sequence.

I looked at my watch for one last jolt of reality. Twenty-five minutes left.

I reached for the door's handle—and found it was unlocked.

2. Shock

A gust of black wind swirled up into my face. I smelled rotting flowers and dead fish. I blinked and blinked, my flashlight jerking in my trembling hand.

At first I couldn't see a thing in the flickering light, but the feeling was overwhelming—a bolt of torment so dark and painful it sent a shockwave down my spine, making my throat constrict and my eyes well up. As dizziness washed over me, my legs faltered. I let out an involuntary gasp as I gawked at something gleaming in the dim yellow beam.

It was a delicate spray of human bones partially fossilized in the hard-packed earth. Part of a femur sunken to my right, half the pelvic girdle to my left, a chain of vertebrae, and the half-moon of a skull. From one of the eye sockets grew a fuzz of mold.

And a few inches to my left, fanned out like some exotic, bleached sea creature, were the remains of a long, delicate craftsman's hand. A hand responsible for many beautiful works of art.

Faustian Aaman's hand.

A chorus of horrible voices erupted in my brain, and all I could think of was the book of rituals. At all costs I must complete the ritual, though my hands shook too badly to find the page.

And that's when I spotted the other body out of the corner of my eye.

At first I thought she was dead, slumped there against the wall. But there was something very weird about the way she was canted against the moist stone, with her arms and legs dangling. She was still dressed in her Public Enemy T-shirt and skin-tight leathers, her clothes damp, torn and filthy. She was alive, just barely, as I could see her stomach heave faintly as she drew in irregular breaths. But I couldn't figure out what seemed wrong about her.

Until I shone my light on the floor beneath her.

Melissa Fallon was floating.

I swear, by God Almighty, that girl was floating several feet off the ground. I stood and stared at her, blinking away my disbelief. The fading flashlight finally flickered off, came back for a brief instant, then died completely.

I blinked again.

And, even through the darkness, I saw why she was floating.

3. Carved out of the Moon

I think I uttered something like, 'Sweet Jesus God in Heaven,' as I fumbled for my ritual book. I couldn't tear my gaze from that apparition only inches away from me.

He was luminous, like a full moon rising in the night, but was neither reflecting nor generating any light. He was like a hole in the darkness. And he was enormous, maybe seven feet tall, and stood there like a totem, holding Melissa's limp body in translucent arms, as though she were floating on a cradle of mist. He made no move toward me, just stood there glaring silently, holding the girl in those impossible arms. Was he intending to kill me? Was he hoping to scare me to death? Infect me? Possess me? All those possibilities streamed through my feverish brain.

But there was something else about him even more extraordinary. In all my years, I had never before seen an apparition up close. I had witnessed a few manifestations here and there, witnessed crockery rattling or flying through the air, seen the phantom stains, and smelled the odors, and come into contact with all manner of evil energies. But I had never encountered a phantom at such close proximity, and it wasn't at all what I had expected. It wasn't ghastly or horrifying at all.

But it was something worse.

It was the bleakest, worst feeling I had ever experienced, radiating off this specter like a stench, and I physically recoiled, cringing, holding my guts as though a sword had just sliced through me. A faint sound suddenly came out of Melissa, a feverish moan, and she stirred suddenly as though caught in the throes of a nightmare. My bloodstream sang with panic, my scalp crawled.

Finishing the exorcism ritual was all I could think of doing.

I glanced down at the book trembling in my hand, barely visible in the glow. ' "Holy-Holy-Holy—Lord God of all hosts," ' I stammered. ' "Be humiliated under the—the—powerful—powerful hand of God!" '

When I looked back up at the ghost, something had changed, something amazing.

A thin membrane of light had formed around Melissa's inert form, like a crust of ice, and I blinked again, my breath sticking in my throat. Melissa's body was covered with the ghost of another woman's clothing, a tattered linen dress from the eighteenth century. I gaped at her face. Another woman's features were materializing, like radiant smoke, over Melissa's. I recognized the phantom face immediately, and it put the squeeze on my heart. A heavier curtain of pain fell over me.

It was clearly Jocelyn Aaman—Faustian's wife.

I fumbled with my ritual book, wrestling with the final lines of the exorcism: ' "Invading enemy, the one named Aaman!" ' I croaked, my insides splitting from the tidal wave of grief. ' "I exorcize you—in—in the name of Jesus Christ—be uprooted! Be uprooted and expelled from this place! And let this child of God go free!" '

Melissa moaned again, louder, and I could hear the terror in her voice.

'LEAVE HER ALONE!' I shrieked at the ghost.

I felt something swooping down at me through the darkness—a slithering, leathery weight on my shoulders—and I jerked away. I snapped my gaze toward the shadows above me, feeling something rough and damp on my face. In that panicky instant I imagined a giant spiderweb, or dirt sifting from the ceiling. But, as I glanced back at the ghost, my throat constricted.

Aaman was slowly floating away, himself several inches off the ground now, but Melissa was groggily writhing in his arms. She was coming awake! And he was taking her down into the black abyss for ever. And I was sure I was losing her. I was losing the girl. She was floating away from me into the black void.

Then I looked up and realized what had fallen on me. And screamed.

4. The Black Tide

It pressed down on my face, a criss-cross of twine smelling of rotting fish, a net from some other era, some other place, some other nightmare.

A phantom trawling net had fallen on me.

And I screamed again, because I could see Melissa still floating away into the darkness, being swallowed up by the underworld, and there was nothing I could do about it, because the netting was too heavy, too impenetrable, and I could smell the stink of the ocean, feel the rough cords digging into my face and arms and back, and the more I struggled to break free, the tighter it tangled around me . . .

And that's when I realized the book of rituals had somehow slipped off my wrist.

I cried out to Melissa, and felt a dagger of pain shoot through me. I gasped again, hunched under the sheer weight of the netting, and I clawed around on the cracked cement for my missing book, and I started to weep. I couldn't find it. And Melissa was being taken away. And a horrible black tide of grief was rolling over me, sucking me down into its dark depths. And I knew I was feeling what Aaman had once felt, and was experiencing what Aaman had experienced, and I knew I was a fake, a phony, and was going to perish down there in the dark. I could feel my heart throb like a busted engine inside my chest, with pain shooting down my arm. I was sure I was suffering a heart attack, and was going to die.

'MELISSA!' I howled in a strangled wail of mingled grief and rage. I started to sob again and, man, I let it rip. It all came out in one thunderous squall of pain—all the shame and heartache and years of self-loathing—and tears and snot oozed down my face, as I shuddered and bawled in the darkness.

'MELISSSAAAHHHHH!'

Then the darkness crashed down on me, and my balance gave way, and I collapsed on my back. But then I kept sinking. I kept sinking through the floor, with the black wave covering me, and all I could see was a narrow porthole, a dim radiance above me—and the horrorstruck invocation of some primal prayer.

Hail-Mary-full-of-grace-the-Lord-is-with-you-blessed-are-you-among-women!

I couldn't breathe. I was being buried alive. I could hear the wall of earth closing down on me, like a giant throat swallowing me, devouring me, and involuntary panic sluiced through my veins. I convulsed and screamed, but could find no breath, so all I could do was heave dryly. I was dying. I was all alone and dying.

And-blessed-is-the-fruit-of-your-womb-Jesus . . .

I could no longer move, which was worse than anything else. The invisible weight was crushing me, till I was running out of fight.

Pray-for-us-sinners-now-and-at-the-hour-of-our-death!

My hand touched something solid.

It was my book of the Roman Ritual!

It was down there with me somehow, lying at my side under the phantom ground, and I managed to crane my neck enough to see it through my tears. It had been inadvertently folded open to one yellowed, dog-eared page. Its heading miraculously visible, despite the pitch dark.

And for the first time I realized the truth.

And all my rage turned to sorrow.

And I felt a new emotion coursing through me, an overwhelming urge to beg God's forgiveness . . .

And that's when everything changed.

Chapter Twenty-Seven

Fate

1. Page 213

All of a sudden, I felt a warmth on my back, and could smell the odors of sulfur and cinnamon. The darkness was opening up around me. The trawling net was melting away, fizzing into nothing like a chemical reaction. I was back up at floor level, in the crawlspace, and the faint yellow spark of my flashlight was still glowing like a dying ember, and gave off just enough light for me to see again my ritual book and the legend at the top of its brittle, ancient page.

I looked around for the luminous outline of the giant apparition. I could hear Melissa's cry fade into the darkness, and my pulse raced so fast I thought my heart would explode. I stared down at the mortal remains of Faustian Aaman, and saw a mosaic of slender bones buried in unforgiving earth, saw the bleached half-moon skull—and I felt a new emotion.

'The wrong page,' I muttered barely above a whisper.

I clumsily twisted around and scooped up the flashlight with a trembling hand, turning it on page 213 of my ritual book. The sudden revelation had revived me, giving me new strength.

The wrong page.

I had been on the wrong page all along.

Of course.

For two hundred years, Faustian Aaman had been trying to tell us—but nobody had listened. There was no need for an exorcism in this house, no need to drive out evil spirits. What that place needed was something quite different. But I had been too blind with fear and anger and prejudice to see it. I had been on the wrong damn page.

Quickly wiping my eyes, with the flashlight held as steady as possible, I began reciting the Last Rites.

' "Soul of Christ!" ' I called out. ' "I do most humbly beseech Thee! As I deliver these rites, deliver this man, Faustian Aaman, from all worldly bondage, and assist him in his passage to eternal paradise!" '

There was a moment of frozen silence.

I closed my eyes. Something was turning inside me, something long buried. I felt it in my gut: I was a priest again—preaching to a congregation of one. And for the first time in twenty years I truly *believed* in what I was doing: The Last Rites, the most sacred of all rites. The ushering of a soul into the afterlife. But the key—the final piece to the puzzle—was an archaic old Church rule buzzing through my mind at that moment, the rule which states that in an emergency the Last Rites can be lawfully administered by *any* Catholic lay person—regardless of clerical status—as long as a few essential guidelines are observed: The recitation of the proper litany, the use of Church-sanctioned icons, and the confirmation of faith by the administrator. And that was when it hit me: My fate, my true destiny.

Of course!

This was why I had been brought to the White House in the first place, and it was why I had put the vestments back on, and it was why I had been chosen. After all, I was the perfect man for the job. I had studied the historical development of the Last Rites while at seminary, studying under that renowned scholar Father Joseph Laurence, and I had written a thesis on *The Catholic Book of the Dead* that was published in *Legourian Magazine*, and over the years I had even administered the Rites to various patients at the St. Mary's Hospital cancer ward. I knew the Last Rites backward and forward, and I cherished them as if they were part of my soul. I was the man, and Dodd merely the agent. A higher power had brought me to that Executive Mansion, that establishment of great men and greater lies. And it was my fate to do one thing only in that place: To perform the Last Rites. This was what Aaman had been wanting all along. To be with his wife in heaven, and to be released from his earthly grave.

And I was the man to lead him there.

My satchel still dangled heavily from my wrist, almost cutting off my circulation. I fished around in it, and felt the larger crucifix in there—a heavy, plated cross cold to the touch—and I dug it out. I wasn't even sure what I was going to do with it, until I held it in my hand. I raised the cross like a beacon.

And gently laid it down upon the ancient skeleton buried in the earth.

Something sparked in front of me.

It looked like a sudden burst of voltage crackling through the air about ten feet away, a shimmer of lightning curling around Melissa. The ghost had turned fluid, like ice melting.

' "O Lord, Beloved Creator, I ask of Thee the greatest of all Thy Graces!" ' I shouted as loudly as my ruined voice would permit, remembering those wondrous lines by heart. ' "That is to say, a holy death for this innocent man, Faustian Aaman! And no matter how greatly we have hitherto abused the life Thou gavest us, grant Your servant Faustian Aaman the grace to end his journey in Thy holy love!" '

Another surge of current crackled through the air—and I saw Melissa slip from the phantom's grasp and drop to the floor with a thud. She was only semi-conscious, and moaning, but fluttering her eyelids.

' "Let him depart this world like the holy Patriarchs!" ' I went on, voice rising, the memory of the beautiful litany pouring out of me ever more quickly and forcefully. ' "Allow-him-to-forsake-this-valley-of-tears-without-sadness! Allow-him-to-enter-into-the-joy-of-eternal-rest! And-let-him-pass-over-like-the-glorious-Saint-Joseph-in-the-arms-of-Jesus-and-Mary-repeating-in-turn-each-of-these-sweet-Names-which-we-hope-to-bless-throughout-eternity!" '

There was a great rending noise above me, almost as though the upper stories of the house were collapsing.

I went on calling out the litany, as though I were born to do so: ' "*Let-him-pass-like-the-immaculate-and-blessed-Virgin-in-the-purest-love-and-the-desire-to-be-reunited-with-the-one-and-only-object-of-our-love! Let-him-pass-like-Jesus-from-the-Cross-with-the-most-lively-sentiments-of-hatred-for-sin-and-of-charity-toward-Thee-O-Heavenly-Father-and-of-perfect-resignation-in-his-agony! Holy-Mary-Mother-of-God-pray-for-him-now-and-at-the-hour-of-his-death!*" '

Air pressure surged around me suddenly, popping in my ears.

I looked up, and my eyes must have bugged out of my head.

I was staring at a miracle.

2. Metamorphosis

The spirit erupted with pure, magnesium-bright light, like a supernova in the catacombs, its radiance engulfing us—Melissa and me—and I had to shield my eyes. A great explosion of sound filled the air and I could smell something hot, like burning metal. It was as though daylight had entered the tunnel, so I could see every pore in the stone walls, every cobweb, every crack, every crevice. I could see clearly for the first time in my life.

I gripped my ritual book tightly as the subterranean winds swirled around me. ' "O Lord and Savior!" ' I hollered. ' "Accept this innocent man, Aaman in his final hour! And by the merits of the Blessed Virgin, and of all the angels and the saints, give him blessed eternity in heaven!" '

I looked up, squinting at the silver sun which was pushing up against the ceiling. In the veins and tendrils of its light, I saw the black figure of the spirit. He was majestic: A giant, slender panther of sinew and muscle, a face of etched onyx, and eyes that glowed with black light. He was connected to the earth with tethers of black vines and roots, but these vines were snapping one by one—like umbilical cords breaking off a mothership.

' "In the Name of the Father—the Son—and Holy Spirit," ' I cried, my mind and spirit buzzing with wonder. 'Amen!'

The white light pulsed suddenly, and the figure of Faustian Aaman shimmered and levitated.

What happened next came near to paralyzing me with awe. All I could do was gape in wonder at the metamorphosis unfolding before me.

Aaman was rising higher, the stone ceiling warping upward like an optical illusion to accommodate him, and his arms were reaching out, Christlike, while two other figures appeared in his arms: An ethereal, angelic woman wearing a headscarf and a tattered linen dress, and a little boy with big innocent eyes. And I began to weep, because there was a fourth figure now materializing in that radiant nebula of light.

It was a second little black boy, with short-cropped hair and button nose.

Eric Rivers.

Sadness washed over me, and I sobbed, and I put my face in my hands and I bawled. 'Lord, I'm so sorry,' I cried. 'I'm so sorry for what I did to that little boy! I didn't mean to hurt his precious little face! I'm so sorry, Jesus God. I hate myself! Please, please, please forgive me. I'm so sorry—'

There was a sudden, deep subsonic blast that threatened to collapse my eardrums.

I glanced up in time to see the final display.

The final metamorphosis.

3. Ascension

As the magnesium-bright flash jolted Melissa awake, she screamed—more out of instinct than anything else. And she buried her face in her hands as the ghostly figures coalesced into a single ball of quicksilver-brilliant white light . . .

And then came the eruption.

Silver daylight flared, followed by an enormous blast of sound that was more of an implosion than an explosion, and I felt a giant fist ram into my midsection, lifting me several inches off the ground and sending me hurtling backward, arms and legs powerless, screaming an involuntary wail. Melissa was still screaming, curled into a fetal position, but sliding across the floor and thudding into the wall.

I slammed into the stone wall near the door, all the breath whooshing out of my lungs. I folded onto the floor, gasping, squinting up at the storm of light. Above me, the ceiling had ruptured open, the silver flames blossoming upward, forming an impossible channel through which the spirit was rising up, up, up through the next level. I could hear the freight-train roar of the fire blazing upstairs, the timbers collapsing, the ancient headers rending apart, mingling with the subsonic rush of phantom energy from below as it ascended. I tried to move, but my body was in a state of shock, wavering in and out of consciousness.

Somehow I managed to make the final sign of the cross, thus completing the Last Rites.

The ceiling cracked open then.

A vast whirlpool of pure light swirled up through the maelstrom, and the sound of it was incredible. It was enormous, it was overwhelming, like being inside the Niagara Falls. I shielded my face and cowered from the light, and I felt like those shepherds out in the field, in Luke 2:8, when the angels came down and said, *'Be not afraid, for I bring you news of a great joy which will come to all the people!'* But I *was* afraid, oh yeah, I was pretty damn terrified—not for my own safety, or even for the fate of the house itself, but for Melissa who was still curled against the wall across from me, shrieking furiously.

I managed to crawl over and put my arms around her, shielding her as best I could.

Soon the silver light started to collapse into itself, like a column of radiant mist being sucked up a tube, until there was only a twister's tail of it spinning above us . . . then fading, fading, fading until there was nothing but the roar of the fire upstairs . . .

The sound of the house being devoured.

4. Right Between the Eyes

After a few excruciating moments of noisy silence, I heard Melissa's strained voice next to me.

'Never again.'

I looked down at her and felt another powerful twinge

of affection for that kid. She was still curled into a ball, her face peering up at me with eyes glassy and dazed, her hair matted with sweat, her skin damp and filthy. She looked like a coma patient awakening after about ten years.

And that's when I hugged her. It was a completely involuntary gesture, a great big sloppy bear-hug full of tears and pain and release. I hugged her out of sheer catharsis for my miserable wasted life, and I hugged her for little Eric Rivers, and I hugged her for all the lost souls buried in unmarked graves. And she hugged me back hard. Hard enough to squeeze yet more tears from my eyes. And I realized that she was probably as drained and traumatized as I was. 'It's okay, sport, it's over,' I said softly. 'And now we gotta get you outta here.'

'He spoke in another language.'

'What?'

She swallowed hard, her raccoon make-up framing a pair of eyes glittering with terror. 'The spirit,' she said, 'he spoke to me in another language.'

I told her it was a Haitian dialect.

The sudden sound of timbers collapsing upstairs sent jagged vibrations through the foundation. The tunnel was filling with acrid smoke, and I quickly rose to my feet, my head spinning. I almost fell back down I was hurting so badly. Another few minutes and I probably would have passed right out.

I helped Melissa to her feet.

She stood unsteadily for a moment. 'He said "never again," ' she murmured. 'It was like I could understand the meaning of it, even though he spoke in another language.'

'Melissa, listen to me, we have to get our butts out of here as soon as—'

I glanced down at my watch and my heart tumbled in my chest.

It was 2:03 a.m.

'Jesus Mary and Joseph,' I muttered, standing there on wobbly legs. I opened my satchel and looked for the black box. It was wedged between my broken cassette player and my caffeine-pill box. I turned it over and studied the indicator. It had stopped on 00:00:00. 'Dear God Almighty,' I muttered, 'I hope Jimmy Dodd and your mother made it out of here on time—'

'He said "never again," ' Melissa repeated, her eyes glinting. And right then it hit me like a bullet between the eyes. I realized exactly what the kid was saying. 'Never again'—a simple phrase that could be taken in different ways. Both positively and negatively.

Never again.

'Come on, kid,' I said, and urged her toward the doorway.

I prayed we weren't too late.

CHAPTER TWENTY-EIGHT

The Freeze-Dried Apocalypse

1. A Filthy Jagged Tension

The sub-sub-level tunnel was now filled with thick blue smoke, so we could barely breathe, and we could barely see, and we could barely hobble along without falling on our faces. But I knew there was another passageway running perpendicular to the main one, so I felt my way along one wall. The noise of the inferno above us sounded horrible, like some gigantic animal in its death throes. I had a feeling the whole foundation was going to give way very soon.

We found another iron door, and I grabbed the handle. It was hot to the touch, but I shouldered it open.

We plunged into an auxiliary tunnel and hurried along through the darkness, limping like a couple of invalids. Melissa kept staggering, so I had to gently guide her along. I needed to get us both out of there as quickly as possible. According to Tooms, this tunnel must run straight north, terminating at the iron ladder leading up to Pennsylvania Avenue. I had no idea how far it extended, and without light everything was guesswork.

Then, thank God, a voice came echoing down the tunnel, only moments later. Otherwise, I'm not sure we would have made it out of there.

'Please identify yourselves!' a male voice called through the darkness.

I yelled back into the void: 'I'm Father Martin Delaney, a friend of James Dodd! I'm with Melissa Fallon, here! Where are you?'

'Straight ahead of you!'

We followed the sound of the voice, till the tunnel widened slightly, the smell of smoke giving way to a cool, moldy odor like a discontinued sewer. An ancient conduit pipe appeared along one wall. We could barely see it in the shadows, but it was a sign we were getting close to Pennsylvania Avenue, so we quickened our pace.

'Over here, sir!' the voice called through the shadows.

I figured it must belong to a secret-service agent, the way it resonated with such precision and authority. But there was also a jagged nervous tension in it. And secret-service agents rarely got nervous.

A moment later we turned a corner, moving straight into a blur of light.

'Hold it right there!' a figure yelled, training a high-watt flashlight on us. As we obliged, I squinted to discern the figure better. Soon I could barely make out the outline of a young man wearing a black parka and bulletproof flak vest, holding something shiny in his other arm. The 'something shiny' was an AK-47 assault rifle—pointing right at us.

He ordered us down on our knees, hands behind our backs. Again we obliged without a word. He came over and quickly inspected my satchel, then helped Melissa to her feet.

I saw Melissa give him a glare. 'You can back off with the Nazi routine, Carl,' she said. 'This is Father Delaney, and he saved my ass, and maybe everybody else's, too.'

The young agent named Carl glanced over at me. Then he helped me to my feet.

'Did Mom make it out of here?' the girl asked.

Carl just stared at her in silence for a moment, then said, 'Come on—this way.'

2. Hotel Purgatory

He led us the rest of the way along the narrow tunnel, till we reached a dead-end and a concrete wall, where an iron ladder led up to ground level. As I instinctively started up it, Carl said, 'Whoa, wait a minute. Not so fast, Father.'

'Why?' I turned to look at him.

'We're not going up there,' he said. Then he pointed instead at an unmarked steel door over to our right. 'We go in here.'

'We're what—?' Melissa began.

But Carl already had his flashlight trained on a small magnetic terminal embedded in the stonework next to the door. He swiped a card through the slot, there was a click and a whir, and then a hissing sound. The door swung open, and he ushered us into a small vestibule not much bigger than a shower stall.

For a second, I thought I was dreaming.

The tiny vestibule was bathed in red light, the sound of air circulators hissing all around us. Somehow, they had gotten power to this little chamber. Melissa was getting nervous. 'Carl, what the hell's going on?' she demanded, but got no answer out of him. He had already closed the outer door, and was now swiping his card through an inner terminal.

'Here we are,' he said finally. 'Welcome to Hotel Purgatory.'

The inner door fizzed open.

The first thing I saw was the glaring white walls bathed in fluorescent light, then a couple of middle-aged agents in down vests and headsets huddled over a computer screen. And then Suzanne Fallon was coming across the room, her face aglow, her eyes red from tears. She rushed towards her daughter, and they embraced in the doorway.

'Oh my God, my God, my God, you're okay, you're okay.' Suzanne hugged her child with all her might.

I glanced across the cavernous room, making instantaneous observations despite my throbbing and traumatized brain. At first glance it looked like a large cellblock, except with benches and dining tables, and restrooms beyond. Then, of course, I recognized the signs that we were in some type of high-tech bomb shelter. Huge air-filtering fans revolved in the ceiling, and the white walls were reinforced with iron crossbeams. There were shelves stacked with neatly organized canned goods, videotapes, books and files. There were banks of security monitors, and even a small gun rack in the corner sporting dozens of military weapons, gas masks and flak jackets, all mounted on pegboard behind a locked glass panel. This was clearly a serious safe house for the First Family and their entourage, during times of war and other upheavals.

Dodd was sitting in the corner, at the end of a bench, with his face in his hands.

My heart sank.

'Jimmy?' I managed to walk up to him and put a hand on his shoulder. 'What happened? Did you get word to the President?'

He looked up at me with a defeated, ashen face. He looked like a man sleepwalking through a war zone. 'We didn't make it,' he said.

I looked around the room. 'What's going on here?'

'We have to stay down here for a while, Father,' he said.

'Jimmy, explain it to me.'

He motioned at the suits. 'They intercepted us in the tunnel, and they told us the launch codes were already received by NORAD. So we never had a chance. These guys are trained to live down here for years.'

I was feeling woozy again, but I fought the disorientation. Was I dreaming? I tried to swallow but my throat was dry as dust. 'Jimmy, we broke the curse—the curse on the house. We broke through it.'

He cut me off with a strange little nod and a weird expression. He glanced at one of the monitors on the wall nearby. 'Cleansed in fire,' he uttered.

I hobbled over to the bank of surveillance monitors, and observed the one marked 'NORTH LAWN.'

On its tiny screen, an eerie black-and-white image rippled amid radiant whirlpools of fire and snow. The vantage point was just beside the iron gate at the corner of Pennsylvania Avenue and West Executive Street, and the White House looked strangely tiny and artificial in the distance, like a dollhouse being gobbled by flames. The north portico was blazing, its giant columns sheathed in fire, and part of the west wing was already a flaming pile of rubble where the roof had caved in. It looked like a toy version of hell—like a freeze-dried apocalypse. An involuntary shudder slithered up my spine. But no fire crews were in evidence there—or the emergency units had all been called away.

There was nobody trying to put out the fire.

I looked back at Dodd. He was now staring at me as though he didn't know what to say next. The others had moved over to gaze at the monitors, too. Melissa stood there, hugging herself as though she might suddenly break apart. Suzanne was lighting up yet another cigarette with trembling hands. The secret-service agents stood stoic and silent, watching us watching the screens. I glanced back up at the monitor.

For a moment I thought I heard a distant siren pierce the night.

I turned to the others. 'Does anybody hear—?'

'It's a civil-defense siren,' Dodd said softly, staring at the floor.

Goosebumps rippled over me. Silence gripped the room.

I turned back to the screen and watched as the blaze consumed the President's house. Around the edge of the video screen was a faint glow, like a premature dawn.

I wondered if it was merely the fire itself reflecting off the snow . . .

. . . or something more distant which was infinitely more dangerous.

Epilogue

THE UNMARKED GRAVE

You have built houses of hewn stone, but you shall not dwell in them; you have planted pleasant vineyards, but you shall not drink their wine.

Book of Amos 5:11

That's it. That's the whole story. I can't think of anything more to say or to add; so I'll just sit here at the end of this dining table, with a half-empty can of peaches and an overflowing ashtray in front of me, and I'll try to drum up some kind of moral to the story.

I'm watching the others, and they're quiet, letting it all sink in.

We've been living like sardines in our tin can for almost two weeks now. We sleep in shifts on inflatable pads in the corner, each of us taking our share of guard duty, occasionally watching the dead monitors in case one of them comes to life again. The screens went blank about twelve days ago, not long after the charred ruins at 1600 Pennsylvania Avenue stopped smoldering in the winter winds. Since then, we've been living on spam, canned fruit, powdered milk and oatmeal. I'm really learning to hate oatmeal. Thank God, they included some cigarettes—I didn't even smoke before getting trapped down here—and some cheap store-brand whiskey that we've been doling out in thimblefuls.

It took me almost five days to write down the whole story. To recall every moment the way I myself experienced it. My memory isn't what it used to be, and I wanted to make sure I told what happened. Every few hours I would pause and

307

take a break, or someone else would pick up the story and tell a part of it from their point of view. But now that it's done, I'm almost sorry I told the damn thing. What the hell are we going to talk about now? I can't listen to these G-men pontificate anymore on the merits of their emergency-preparedness system. Who cares? And, for that matter, why keep the First Family on ice down here if there's nothing but burned rubble and toxic waste to go upstairs to? My patience is even wearing a little thin with Suzanne. If I hear her bad-mouth the Pope one more time, I'm going to slap her. Oh well.

Thank God, Melissa's down here with us. The girl is still a never-ending source of entertainment, going off on her hilarious rants about being the 'First Daughter' in a post-literate America, or about going to see James Brown at RFK stadium when she was only ten years old, or sneaking mari-juana into the crème brûlée during a reception for the Jamaican ambassador. I love that kid, and I'm glad she seems to be healing from her ordeal. She wakes up screaming in the middle of the night sometimes—actually, I'm not sure if it's night or day down here—but on the whole she seems to be recovering.

It's Dodd I'm worried about. I think he's lost hope. He never even glances at the surveillance screens anymore, and he never talks about the possibility that the weapons launch might have been intercepted or canceled, or that the mis-siles might have been averted. He doesn't sleep. He doesn't even eat much. All he does is sit in the corner, playing solitaire and smoking cigarettes. I think the house has got to him, and I think it's going to take a lot of work to get him back. I still love him, though. I love him for believing in me.

Finally Melissa looks at me and says, 'Pretty cool story. Only problem is, I don't like the ending.'

I manage a tired smile.

Suzanne is sitting across the table from me. She lights another cigarette. 'Let's hope the story's not over yet,' she says.

Carl pipes in from across the room. 'The system will tell us when it's all clear to go upstairs.'

Dodd's voice comes from the corner, barely a murmur as he ceaselessly deals cards to himself. 'If it's ever clear.'

I don't say anything.

Instead, I get up and walk over to the monitors. There are eleven screens in all, programmed for catastrophic emergencies, to show eleven different angles of the interior and exterior of the White House, as well as two separate views of the Mall along Independence Avenue and the Capitol building.

Those great monuments to our lofty, abstract notions of civilization . . . reduced to a shimmering nothingness on a video screen. I stare at the monitors.

There are no more phantom faces in the electronic snow.

The screens are blank, and the ghosts are gone.

And now we inhabit an unmarked grave.